THE GHOSTS OF GREYSTONE

Prologue

(Millie-September, 1917)

I am headed to the sea again. Down the short path that cuts through the woods from the house. The leaves are falling faster now...copper colored to brown...to dust...to nothing as we all will be given time or circumstance. I walk among them listening to their crunch beneath my feet...feeling them swirl around my ankles. The moon is rising over the mountains, and the birds are no more than dusky shadows seeking their havens from the encroaching darkness.

The trees now thin around me, and I can hear the pound of the waves rolling up on shore. Leaves become sand, and I kick off my shoes and let them lay where they fall. Closer and closer I walk to the darkening water then climb up on a granite boulder already cold with night. It is a history book of this place...of the eons of time that embraced it and have yet to let it go. A place of my memories. I hug my knees for warmth and gaze up at the crescent moon and a million stars... jewels scattered on the fabric of infinity. I feel small. Smaller than small.

2

I lie now on my back and study the sky as an intense loneliness drifts down from the heavens that finds its echo deep inside my being. I had been lonely for a very long time, but not the kind he left behind. Now I call to him on nights like this...send my love across the vast, cold sea that carried him away and wonder who I am without him. No longer whole. No longer me. He changed me forever the day he walked into my life and lifted the bleakness from my soul. I remember every minute.

It had been a blustery day along the coast, and the gray sea churned restlessly flinging its waves high on the shore. The sky was thick with dark clouds smudged with purple and rimmed in light where the sun revealed its hiding place. It was cold then, too. I had set up my easel in the shelter of these very rocks and been painting for a while trying to catch the somber ambience when someone intruded on my solitude. It was a man and his dog walking along the edge of the water just above the waves' reach. He stopped every now and then to pick up something from the sand or to call back his dog that was chasing the sea gulls squabbling over something netted in the tangle of seaweed that the tide had brought in that night.

From my place of concealment, I watched him come closer. He was tall with dark, wind blown hair. His coat collar was turned up to ward off the biting cold, and he was smiling as his narrowed eyes scanned the endless sea. His dog found me first. A golden retriever whose excited barking revealed my hiding place. I remember his words when he reached me. Every single one.

"Sargent's great at finding things when we beach comb, but this is the first time he's found a mermaid disguised as a red headed painter with a smudge of blue on her nose. Aren't you freezing?"

I hadn't realized it till then, but he was right. I refused the offer of his coat but accepted the hot chocolate he offered from his Thermos. He asked my name, and when I told him it was Millicent Grey, he smiled then said "Millicent is much too prim for a lady with paint on her nose. My name is Eric Sanders. I'm going to call you Millie or Smudge. Which do you prefer?"

I shake my head to clear my thoughts. I can't let myself remember. Let the pain of his absence trickle past the cocoon of numbness I've tried so hard to weave around my heart since the day I watched him walk away. He promised to return, but the war could change that. His death might be the price paid for our secret happiness. He's been gone almost two months that seem like an eternity, but I will wait no matter what happens or how long it takes. He is my forever love and nothing...not even death...can part us.

CHAPTER ONE

(Jodie-The Present)

I woke up and looked around the near dark room. Through a thin opening in the drapes, I saw a flash of red neon...the vacancy sign out front flashing its announcement. A quick peek at the digital clock told me it is almost time to get up. Almost. I still had time to think about how I had come to be at a place called Courage Cove. A place that had been described to me so many times, it had felt like home

4

when I drove down Main Street past the red brick buildings with their green shutters to this Pine View Motel and tucked in for the night. I had never had a 'home' in the real sense of the word until all that changed one rainy day when she walked into my life. The formidable Miss Allison Shield.

I was all of fifteen and had just been brought back to the group home again after running away from another family that had fostered me. I was waiting for a social worker to tell me for the umpteenth time that I was both incorrigible and ungrateful when she walked through the door. Dressed in unrelieved black, she was somewhere in her 80s with silver hair piled on top of her head and laugh wrinkles fanning out around her amazing green eyes. She took the chair across the table from me...propped her chin on her hands and met my eyes squarely. I was the first to look away.

"I am Allison Shield. Allison will do. You, young lady, are headed for the worst kind of trouble, but from what I've heard and read you are smart and have potential. Don't get me wrong. Your grades are disgraceful except in English where your essays are provocative to say the least, but well done, incisive, and show a great deal of imagination. What interests you?"

I had refused to answer as I stared in fascination at the intricate mermaid pin stuck in her lapel, so she continued, "Apparently, as they say...the cat has got your tongue. I have a cat. Her name is Cinda. Black as night and the best judge of character I know. You are coming home with me and there you will remain until you are a proper age. I expect you to be respectful of my rules, and we won't have any problems. What do you say to that?"

"What's with the mermaid?" I had found myself asking almost against my will.

She might have smiled. It came and went so fast I couldn't be sure. "An interest of mine. I am a sea person. Go gather your things while I take care of the paperwork and settle a few details."

I had learned later that she was a big supporter of group homes and supplied all of the extras the state wouldn't fund including field trips to museums and other places that would "broaden our horizons". Her interest gave her access to my file. I can't imagine what she saw in those pages that would attract her. Quite the opposite. I had been a ward of the court for as long as I could remember. A "difficult placement" and had run away four times from foster care, but she took me home with her anyway.

It was a limo that took us there driven by an aging chauffeur named Oliver while she sat stiffly next to me in her somber black suit. She smelled of something sweet I couldn't name. Not a word was said though Oliver smiled at me in the rearview mirror. I remember my surprise when we pulled up in front of what was to be my new home. It was enormous...a sprawling stone mansion set among impeccable grounds bright with flowerbeds in a riot of colors.

I know my jaw must have dropped because she told me, "It's just a pile of rocks that needs a helluva lot of upkeep. The heart of any house is the people who live and have lived there imprinting it with their history. Their laughter. Their tears. Their triumphs and their tragedies. That stone pile has seen more than its share. Let's get inside. Ollie will bring in your things."

She marched on ahead of me pausing to introduce me to Anna, the plump, dark haired woman with the kind eyes who greeted us at the open door. From there, we stepped into a grand hall with a lofty ceiling and a dangling crystal chandelier that sparkled like icicles in sunlight then up the sweeping staircase to my room where she opened the door and waited for me to step inside.

It was painted in the same azure blue as the seascape over the fireplace and way beyond anything I could have ever imagined. There were bookcases, and a soft rug, and a window seat with a view of the trees and sky. There was a desk in the corner and a four-poster bed piled high with ruffled pillows in blues and turquoise that happened to be my favorite colors.

She waited by the door as I walked around touching everything to see if it was real. Secretly, I pinched myself and was surprised when I didn't wake up and discover it was all just a dream.

"You have your own computer over there on the desk. Many of the books are classics as well as some authors that might interest a young adventuress such as yourself including one or two written by yours truly when I toyed with that genre. There are far more in the library downstairs. We will sort out your wardrobe tomorrow. Perhaps a nap is in order now."

I shook my head. "I'm not tired."

"But I am. We will see you at dinner. You'll hear the gong. Good day."

I spent the rest of the afternoon exploring the many treasures found in that room until the sonorous gong reverberated through the house. I had been surprised when Oliver and Anna joined us at the table. That surprise must have been apparent, for she told me, "We are all friends here. Anna has worked hard to make this lovely meal. We will give thanks to God first and then her."

I was clumsy with all the unfamiliar cutlery, and when I dropped my fork and knocked over my water glass, I was expecting the worst and not, "No harm done. See! There goes my knife and spoon right into my lap. We'll work on navigating all this stuff as we go along. Now eat up! Anna's made a chocolate cake in honor of your arrival. Sometimes we even have one for breakfast."

I remember that first night lying there in my huge bed looking out the window at the trees back lit by the moon. Occasionally, a car would pass on the street out front, or distantly I heard a siren, but not the squeak of my bedroom door which meant I had to hide, run, or scream and fight my way out of there. Most nights, I had hid under the bed in the different places I had stayed. Sometimes it was the other 'fosters' who tormented me...sometimes it was an adult with bad intentions...sometimes it was both. Reporting it only made things worse, so I kept my mouth shut until the situation left me with no choice but to run.

I soon found out that the outside world had its own predators. Somehow I managed to escape from them more by luck than anything. I was always cold and afraid. Had slept under porches or empty sheds and avoided places where others gathered. Rummaged through dumpsters behind restaurants, but often went hungry. The last time I was caught scrounging for food behind the Chicken Shack. A cop had hauled me in then back to the 'system'. Allison had rescued me, but as I lay there that first night, I wondered what her angle was. By then, I had come to think everyone had one.

Sometime during the hours that followed, I climbed under the bed again, and she had found me there the next morning. To my surprise, she climbed under it with me then said, "This isn't too bad for a hiding place. I used to do this very thing back in the day when dinosaurs roamed the earth, and I was in a place like I found you. Lots of things scared me back then. That will change for you just as it did for me...with time. When you learn how much you are loved and wanted here by us. How about some breakfast? Anna can whip up anything that strikes your fancy."

I had learned later that she had been a foundling, too. Had lived since infancy in an orphanage called Second Chance in a small village renamed Courage Cove after a sea disaster that happened more than a century ago. A fierce storm had driven a ship called the *Morning Star* onto the rocks far offshore, and the villagers had risked their lives trying to rescue the passengers and crew. Some had died. Had been swept out to sea and never found. Those who survived knew it had taken a miracle.

I had also learned from the photo albums she kept that she had helped other orphans through the years, but I was the only one she took home with her and adopted. Had pulled a few strings and made it happen despite her age. A rebellious orphan with no known last name except the one they pinned on me became Jodie Shield...adopted daughter of the famous Allison Shield whom I hadn't known was famous at the time. She was just someone who opened the door to a whole new way of life. I loved her for that, and I loved her even more for becoming the mother I had always wanted....always needed. Someone who gave me a sense of *belonging* I had never thought I'd find.

The phone rang interrupting my lengthy reverie. It was a wake up call from the office. I hadn't wanted to oversleep and be late for my meeting with a local Realtor...one Helen Goodall...who was going to show me rentals with a view of the sea. I had promised Allison two things on the night she died three months ago in Greece: I was to write her bio which meant uncovering the mystery of her birth and look after her much loved cat.

She was now with me. I reached for her, but she was gone from the spot where she usually snuggled. Turning on the light, I found her curled up in her portable litter box as she sometimes did when she was stressed.

"Come here, baby girl," I whispered to her as I lifted 15 lbs of geriatric black cat into my arms where she purred loudly like a bumblebee trapped in a bottle.

Disengaging her kneading claws from my pajama top, I lowered her to the bed, stroked her soft fur then opened a small bag of kibbles. "Ocean fish this morning. Doesn't that sound yummy?"

She blinked twice then jumped down and sat by her bowl. "Okay, we have a meeting with the Realtor in less than an hour, so while you chow down, I'm grabbing a shower then see what I can do with this hair."

While she settled down to eat, I did just that then left the motel a short time later with Cinda in her carrier. Leaving her behind was not an option. Her loud, mournful vocalizations when left alone since Allison's death would not be welcome.

I drove through the quaint village that was just stirring to life. Again, I marveled at how little it seemed to have changed from Allison's description despite the length of time that had passed. The Realtor's office was in one of the gray saltbox houses at the far end, and she met me at the door. She was short...compared to my 5'10". Her too black hair was arranged like a steel helmet, and she was dressed to impress. Her eyes narrowed as she looked me over in turn...me in my jeans, sneakers, hoodie, and ponytail. None of which screamed "Money!" and I could tell she thought I was wasting her time.

"I don't think we have what you want, Miss Shield. Rents are still very high this time of year and...." she began until I cut her short.

"Not a problem. It needs to be close to the ocean...preferably on the water...older with lots of personality and a bit of land around it." I'm not at all sure what made me say all that, but I knew as soon as those words left my mouth that was exactly what I wanted.

Her eyes narrowed a second time. "Nothing comes to mind on the rental market."

My mouth opened again and these words came out, "It doesn't have to be a rental. I will purchase what meets my requirements."

"Very well. I hope you realize with the market these days, the down payment is thirty percent and then of course there are all the other fees."

"Of course. Where are we going first?"

"I do need to get back here before too long. Another client is coming up from Miami."

"Then we better get moving," I replied with a smile.

"Why don't I show you this condo that would be perfect for you? One of several in a new construct with special incentives to..."

"Not interested," I cut in sharper than I had intended. "Let's get started. I'll take my own car."

I followed her through the village to a string of cottages across the street from a very blue ocean. I was surprised when she pulled up in front of the one on the end. It was older, but remodeled. It did have a sea view if you didn't mind looking over a busy road at what would be a jam-packed beach come summertime. None of which appealed to me.

Climbing out, I reached her as she fiddled with the lock box then told her, "You're wasting your time and mine. You know what I want. Let's keep looking."

From there, I followed her to one of the condos she had tried to unload on me insisting it was a "must see for a single woman". I disagreed and the hunt continued.

Finally, she told me, "Look. That's about all our current offerings that come even close to your requirements. I do have one just listed with us that I haven't had a chance to view yet. Right off the bat, I'll tell you it's not on the water. Is that a deal breaker or am I wasting my time dragging you way out there?"

Again, I'm not at all sure what made me tell her, "I want to see it and then decide."

Clearly annoyed with me by then...especially since she had to hand off her Miami client to another agent, I followed her out of the village then through the countryside along a dirt road that paralleled the shoreline. A narrow lane took us back among the trees that pressed close from both sides. A curve brought us to the house.

I pulled to a stop behind her car and just stared at the house that vaguely reminded me of Allison's. It was enormous, old...probably the late 1800s or even earlier and made of weathered gray stone. A mossy slate roof was topped with multiple chimneys ...several of which had collapsed. Broken windows pockmarked the front. A huge, tangled mass of late blooming red roses climbed up one side and along the roofline. Its profusion of blooms scented the air as I stepped out. Her scent. An errant thought crept into my mind. Maybe she had sent me here?

"This property is really not presentable for showing and certainly not suitable for a young woman all on her own," Helen called to me as she picked her way, gingerly, through the tall weeds and dead leaves that had accumulated over many years. "As you can plainly see it needs a lot of repairs. The location is close to the water, but not *on* it, which was one of your main requirements. However, I was told by the sellers that on a windy day you can hear the surf from here. The original family...the Greys... died out, and it went on the auction block back in the 40s. The current owners want it gone."

"It could be beautiful again," I murmured.

She shook her head. "That's clearly a matter of personal taste. Most would bulldoze it and break up the property. There's twenty acres that could be divided into lots. The land closest to the water is state owned...seized from the owners for a state park by eminent domain in the 80s, so no one can build on that which is a plus."

"It looks so unloved. Who are the owners?"

"The Bainbridges. My understanding is that the property was bought for a summer home, but never lived in. They're scattered all over the world now and have no interest in this place. They had tried renting it, but no one stayed long. Occasionally, squatters were found here and did some damage. I don't know the details. I probably shouldn't say this but a cash offer could steal it though it would have to be a sizable one to compete with the investors who will be sniffing around once they hear it's gone on the market."

"Let's go inside. I want to look around...get a sense of it."

She looked at me like I was deranged then told me, "Don't tell me you're one of those ghost hunters."

"Because?" I prodded.

She sighed then told me reluctantly, "I suppose, ethically, I must divulge what I know...or rather heard though it's no doubt all nonsense."

14

"Which is?"

"It's haunted. At least that's what they say."

"*They* being?"

"Locals...the renters who never stayed long. A rumor only and one I couldn't verify with the Bainbridges when they listed the sale."

The scent of the roses seemed to grow stronger. "Let's go inside."

"No lock box yet, but the key is supposed to be under a rock somewhere. I'll wait right here while you look for it."

I never found the key but did find a broken windowpane in the back door. Reaching inside, I unlocked it then entered the shadowy kitchen. Cobwebs drifted lazily like strands of gossamer from the overhead beams as I carefully stepped through the dust and garbage that littered the floor and looked around at the antiquated appliances and plumbing. Plywood covered a brick fireplace in the back wall. Across it, a crude skull and crossbones had been drawn in what I hoped was red paint. In the middle of it all, an oak table lay on its back with its legs outstretched like a dead animal, and I wondered where that thought had come from.

Pushing through the swing door, I followed the dark hall dimly lit by open doors on both sides that offered glimpses of rooms equally derelict or worse. A shudder ran through me. It felt sad...lost...lonely, and I questioned my sanity for even thinking about buying the place. It was already having an effect on me that didn't seem healthy.

Reaching the front door, I unlocked it for Helen who was examining a hole in her panty hose with a moue of distaste.

"Thank God I keep an extra pair with me," she murmured as she stepped inside where we both looked around.

At some time in the past, vandals had smashed a large ormolu mirror, and shards of glass were scattered among the dirt and debris that littered the marble floor. The rose wallpaper was peeling away from the left wall where an elegant staircase swept up to the second floor. Like the sword of Damocles, a crystal chandelier had pulled loose from its moorings and now dangled from its wires high above us.

"I know someone who had one quite similar," I murmured. "That one is in really bad shape, but it can be restored."

She wrinkled her nose in distaste. "This whole place is a colossal money pit with nothing going for it."

"Why was this built here and not on the water? From what you told me, the Greys owned the needed land back then."

"The very thing I asked the owners since it would have commanded a much higher price. Their grandfather had researched its history after he bought it. It seems that Horace Grey was on the ship that sank off these shores. The *Morning Star*. You may have heard of it?"

At my nod, she continued, "He was the owner of the shipping line, and the ship was on her maiden voyage. His young wife and infant son had accompanied him. He and his wife survived, but the baby drowned, and his body was never recovered. Afterwards, he wanted to live close to where the tragedy occurred. His wife, Hannah, couldn't bear to look at the sea. The house was built here as a

16

compromise. Local legend claims he was often seen walking along the shore and calling his son's name. Perhaps hoping he would return by some miracle. She went quite mad after little more than a year. Claimed she kept hearing her baby cry. She died a short time later. I don't remember the particulars."

She had related the whole story in a flat monotone without emotion unless boredom could be considered such. "This house was built on a foundation of loss and sorrow, no wonder it feels so sad," I whispered as a shiver ran up my spine for a second time.

"It's just an old house that's falling apart and nothing to romanticize about. Let's move on, shall we?"

"No. I'll take it 'as is'. No inspection," I found myself saying again without knowing why.

***

Everything went smoothly with the sale, but the house needed a few things checked out and repaired before I could move in even if I roughed it for a while. The few turned into many before I would have running water, power, heat, and a working toilet. The place was soon alive with workers...hammering...sawing...and reporting all the small and large disasters they had found from mold to termites...broken pipes...a furnace that was beyond repair, and wiring that needed to be replaced before the whole "damn thing burned up".

I was there every day checking on things and doing what I could despite the disapproval of my contractor, Big Joe Albright, who claimed I was more of a distraction than a help. Not that I listened.

I was healing the house, and it mattered to me that my hands were doing some of the work.

The second week in, Joe told me they were going to cut down the climbing rose because it was rotting the soffit and loosening the slate shingles. It was an antique rose, and I told him not to touch it. That I would handle the trimming and set to work. It was a huge, twisted, tangled, thorny mess. Despite my canvas gloves and long sleeves, I was soon covered in scratches when a vintage pickup truck pulled in front. An elderly man in a red flannel shirt, jeans, and a baseball cap climbed down and headed my way.

"Mornin', Miss," he called up to me on my ladder. "Looks like them roses are getting' the better of you if you don't mind me sayin' so. They been here since before I can remember. Heard tell it was the first Mrs. Grey what started them...the second kept adding more."

I climbed down, carefully, since I had never liked heights or did well on ladders. "Just needed a bit of a trim," I told him wryly as I stripped off my gloves and offered him my hand. "I'm Jodie Shield, and you are?"

His hand was rough with calluses and freckled with age. His grasp was warm and firm. "Pleased to meet you, Jodie Shield. I'm Henry...Henry North and live over yonder a bit. Been hearin' about you in the village and thought I'd drop on by to be neighborly and nosey. Looks like you got your hands full here with this place. Got a good contractor though. Big Joe is as honest as they come, but I'd keep an eye on that Bob French. Not much for putting in a full day."

I smiled back at him. "Joe will handle it, but thanks for the tip."

"When are you movin' in? Looks like there's still mor'en a mite to do yet."

I sighed. "As soon as I can manage to live here without me or my cat falling through the floor. The basics are almost finished...or so I've been told once or twice. How long have you lived in these parts?"

"Most of my life. Don't want to go nowhere else."

"Then you know the history of this house?"

He smiled crookedly and nodded. "That's what has me wonderin' why you or anyone else would want to live here."

"I feel its sadness."

"It's got a lot to be sad about. It surely does. There was the shipwreck for starters and then this house was built for reasons most thought mighty peculiar to say the least. Other bad things happened here, too. Early...tragic deaths. Some say their ghosts still linger."

"Heard about the shipwreck and why this house was built but not the other stuff. Do you believe Greystone is haunted?"

He hesitated for a long moment before he replied. "Do know I would never go in there after dark. Don't mean to be scarin' you none. I'm just an old man who's heard stories about that place for as long as I can rightly remember. Just be mighty careful if you won't reconsider the whole thing."

There were so many questions I wanted to ask him, but he tipped his hat and left a moment later. His words left me with an uneasy feeling, and I decided to check on Cinda who had been confined to

19

the dining room that was still in reasonably good shape. I found her sitting on the window seat and joined her there.

"Would you tell me if you saw a ghost?" I asked while I stroked her soft fur and listened to her rumbling purr. I had read somewhere that animals could see spirits and wondered if she had been gifted with that ability. I found myself hoping she hadn't. It would be very unnerving to see her staring at someone or something invisible to me.

I spent some time playing with her then went back to trimming the roses. The sun had settled low in the sky when I finished doing what little I could then watched Joe and his crew leave for the day. Suddenly, I realized I had never stayed that late before, and now I was all alone in a place no one wanted to be after dark. It wasn't a good feeling.

Dropping my pruning shears, I hurried back inside. The kitchen was already filled with shadows that were making me all kinds of nervous, so I sped to the dining room where I found Cinda lying in her litter box with her ears flattened, and her pupils dilated. Something had frightened her. A something I couldn't see. Suddenly, I heard the sonorous chime of a big clock echo through the house twelve times. A shiver shot through me. There was no clock, so what had I just heard? Was it some sort of residual...some imprint from past lives?

I loaded Cinda in her carrier and headed for the kitchen at a run. From somewhere down the back hall, I heard sibilant whispers and felt a shivery awareness sweep over me. Someone was watching me from the shadows. Cinda's hiss told me she sensed it, too. Flinging open the door, I sprinted to my car where I shoved the carrier in the front seat, climbed in next to it then stepped hard on the gas sending gravel flying in all directions.

In the rearview mirror, I looked back at the sprawling mansion I would be living in soon if Joe stayed on schedule. There was a glimmer of light in the kitchen I had left dark. I took a deep breath to steady my nerves. It had to be a trick of my overactive imagination. Greystone was now my home. I needed to face my fear. More than ever...with each day that passed...I felt I was meant to be there.

Suddenly, the scent of roses filled the car and I heard a voice...or thought I did. "Don't be afraid. I am with you." It was Allison although it didn't *exactly* sound like her. Did she have the power to protect us or was that asking far too much even from her?

***

As it turned out, the official move in date was now a firm three days away, which gave me the time I needed to finish my last minute shopping for things I kept adding to my list of necessities. What I had accumulated so far had either been hauled out to the house or stockpiled in my motel room. The appliances and few bits of furniture I had purchased had already been delivered to Greystone.

Finally, it was time to check out of the motel. As I drove away with Cinda in her carrier wedged between the boxes in the back seat, she uttered a profound and eerie cry I had never heard before. It almost felt like a warning. As though she knew somehow that I was making a very big mistake.

"It is what it is." I told her as I watched her in the rearview mirror. "We're going home, and we will both love it." I had added a very fervent "I hope" under my breath. I wasn't at all sure either one of us was going to like our first night all alone at Greystone even with Allison's protection.

We arrived while the workers were still busy, and I carried some of the boxes I'd need up to my bedroom then went back for Cinda's carrier. By then, Joe had seen what I was doing and offered to help. Between us, everything got dispersed rather haphazardly, but it would do for now. He and his crew left a short time later just as the sun was disappearing behind the trees in a raspberry red sky.

Shadows were creeping in from the corners as I looked around the beautiful room I had decided would be mine the first moment I saw it. I was looking forward to a fire in the white marble fireplace that actually worked once the dead raccoon was pulled out of the flue. The bed was the perfect choice for Greystone. It could well have been the same age...a rich dark walnut beauty with carved roses on the very tall head and footboard. The almost matching armoire was found in another antique shop...a serious necessity since there was no closet and the dressing room was now my new bathroom. A side table, small dresser, a real Tiffany wisteria lamp, and a chair bought from a third village antique shop completed the furnishings.

The sun had set by then, so I switched on the light then put the finishing touches to the bed. I had chosen sea colors...blues...aquas...and teal for all the bedding right down to the mound of ruffled pillows. I had just plumped up the last one when Cinda jumped up and found a spot among them. I was smiling when I took a seat next to her then wriggled my bare toes in the soft rug that was almost identical to the first one I had long ago.

"Time to head downstairs and try out the kitchen," I told her as I scratched behind her silky ears. A sudden feeling of dread settled over me. It would be dark down there by now, and I remembered all too well the whispers I had heard only a few days before.

"Stop being such an idiot!" I told myself firmly. "You can do this!"

Jumping to my feet, I grabbed a flashlight from the bedside table, slipped back into my sneakers, and headed for the door with Cinda right on my heels. Out in the hall, I flashed my light in both directions and thought about which route I would take. The main staircase was closer but the service stairs led directly to the kitchen. Joe had warned me they weren't all that safe. Repairing them was still on his 'to do list' which only seemed to grow longer instead of shorter. Greystone was the mega 'money pit' Helen had warned me about, but thanks to Allison I had the funds I needed.

Deciding better safe than sorry, I headed for the main staircase with Cinda now running just ahead. I followed her down the sweeping stairs to the entry hall below where the silver light of an early moon found its way through the sidelights and transom I had spent a long time cleaning. There was still no power to most of this floor, so the hall off to my right was the kind of dark that made me very uneasy.

Taking a deep breath, I flashed my light in front of me and ran past each door, remembering what I had seen behind them...rubble, rat droppings, an occasional bird or animal carcass, and decades of dirt and dust. In many, broken windows had let in the rain and snow, so the floorboards, paneling and plaster walls were being repaired or replaced. I smiled ruefully as I remembered one of the rooms had had satanic graffiti covering its walls, and Joe had it painted over before I could see it.

Reaching the newly rewired kitchen, I snapped on the lights then smiled at the difference time and effort had made. The walls were now a cheerful yellow with a sunflower border running around the top. The uncovered fireplace had been cleaned out and now housed a struggling English ivy in a copper pot. Every cupboard and cabinet that could be restored had been restored...everything else replaced with hand crafted replicas. The oak table had been salvaged and repaired by a retired veteran...Hank Crenshaw... who supplied four matching chairs if you didn't look too closely. Not that I cared all that much. The entire house would have an eclectic mix of everything before I was finished with it.

Cinda wound around my legs and head bumped my sneakers until I filled her bowls to her satisfaction.

"Maybe an omelette and an early night for me," I murmured to myself as I rummaged through the contents of the double door fridge that looked so out of place. I had decided to keep the old side oven electric range. Once cleaned and polished, it was a real beauty and looked quite content like an old broody hen on her nest.

The omelet was quick and easy. I shared a bit with Cinda then cleaned up. By then, I was feeling increasingly uneasy...as though I was being watched again.

While I washed the few dishes, I glanced out the window where the night pressed against the glass. It was darker than dark, and I realized that this was the first time I had lived some place without streetlamps or the glint of a neighbor's lights shining through the trees. There was nothing out there, and yet I sensed there was. My uneasiness hiked up another notch, and I checked the back door to make sure it was locked. Not that that would stop someone who was determined to get in as I knew all too well. It was not a comforting thought.

I decided to leave the light on when I grabbed my flashlight and headed down the back hall with Cinda running alongside. I wanted to check out the service stairs this time and see just how safe they were safe in case I needed them for a quick get-a-way. I knew what was behind the doors I passed: storage rooms, the cellar, a laundry room with its brand new washer and dryer that still lacked power. Opening the one at the far end, I flashed my light up the narrow staircase. More than one of the treads was cracked, but seemed stable, so I kept climbing.

Reaching the top, I pushed open the door and pointed my flashlight down the hall that was inky black except for the light that spilled from my open bedroom door near the far end. Something or someone was between me and that light. A thick heavy shadow that moved ever so slightly when Cinda hissed at it.

"Okay," I told her as my heart rate soared. "It's a shadow. No big deal. We are going to run right through it. Ready...set...here we go!"

I scooped her up and sped down the hall. Whatever it was thinned then dissipated completely before we reached it, but left a scent I couldn't quite place...and then I did. It smelled of the sea. Reaching my room, I slammed the door shut and locked it behind us. Whatever had been in the hall hadn't followed us...I hoped...but there was a long night ahead.

"Yet another comforting thought," I murmured as I shoved my one and only chair under the knob. Somehow...some way I would have to deal with my fear, if I was going to stay at Greystone.

"Don't be afraid. I need you here" the voice spoke again...the one that sounded like Allison, but not quite.

"Why all this?" I found myself asking. "Who or what was that out there, and why do you want me here?"

There was a long, heavy silence before the voice whispered close to my ear, "I don't know, but time will tell."

Which wasn't really an answer, but despite my continued questions the voice was silent. Allison was gone.

I prepared quickly for bed then lit a fire to ward off the increasing cold that permeated the entire room. Cinda joined me when I climbed inside the covers. I left the bedside lamp on as I lay there listening to the sounds in the old house. The mystery clock chiming midnight...the sound of whispers outside the door...the knob turning…the weak cry of a baby somewhere in the walls. The wind had picked up and wailed mournfully as it forced its way through the cracks around the dry rotted window frames. I watched the flickering flames...feeling drowsier and drowsier...until sleep claimed me. I'm not sure when or what it was that sent me scurrying under the bed some time during the night, but that's where I woke up when morning found me.

***

Everything looked so different in daylight. As Cinda and I headed down the back stairs to the kitchen, I could *almost* believe what had happened the previous night was due to fatigue and an overdose of imagination. Soon I had coffee brewing and breakfast started. I was eating when Joe's crew arrived. He was the first through the door and seemed very glad to see me.

"Wasn't sure how you'd do," he told me. "Been mor'en a mite worried. We all have."

I forced my brightest smile. "I'm just fine. How about a cup of coffee?"

He grinned back, but his eyes were troubled. "Look. You could sell this place. Why sink more money in it when you could let it go 'as is' and move on to some place not so...."

His pause had me supplying, "Haunted? It appears those stories may be true, but I'm still here and have no plans on leaving. We've never talked much about the history of this place. What do you know about it?"

He leaned against the wall and sighed. "Just rumors mor'en anything. A bad luck place where things happened. Best person to ask is your neighbor. The one I saw drop by a few days ago. Old Henry North might answer your questions, if you give him that smile of yours."

"He said he lived close by, but not exactly where."

"Instead of goin' towards the village, head left. His place is about two miles or so up the road. Impossible to miss. There's an old tractor and a carnival Tilt-A-Whirl in the field next to it. Name's on the mailbox. Best be gettin' back to work. Thanks for the coffee offer, but the missus always packs me a Thermos."

I watched him head down the hall as I thought about what I would do next. If Henry had the answers I needed, I would pay him a visit.

It didn't take long to get ready which included confining Cinda in the dining room again with all her necessaries till I got back. As I made a left turn at the end of the drive, I wondered how Henry would feel about me dropping in out of the blue and hoped he was a morning person. Just as Joe had said, his place was impossible to miss. He was standing on the front porch of his cabin when I pulled up and parked. I joined him there wearing the best smile I could manage.

"Just checkin' out the new day when I heard you comin' down the road. Was about to make a fresh pot of coffee," he told me with a grin just as a beagle hound came around the corner and flopped down next to me. It was apparent she was nursing a litter. "That's Bella. She's tired of them pups pesterin' her and needs a break.

28

They're 'round back in the shed if you've a mind to take a gander. Follow that path through the weeds. When you finish, I'll be in the kitchen."

Tail wagging, Bella led me past the Tilt-A-Whirl to a rickety shed. Inside, on a pile of straw, was a heap of beagle puppies snuggled in so tightly it was hard to tell where one began and the others ended. One woke up when he heard us enter and whimpered when he saw his mother. She settled down next to them, and I did the same. They were so warm...so tiny. Before long, I had a lap full of six wriggling, nuzzling puppies and forgot all about Henry until he joined me there. Hunkering down next to us, he pulled a bit of straw out of my hair and smiled.

"Might be you could use one of them when they get old enough. Make a good watchdog. Got a voice like a bugle. Don't hunt no more, and Bella is about all the dog I need. Whichever one you choose is goin' to be right smart like his mama. Goin' back inside. Join me when you're good and ready."

"Coming now," I told him as I stood up and brushed off my jeans. I followed him back to his cozy kitchen with its knotty pine walls and cupboards. A wood-burning stove crouched in the corner. Next to it were two rockers with matching cushions and a basket of yarn, which made me wonder where Henry's wife was.

"Take a load off and tell me how it's goin'," he told me as he pulled out a chair at the table for me and took the one next to it.

"Well, last night was my first one there," I began to tell him as he poured the coffee and shoved a mug my way.

"And how did that go?" he asked as his bright blue eyes watched me closely.

"Not so well. Heard things."

"Like what kinda things?"

"A clock chiming...a baby crying...whispers...that kind of thing. Saw a shadowy something that smelled like seaweed. I really need to know more about the house, and the people who lived there."

"You told me you already knew about the shipwreck and why the house got built where it did. The missus went crazy as a loon after they moved in there. Kept hearing her babe what had been lost at sea cryin' at night. Began carryin' a doll around with her and talkin' to it. Ended up hangin' herself in that front parlor on his birthday."

He hesitated then continued. "Horace remarried 'bout two years later. It were said she was a prim and proper madam. Most wondered how it was she ever gave birth to a daughter. Ever let old Horace.... Well, you get my drift. Anyway, her pa treasured her. She could draw most anything as soon as she could hold a pencil, and he encouraged her painting. Her ma was another story. Was said to be jealous...spiteful. Drove the old man away with her constant naggin' and complainin'. Left on the morning of his daughter's sixteenth birthday and never returned."

He hesitated again then added, "The next part is God's truth...no rumor...no village gossip. I can't quite remember how the daughter was called, but it will come to me. Anyway, she... Maddie....no, Millie found herself in a family way with no husband. It was during the first World War, and she'd fallen for a soldier who never came back. Kept mutterin' during the birth that his ship had been torpedoed just before Christmas, and he drowned. Her baby was born dead. She bled to death a few minutes later. Her ma kept it all hushed up 'cause of the scandal and no proper doctor was there though that was not uncommon back then. The midwife was someone she knew would keep her mouth shut for a price. Maybe it's this Millie's baby you hear?"

An overwhelming sadness had settled over me as he told his tale of loss and death. There were tears in my eyes when I asked, "How do you know all this, Henry, if it was such a big secret?"

He sighed heavily. "That midwife was my ma. She was educated but took to midwifin' after her family lost their money. Married Pa for some reason she soon regretted. This here house was where I mostly grew up when we settled down. She used to sit by the fire over there and talk to herself whenever she drank too much. Kept sayin' it were a secret she swore to keep. That there was far more to the tellin' that would never pass her lips. I used to listen from the hall. Never told no one what she said till now."

"And you never asked her what that was? Confronted her?"

He shrugged. "My ma weren't someone you *confronted* especially when she'd been drinkin'. 'Sides, they were all dead, and it didn't seem to matter none, so I let it be till now. There's been others that died there, too, including a couple of homeless guys in the attic. Natural causes it was said though there were those who thought differently."

31

"The Realtor didn't tell me about them or how Hannah Grey died," I told him wryly.

He snorted in disgust. "She wanted to unload the place, so she'd tell you most anything but the truth."

The conversation drifted on to other things. The grandson coming for the holiday. The *Old Farmers Almanac* predicting heavy snow earlier than usual. I was only half listening. At least five people including an infant had died in that house in hideous ways. It was a very troubling thought.

As I headed back home, I felt a strong tug of reluctance. Maybe I should just grab Cinda and get out of there while I could. Have it demolished and sell off the lots. I sighed. I couldn't do any of that. Someone wanted me there. *If* it was Allison as I hope and prayed it was, I owed her everything and wouldn't let her down. Just then, the house loomed up before me and a sudden coldness seemed to settle around my heart. It looked positively sinister. I had the distinct feeling it knew exactly what I was thinking. That it had been waiting for my return. That it wouldn't let me go that easily.

I checked on Cinda as soon as I got back. Cuddling her close, I wondered what might happen to her if we stayed and then remembered she had been Allison's cat. If she wanted me here, she wanted Cinda with me for whatever reason. "Or am I mad to think there is a rhyme or reason to any of this?" I asked her as I rubbed under her chin.

While we were sitting there, Joe entered and seemed clearly uncomfortable with what he was about to say.

"We all talked while you were gone. Seems this here house of yours is takin' a lot more time than any of us figured on when we first got here. Been findin' one thing after another and...." He sighed then continued, "There's another job we promised to be at by now. Up north where it's winter already. Shouldn't take mor'en a couple of weeks. We'd like to put this on hold and get back to it when we finish up there, but me and the boys don't like the thought of you all alone out here."

I was surprised at how his words had affected me. I felt bereft...lost. He had always anchored me with his no nonsense *let's get 'er done attitude* and now he was leaving.

Pasting on my most reassuring smile, I told him, "I'll be just fine, Joe. Not to worry at all about me. I spent last night here and came back for more. I'm a writer, and this old place is jump-starting my imagination. Maybe I'll write a best seller about the supposed ghosts of Greystone. When will you be leaving?"

"Like to leave tomorrow, which means we'll be packin' up at the end of the day. You have all the basics to keep you goin'. Furnace is workin' just fine. Should be plenty of heat in the rooms with the new vents. Might want to close off any you won't be needin'. I called Henry last night to give him a heads up. He'd be mor'en glad to drop on over if something gets broke. He can fix about anythin' and don't have to come far to get here."

I smiled again. "I paid him that visit and have his number now. I was wondering about his wife. I didn't see her there."

"She died a long time ago. He never got over it."

"How heartbreaking for him," I replied remembering the basket of yarn sitting there as though she had just stepped away for a moment that had turned into years. "They must have loved each other deeply. I'll give him a call if I need him once my phone is working. Stop by on your way out, Joe, and I'll write you a check that will catch us up to date."

"No need. We'll settle up later. I know you're good for it. Just be safe!" He looked at me as though he wanted to say more but shook his head and left.

I hugged Cinda again then told her, "Looks like it's just you and me now. Wait here while I close those vents. Some of the rooms really give me the creeps, so I'd rather have Joe still here while I do it."

I left Cinda curled up on the window seat, closed the door then headed down the hall checking the vents as I went till I reached the front parlor with its big bay window. It faced east, and I'd been hoping for a view of the sea when the trees were bare. Now I knew the first Mrs. Grey had died there.

Suddenly, it struck me. I had never taken that trail that led to the sea and wasn't sure why. It should have been the first thing I did! Now the urge to go there was nothing short of overwhelming.

I left through the front door and headed for the leaf-covered trail that cut through the trees. The wind had a sharp edge, and I was glad I wore a warm sweater. Off to the left, the mountains were half hidden in a blue haze and capped with a ridge of dark clouds. I passed a sign that read: *State Land No Trespassing* and continued on. With each step, the sound of the surf...the smell of the sea grew stronger and then there it was! An immense stretch of indigo blue water that rushed up on shore in a froth of white leaving a mirror for the sky with each wave's ebb. I found a large boulder to perch on out of their reach and smiled. It was so beautiful. A painter's dream and then I remembered that Millie had been an artist. Millie who had died in Greystone. She must have come here often. I could almost picture her...wind blowing her copper colored hair...her gray eyes narrowed as she scanned the endless expanse of water that seemed to touch forever.

I laughed. I had no way of knowing what she looked like. It was me I had imagined. I had put myself in her place. Suddenly, an intense feeling of loss and despair settled over me. She had loved and lost both her soldier and his stillborn baby, but she must have had a life before that. A happy one if her father loved her. I never had a father I remembered or a mother until Allison found me. She had loved me very much, and I had a promise to keep that for some reason had brought me to Greystone.

Jumping down from my rock, I reluctantly headed back to the house where the night with its ghosts would come soon enough.

CHAPTER TWO

(Millie-April, 1918)

*A full moon rides the night sky lighting this place where I stand
with its strange bright clarity. I don't remember how I got here, but
I am back on the shore... listening to the fierce pound of the timeless
waves...the shriek of the wind off the icy water. I should be cold, but
I'm not. It must be a dream, I think, as I look down at the snow
covering my bare feet. There's blood there...blood on my
hands...blood down the front of my nightgown. Where had it come
from? Something bad...something new and terrible had happened I
can't quite remember. It's there...teasing me...a shadowy memory
that comes and goes without distinct shape or form. I sigh. It will
come when it comes, and I will regret it...of that I am sure, so I turn
my attention to the endless stretch of turbulent, moon silvered water.*

*I had often turned to the sea for solace. Escaped to it every chance
I found. Sometimes I just sat there absorbing its intense, awesome
beauty. Sometimes I walked along the edge letting the incoming
waves lick at my bare legs or waded out into its depths. Sometimes I
explored the caves.*

*One was above the reach of the waves and high tides that came
with the new and full moon, so I had chosen it for my secret place.
My sanctuary where I could escape from her. Bit by bit, I had
brought the things I needed...a lantern...blankets...a discarded
chair...an old comforter I painstakingly ripped open and stuffed with
straw to form a makeshift mattress. I had kept my art supplies there*

well covered from the elements and safe from her. She had always hated my painting...called it "the devil's work", so after Papa left......

I shake my head to clear my thoughts from the dark place they were headed and let my mind drift back to the time spent with him...my Eric.

From the very beginning, it felt like our stars had destined us to meet and fall in love. He had visited Courage Cove often as a boy and had friends there he wanted to see again before he reported to duty. The golden retriever he was walking that morning had belonged to one of them. We had met every day after that. I showed him my secret cave where we lay in each other's arms as he shared bits and pieces from his world, because there was little to tell of mine, but soon we began to share our secret thoughts and dreams. When the war was over, he wanted to build us a house by the sea. We planned it room by room. Our some day house.

I was far happier than I had ever dreamed possible. She must have noticed the change and began to watch me closely...check on my movements. It became more and more difficult to escape except at night when she slept. Each of those long summer nights was precious to us. Sometimes we danced at the water's edge or shared a bottle of wine in our sanctuary and watched the storm thrashed water below... the lead bellied clouds tearing across the sky...tasted the salt spray on our lips when we kissed.

It was on our last night together that I asked him to make love to me when he had wanted us to wait.

"I don't care about the consequences," I had told him as I pulled him into my arms. "I need to remember this night forever."

We had made love through the hours that followed with the sound of the restless sea all around us. The sea that claimed him just before what would have been our first Christmas together if there hadn't been a war. But he had unknowingly given me his gift before he left. The life within me and....

Suddenly, I remember it all! The reason I am here! The reason I am covered in blood! I had just given birth to the fruit of our love...a stillborn son...the precious baby who had kept me alive when I had wanted to walk into the sea. I had followed him in death. We were beyond her reach now. She couldn't hurt us any more.

A bubble of grief wells up in my throat. As though from a great distance, I hear someone wail. It must be me. That woman who screams, and shouts, and cries. That woman who lost everyone she had ever loved. Now all she can do is wait and pray their spirits will return by some miracle, for that is what it would take. May God be merciful.

(Jodie-The Present)

Joe and his crew were loading their trucks around back when I returned. "Thought we'd take off a bit early," he told me when I reached them. "Got quite a drive ahead of us. Don't hesitate to give Henry a call. He's a good guy...honest and reliable... or I wouldn't be tellin' you that. Be back soon as we can. Just be safe. Ain't no shame in you gettin' the hell outta there if something bad happens."

I wished him safe travels and watched them drive away then looked up at the house. Much had changed since the first time I saw it. Broken windows had been replaced...the chimneys and roof repaired. The thick tangle of now winter dead roses had proved impossible to cut back. I admired their tenacity and wondered how many blooms I would have next year after my amateur pruning efforts. I smiled ruefully. Would I even be here next year or for that matter last the night?

I was delaying going back inside, but Cinda was now alone in there. Taking a deep breath, I headed for the kitchen door then made my way to the dining room where I found her still lying on the window seat. She always reminded me of Allison. Of course she was her cat and that was only natural, but it was more than that. Sometimes it seemed like she was *inside* her looking through her golden eyes, and I wondered if their souls had fused after her death as absurd as that sounded even to me.

"Looks like it's just you and me, kitty, for the foreseeable future," I told her as I scratched between her ears. "Let's go check out my computer and see if *someone somewhere* did *something,* and we finally have Internet."

She chirped once then followed me out the door with her black tail raised high like a pirate flag till we reached the small study that had been turned into my work station. The landline was now active, but I still had no Internet, which meant research from that source would have to wait.

"But the library in the village must have computers," I told Cinda who had perched loaf style on top my printer. She blinked once as though she understood, and I smiled. "Let's head there and see how that works out. Might grab us a pizza on the way home. You know how much you love the cheese."

I loaded her and the things she would need in her carrier then carried it out to the car since I would never leave her alone at Greystone. By then, the temperature had plummeted, and clouds now covered the sun, so I flipped on the heater as soon as I slid behind the wheel.

In the time it took to reach the village, I thought about what I hoped to find regarding Allison's roots. To date, I knew that the orphanage where she had been 'dumped' as an infant had been destroyed in a fire that killed eight children and two caregivers. The memories she shared of that place were sketchy at best. It was a painful time she didn't want to relive, and I understood perfectly. She had told me I would find what I needed for her biography inside the pages of her journals that had yet to reach me. I had delayed sending for them, because I hadn't been ready to reopen Allison's past when I couldn't move past her loss. Now I was.

Reaching Main Street, I drove past the little shops where few tourists were visible. Summer vacationers and autumn 'leaf peepers' were long gone, and it was too early for skiers though that could soon change if the temperature dropped much lower. I took a side turn just past the flower shop and parked in front of the old Victorian house that served as the library.

"I can't leave you out here in the cold, so I'm going to try the impossible...talk a librarian into breaking the rules," I told Cinda as I unloaded her carrier and headed for the front door where I pushed my way inside. From there, I made my way to the front desk and I told the prim looking Librarian with the sleek gray bun and wire rim spectacles, "I need to use your computers and can't leave my cat in the car. She's very well behaved. Won't make a peep and....."

She broke in at that point with, "Of course, you can't leave your kitty in the car. She'd freeze her whiskers off! I'm predicting snow by morning. You can leave her behind my desk, and no one will be any the wiser."

My face must have reflected my astonishment, because she smiled and tapped her nametag. "I may look like a stereotype, but I'm far from it. I'm Alice Cooper...no relation to the rock star of the same name...and known as the Crazy Cat Lady of Courage Cove. You haven't been here before, so here's a membership form. You can hand it in on your way out. Meanwhile, Puss Puss and I will get acquainted."

I introduced myself and Cinda then headed for the computers sandwiched between rows of bookshelves. After I signed in, I took the only empty seat and began my search which soon turned up a photo of the grim looking orphanage named Second Chance...a few black and whites of unsmiling children lined up in orderly rows, and a head shot of a dour Mr. and Mrs. Flint who ran the place for years until their grandson took over. It was on his watch the fire occurred. Faulty wiring according to the fire department's report I read. It had gone up quickly during the night, and it had been nothing short of a miracle they had managed to save as many as they had. The building had been leveled...nothing had survived the fire.

I printed out everything that might be useful which wasn't much. I had been hoping that the records had been saved by some miracle. That her file would give me a description of what she'd been wearing...her physical condition...her estimated age when she had landed on their doorstep plus other information about her that would have been immensely helpful. Now I had next to nothing.

My disappointment must have shown, when I returned to Alice at the front desk. "Looks like you didn't find what you want, Jodie. Meant to ask if you were a relative of our Allison Shield. A famous writer. Grew up in the orphanage here and became the pride of this village."

I told her I was her adopted daughter and looking for information, so that I could write her biography. She nodded then smiled and told me, "Just happen to know someone who could help with that. My mother spent some years in Second Chance. Seems her folks couldn't care for her and left her there till their circumstances improved... which they didn't. She might be able to tell you more if you catch her on a good day. She's near on ninety-four and has dementia. Breaks my heart. Used to be sharp as a tack. Still has flashes of lucidity."

"I'd love to meet her. I'm staying at Greystone and can be here any time that's convenient for her."

She pushed up her glasses with her forefinger and shook her head. "I'll bet there's not a person in this whole village that doesn't know you're out there and wish it weren't true. It's a sinister place on a good day...never mind what it is at night. I know you already sunk a fortune in it...restoring it and all...but you're only waking the devil. There's evil there, child, and that's not this old woman's wild imaginings."

She tried for fifteen more minutes to dissuade me...even offered me a room in her own house till I found something more appropriate...but I shook my head and told her, "I need to be there. Not sure how I know that, but there it is. When would be a good time to see your mother?"

We arranged a time for tomorrow, which was Saturday. Gathering up a sleeping Cinda, I thanked Alice for all her help and headed back outside. It was much colder, and I feared her prediction would come true. There would be snow by morning if not before. I had grown up where there was snow, but hadn't driven in it. Oliver had taught me how to drive the limo that first summer, and I had honed my skills in warmer climes adventuring with Allison when she didn't want to take the wheel.

Since I had stayed longer at the library than I had intended, dark was closing in fast when I stopped for a carry out pizza. We had just left the lights of the village behind, when the first snowflakes drifted lazily down. Reaching Greystone, I lugged Cinda's carrier into the kitchen then returned to the car for the pizza. I was just heading back when I saw a flash of light in an upper window. I couldn't quite place the room...just knew it was one we hadn't renovated yet. Someone or *something* was up there, and a cold shiver raced up my spine that had nothing to do with the now sub freezing temperature. All of me wanted to get back in that car and keep driving, but Cinda was inside and not alone.

I was running when I reached the door and threw it open. To my surprise, Cinda was sitting on the counter when I had left her inside her carrier. She was purring, loudly, and dividing her attention between me and something in the far corner.

"Who's there?" I called hoping with all my heart no one would answer. No one did. By then, Cinda had turned her attention to the pizza box I still carried. She was back to normal, and I breathed a sigh of relief. Had it been Allison in the room with us? Whoever it had been wasn't evil, or Cinda would have reacted differently.

I sat at the table and ate a now cold pizza while Cinda, alternately, chowed down on her kibbles and begged for cheese. Sticking the leftovers in the fridge, I made sure the outer door was locked then grabbed a flashlight and headed for the back stairs with Cinda sprinting on ahead. I remembered all too well the light I had seen in the window earlier as I reached the top and looked around. The hall was totally dark when I had left the lamp on and the door open to my bedroom that morning. Again, I sensed a presence. Cinda did, too. Uttering a long hiss and a low growl, I felt her tail twitch against my ankles just as the dark shadows at the edge of my light solidified into a human shape. It was distorted...constantly shifting and changing. Only the eyes remained the same. Red and malevolent.

44

"It will not be now. I will choose the when and where," came the hoarse whisper from the roiling mass of darkness as it began to wrap itself around me then thinned and vanished.

Heart hammering wildly, I sped down the hall at a flat out run with Cinda leading the way. Reaching what I hoped was safety, I slammed my bedroom door shut, locked it, and turned on the light. Cinda had disappeared under the bed. I joined her there a few moments later after stuffing the rolled up rug under the door to prevent shadow seepage.

Lying there with a still badly frightened Cinda, I thought about what I had seen...felt. It was a different entity than the one in the kitchen, or the one I had seen the previous night. This one was pure evil, and I wanted it gone.

"Maybe Alice will know someone who does 'cleansings' or whatever they call it," I murmured to myself just as something brushed my cheek. At first, I thought it was a long thread snagged in a splinter, but on closer examination it turned out to be a human hair brittle with age. Time had faded the color till it was indiscernible. It might have been brown or even some shade of red. Apparently, I wasn't the first to take refuge under this bed. I had chosen it for its carved roses. Could it be that it had once belonged here, or was that further wild imagining on my part? The odds were certainly against it, but still?

I remained where I was with Cinda snuggled against me, as I listened for noises in the room. There were none. Whatever had been out in the hall hadn't followed us inside...thankfully. I hesitated for a long time then took a deep steadying breath and crawled out from underneath.

"Jodie Shield!" I told myself sternly as I rose to my feet and looked around, "You are not a frightened child any more! You will sleep on top the bed like a normal adult. It is your room...your house and no one is going to make you leave."

Of course, my pep talk was based on a lie. I was terrified, but I had made a promise and planned on keeping it. Alison wanted me here at Greystone. Of that, I was *almost* certain though there was no possible connection that I could see except her love of roses.

Still dressed, I kicked off my sneakers and crawled beneath the heavy covers where Cinda joined me. I stroked her silky fur and listened to her rumbling purr that stopped, abruptly, like a thrown switch when she fell asleep a few minutes later. Somewhere very close, I heard a baby cry and then nothing more as sleep claimed me.

It was sometime during the night that a dream found me only half remembered when I woke up to the pale gray light that pushed through the frosted window panes. Something to do with a cave overlooking the sea...something to do with a young woman who felt like me, but wasn't. Was she this Millie Henry had told me about?

"It was just a dream," I told myself as I crawled, reluctantly, from the warm comfort of my bed.

Taking the top cover with me, I padded to the window and looked outside. Everything had been transformed by a thick layer of snow that had fallen silently all through the night. It was beautiful. A magic blanket that hid all that was scarred or ugly.

It was then I noticed Cinda had jumped down and was playing with something on the floor. It was a seashell that I picked up and turned over in my hand as I wondered who had left it there for me to find. Was it the one in my dream? Was it this Millie who had died here and might still remain? Or was it Hannah Grey whose baby had drowned not far from here? All I had to date were questions and lots of them. What I needed were answers and hoped I would find them before I ran screaming out of there.

Still wrapped in my blanket, I made my way down the hall to the service stairs with Cinda racing on ahead. It was almost warm in the kitchen. While I made a quick breakfast for both of us, Cinda headed to the dining room and litter box number 2. She was as regular as clockwork, which made it much easier on both of us since I had to take her everywhere I went including the upcoming meeting with Alice's mom. It had been arranged for 9 am, and I wondered if I would learn anything new.

"If all else fails, maybe one of them knows someone who can help with the haunting here," I told Cinda when she returned a few moments later and began munching her kibbles after she checked out what I had on my plate.

I left the dishes and headed upstairs where I dressed quickly. A short time later, we were out the door. The snow wasn't deep...maybe six inches...though it had drifted much higher in places. From the gray clouds churning overhead, I knew there was a good chance more would come. As if the sky had heard my thoughts, a few flakes floated down as I loaded the carrier and threaded the seat belt through the bars to keep it in place should something happen. Taking a deep steadying breath, I climbed behind the wheel and slowly pulled away.

After a few miles, my confidence grew, and I dared take my eyes off the road long enough to look around at the transformed landscape. It was beautiful. The snow had added a special kind of magic to everything it covered. The world had become one giant snow globe. I smiled at that image then frowned. What a horrible fate that would be! Trapped forever inside a prison of glass. Would I end up trapped forever in a prison of stone? It was a troubling thought that had come out of nowhere and haunted me till I reached the village.

Main Street had been plowed, but snow still covered those sidewalks that hadn't been cleared yet. Alice's house was just on the outskirts, and I pulled up in front of a gray cottage with blue shutters. I was a bit later than planned and hoped that wouldn't be a problem. Unloading Cinda, I carried her up the shoveled, but still slippery steps, to the porch where Alice greeted me at the door.

"Hurry on through, so we can shut out this dang cold," she told me as she ushered me inside. "I told Mother to expect you. She's having one of her good days. Glad you brought Cinda with you. Wouldn't want her out there at Greystone all by her lonesome."

"Nor I. We had a bad experience last night, but then another not bad at all."

"You can tell me all about it after I take you in to meet Mother. She gets agitated if she hears unfamiliar voices in the house. Why

48

don't you open that carrier and let Cinda roam about? No mischief she can get into, and my old cats would be glad of a new face."

I opened the door, but she seemed content where she was, so I left her there and followed Alice into the kitchen. A very elderly woman in a shocking pink robe was sitting at the table cradling a cup in her hands and talking to herself. Her blue eyes were bright with curiosity when she noticed me standing there.

"Come sit by me, pretty thing. Did you come to clean the house or rob it? Not much here worth taking. Used to be. Come closer. Promise I won't bite. Haven't got the teeth for it these days," she told me with a chuckle.

She didn't seem all that lucid to me, I thought, as Alice introduced us then said, "She's the girl I told you about, Mother. She wants to know about Second Chance and what you remember of Allison."

Her eyes lost their focus, and her blue veined hands fiddled with her spoon.

Alice sighed. "She's off for a bit, but she'll be back. Take a seat while I make us a fresh pot of coffee."

I sat down next to her mother and watched her out of the corner of my eye. She was muttering something now I couldn't hear and then she grabbed my hand. Her grip was surprisingly strong, and I was afraid pulling away would tip the scales in the wrong direction, so I folded my other hand over hers then told her, "Everything is all right. You are safe and at home with your daughter. I'm a friend. Allison sent me."

She smiled. "Ally. They found her on the doorstep like in some book. I were about four or five...don't know which. She weren't more than a tiny babe. Weak and skinny. They didn't think she'd live, but she fooled 'em all and did. She sent me letters sometimes after we both grew up and left. Calls herself Allison somethin' or other I can't remember, but that's not her real last name."

"What was her real name? Did she have any identification on her when she was dropped off?"

A puzzled frown drew her thick brows down to a 'v' and then she said, "There was a note pinned to her. I heard the Matron say what it was, but I can't quite remember."

"Please try! It's very important!"

She shook her head. "It's there and then it's gone. No wait! She said...'there weren't no Bogarts in this neck of the woods'. Tea's cold. Ready for my program now. Alice!" she bellowed then struggled to her feet.

Alice thrust her cane in her hand then led her towards the door as she told me over her shoulder, "Let me get her settled. Be right back."

I leaned forward with my head in my hands. I had learned that her name had been Allison Bogart *if* Alice's mother remembered correctly. At some point in time, she had it changed to Allison Shield. No doubt I would learn more about that in the journals when they reached me.

I remembered she had told me more than once that they contained names best not mentioned though all were now dead. "There were

50

mistakes made...lessons learned and not learned. I have a history I hope some might find interesting if a bit salacious...maybe more than a *bit*. It will be your job to piece it all together."

Increasingly, she repeated what she wanted me to remember as though I would ever forget. I had been holding her hand on the night that she died when she finally told me, "I should have gone back to find my roots years ago, but it was too painful, and I am a coward. Find out who I am, Jodie...who my parents were then make me live again between the pages of your book."

My eyes had filled with tears when Cinda walked into the kitchen followed by two very large ginger tabbies and a small black and white cat with three legs. She jumped into my lap and looked up at me with her golden eyes. It was almost as though she knew where my thoughts had been and wanted to comfort me. The moment was brief. After a quick head butt to my chin, she jumped down and ran back out the door with her entourage in close pursuit.

Alice passed them in the doorway. "Looks like she met the tribe," she told me with a smile. "She'd be more than welcome to stay here whenever you need to leave her."

"Lugging her around isn't making either one of us happy, so I probably will take you up on that. How's your mom?"

"Tucked her in her recliner and put on her favorite TV quiz show. She'll be fine till lunch and then a nap afterwards. I have someone stay with her when I'm not here, or she'd turn on the stove and burn the house down," she replied as she poured us both a cup of coffee and sat down across the table from me.

"The only real information I got from your mom was that her name had been Allison Bogart when she was dropped off at Second Chance. That she wrote to your mother over the years. If she still has those letters, they might be very useful."

"I'll see what I can find and get them to you if they still exist. Now back to what happened last night at Greystone. Tell me everything."

So, I did....well, most of it. I wasn't proud of crawling under the bed. She was quiet as she listened and then took my hand in hers. "There's evil there, and you met it. Surely, you won't go back. There's plenty of room here... even a place where you can work on Allison's biography undisturbed till you find a place of your own, and Cinda has already made herself quite at home."

I sighed. "I don't know why I'm at Greystone. I only know...or think I know that Allison wants me there. But I would really, really like the evil purged if there is a way."

It was Alice's turn to sigh. "Well, child, I might know someone who could help. Name's Jennie Tanner. Lives a couple of blocks over and should be there since it's Saturday. She might know a way to get it done or at least offer some suggestions on how to protect yourself. Finish your coffee and I'll give her a call. Might mention, she's a 'dog person' with an oversized Irish wolfhound boxer mix she found at the shelter. Best you leave Cinda here."

I had no trouble finding Jennie's place when I left a short time later. It was a simple brick ranch, which came as a surprise. For some reason, I was expecting her to live in a rambling Victorian that looked haunted. She was even more of a surprise. Nothing supernatural or mysterious about her, I thought, as she greeted me in sweatpants and a heavy sweater with a patch on the sleeve.

"Come on in," she told me. "Watch out for Brutus. He can be a bit much if he likes you."

Apparently, he did as he barreled out of the hall and jumped up on me nearly knocking me over. His yellow eyes were level with mine when Jennie told him sharply, "Down, Brutus!"

He looked from me to her then complied with every sign of reluctance. "That's some dog you have there!" I somehow managed to tell her.

"He's just a big overgrown baby no one wanted. Alice told me why you're here. Let's go back to the kitchen and grab a cup of coffee while you tell me all about it."

I didn't want to tell her I was already on caffeine overload, so I followed her to her little kitchen painted a warm terra cotta.

"Have a seat over there at the table...just push aside the junk piled up. Doing some crafting for the Christmas Bazaar down at the church."

I carefully moved the Styrofoam balls dusted in glitter and the bits of felt she'd been fashioning into angels. She joined me a moment later with two earthenware mugs in her hands.

"Cream and sugar?" she asked brightly as she studied me closely.

"Black is fine," I replied with a smile.

53

She sat down across from me and dug under her craft pile till she found the sugar bowl then added three heaping teaspoons to her own mug. As she stirred it in, she told me, "I don't like the idea of you staying at Greystone any more than Alice does. It's a bad place."

I smiled ruefully. "No one seems happy I'm living there. Please tell me what you know about it."

She sighed then began. "I was about fourteen when a bunch of us the kids from school went out there on a Halloween dare. It was spookier than hell. We all camped out in the front room with the bay window. Curled up in our sleeping bags and waited to see what happened. There was a clock chiming somewhere, and a baby crying. I was the only one who heard any of it, and the others told me I was just making it up to scare them. I also saw shadows moving around and heard whispers no one else did. Suddenly, I felt a sense of profound evil. The really, really scary kind. I was beyond terrified, and about to warn the others, when Jasmine Hodge screamed and headed for the door at a run. The rest of us were right behind her. She told us later that someone had touched her...a cold, bony hand. It took two weeks for us to get up the courage and return for our gear. Even in daylight, that old house felt malevolent."

"I know exactly how you must have felt. There is evil there, but also something else. A presence I think may be my adopted mother, Allison Shield."

"The famous writer. Alice told me you were related. I read some of her books. A bit over my head at times, but she had a way with a story. Alice told me she'd been an orphan at Second Chance, but why would she be at Greystone?"

"I've felt ever since I first saw that house that I am meant to be there. That she wants me there though I don't know why. I think she's trying to protect me from the evil that's within those walls, but don't know if she will be enough. Is there some way to cleanse the house...purge it?"

Her mouth tightened, and her brown eyes were troubled. It was a long time before she answered me. "You could try having it cleansed with burnt sage. Sometimes that works. Another might be to hold a séance and see who turns up. Find out what they want. I'll tell you flat out that this chick won't be doing any of that. I won't set foot inside that house ever again!"

For a moment, I'd been hopeful. My acute disappointment must have been evident because she told me, "Sorry to tell you that. You seem like a nice person, and I would like to help you. The best I can do is give you the number of someone called Simon North. He *might* help but there's no guarantee. He's into paranormal research and occasionally does some investigating."

"Any relation to Henry North?"

"His grandson."

I smiled wryly. "'*Might be helpful*' suggests I can't rely on him. Is there some way I can protect myself and my cat?"

"So, you're a cat person," she told me with a smile. "I will tell you they can see what you cannot. Be very sensitive to changes in its behavior and pray you are right about your mother. That she is there to look after you."

We talked a bit after that. She told me about some of the other hauntings she had helped with then gave me this Simon's number before I left.

Back at Alice's, I stayed for lunch and related everything Jennie had told me.

"Too bad that didn't work out the way we both wanted," Alice told me when I had finished. "Jennie doesn't frighten easily, so I can only imagine what you must be going through out there. Please reconsider and stay here with me. I would be very glad for the company. As you saw, Mother, isn't much of a conversationalist these days. You can have Daphne's room. She was my daughter."

There was so much pain in her eyes when she uttered those four words that I knew something tragic had happened. A moment later, she drew in a deep breath and confided, "She was killed by a drunk driver the night of her senior prom. Her room is just as she left it. I know she wouldn't mind sharing it with you."

I thanked her but declined. I had to go back to Greystone and wanted to get there way before dark. She delayed me as long as she could hoping she would change my mind, but finally I collected Cinda and headed out.

The snow had been light, and there was no significant accumulation as I drove through the village and cut through the countryside. The snow globe image crossed my mind again. The magic had taken on a sinister dimension I was hoping would dissipate with time, or it would be a very long winter. When we finally reached Greystone, I saw two sets of tire tracks and wondered who had come and gone. The phone rang a short time later, and my question was answered.

"Came by to check on you," Henry told me. "Joe said he had to leave for a spell, and I thought I'd stop on by and see how you're doin'. First real cold snap and snow we've had. Good thing you got yourself a new furnace."

I found myself telling him what Alice's mother and Jennie Tanner had told me including what I'd learned about his grandson. He listened quietly then replied, "Looks like you got some useful information if you can figure out what to do with it. Simon plans on stayin' with me for the upcomin' Christmas holiday, so he might know a way to help you out. Worth a try any way."

Before we ended the call, he promised to drop by for dinner tomorrow night. I found myself smiling. Surely, his grandson would help me if Henry asked him to and then I remembered how many long nights I'd need to survive at Greystone till Christmas rolled around. A lump of dread settled in the pit of my stomach.

I finished up the leftover pizza for supper then went to my study where I snatched up a biography I planned to read and headed upstairs with Cinda running on ahead. We took the main staircase this time. It was already getting dark, and I didn't want to risk bumping into the terrifying entity we'd encountered last night in the upper hall near the service stairs.

Once inside my room, I took the usual precautions the headed to the bathroom where I picked up the shell I had found earlier and left on the sink.

Picking it up, I looked it over then noticed Cinda behaving strangely. She was staring at a spot just to my left, purring loudly then head butting an invisible someone only she could see. The temperature plummeted, and my frozen breath hung in the air. Suddenly, the fogged over bathroom mirror cleared, and I saw Allison, as I last remembered her, standing right behind me.

"Be warned, my child. There is great evil here that wants to harm you both," she whispered then vanished.

"Don't leave me!" I cried as I pressed my hand against the cold glass just as another image appeared.

She was about my age and wearing a long, white nightgown soaked down the front in what could only be blood. Her tangled, copper colored hair framed a pale oval face, and her eyes were the saddest I had ever seen. Then she, too, was gone, and I was staring at my own reflection.

"You must be Millie Grey," I called after her hoping she was still listening. "Henry told me about you and what happened here. My name is Jodie. I won't harm you. Perhaps we can be friends?" There was no answer. Not that I had really expected one, but she could be of immense help in solving the mystery of Greystone *if* she would trust me enough to share what she knew. It was then I remembered my dream of the sea. Maybe she was trying to do just that.

A short time later, I was in bed with my book and Cinda. The biography I was reading was well written by an author I knew. I had been curious to see how it was structured, since I would be starting Allison's soon. The opening had been strong...the following chapter less so. Drowsiness overtook me, and the book fell from my hands. Soon I was fast asleep.

CHAPTER THREE

(Millie-The Present)

I had showed her what I looked like in the mirror, and she hadn't been afraid. Now she lies curled up in my bed with her cat. This Jodie who wants to be my friend lives here now when I am no more than a wraith wandering through these halls. Perhaps I will leave now for a while and go to my secret cave. Away from this mausoleum...this crypt. Perhaps he will be there this time. His lost spirit returned from his watery grave. I remember the day I learned the news of his death.

I was headed home from the shore on a cold December day. The house had just come into view, when I saw a black car pull away. There were two men inside wearing uniforms. Khaki colored Army uniforms. My heart seemed to stop. They wouldn't have come unless he had died. Screaming, crying I began to run back to the sea. I would walk into its cold waters. Join him in death and then I felt the first stirring of life inside me. The tiniest flutter. The awakening of the son I knew I carried.

I had turned around and walked back to the house. Mother now knew my secret, and I feared what she might do. I opened the front door, quietly, hoping to escape to my room, but she was waiting for me. I remember her words. Every one. Her eyes were like chips of blue ice when she said, "Filthy, deceitful sinner! Your so-called fiancé is dead. Hideously burned then drowned when his transport ship was torpedoed by a U-Boat. That ends that. Should there be any consequences of your illicit liaisons, I will handle it. Meanwhile, you will not leave this house. I would rather see you just as dead before there is a hint of scandal attached to this family."

I wept myself to sleep that night and all the nights that followed. Each morning, I woke up to the reality of his death sitting there grimly waiting. The dreams in between were all I lived for...dreams of him and our secret life that was a secret no more. I was locked in my room as soon as I began to show. This room. That could be me lying there in that very bed that somehow found its way back here as impossible as that seems.

She is getting sleepy now. This Jodie who promised not to harm me. The book she was reading just fell from her hands. I will not leave her tonight. I will stay and watch over her. Help her if my mother comes though I will need the aid of the others here. The lost souls trapped between these walls. Some of them are angry...some merely sad. I cannot let this Jodie join us.

60

Ah, she just fell asleep, and I will kiss her cheek ever so softly...stroke the cat that snuggles next to her and watches me with her golden eyes. The first living things I have touched in a very long time. Funny how time becomes of little consequence. The hours, days, minutes, years all meld into nothing. There! The clock chimes again as though it heard my thoughts. The grandfather in the parlor that is no more. Calling out the hour of midnight. The time of birth and death. I still have not found my baby's spirit...Eric has still not returned...but now I have a third reason to stay in this evil place. These two precious beings I already love.

(Jodie)

I don't know what woke me. The bedside light was out when I knew I had left it on as I always did. "Maybe there's a power outage," I told myself as I lay there with the dark pressing down on me like a physical thing. I searched for Cinda and found her huddled next to me. She hissed loudly then growled that strange kind of low growl cats do. She was terrified. Something was there with us.

"It's okay," I murmured to her as I offered her refuge under the covers, which she refused. It wasn't anywhere close to "okay" but neither one of us needed to hear that.

Listening intently to the sounds around me, I tried to label each one. *That* howl was just the sound of the wind finding its way inside every crack and crevice. *That* was the settling creak of an old house, which reminded me Joe had said there was a problem with the cellar wall. *That* was the mystery clock striking somewhere in the house. It was always midnight in whatever realm it was keeping score.

61

Okay. Nothing out of the ordinary at least in my room, I thought, and then I heard someone laugh. It was maniacal...the cackle of the truly insane just as a glowing, red mist began to form at the foot of the bed. Slowly, it took human shape. Churning and sending out shoots of red light in all directions, it rose slowly until it hovered over me. The stench was terrible! Dead things. Rotting things. Narrowed red eyes peered down at me as closer and closer it came until less than a yard separated us. The rest of its face was a blur like something seen through a fog and then it spoke in a sibilant whisper, "I want you dead like us. You and that filthy beast."

Tail thrashing, Cinda hissed and launched herself at the glowing entity that caught her midway and tossed her to the floor. Despite my intense fear, there was no way I would let it hurt Cinda.

"Touch her again!" I shouted, "And I will...."

"What? Kill me? You stupid girl! I am going to suck the life from you. You will stay here forever just like the others until the time comes to end you all."

Its face began to take shape. The enraged face of a woman, or what was left of one, which wasn't all that much. Just bits of flesh and white hair clinging to a skull. Drool dripped from her now gaping mouth. Every tooth was long, pointy, and yellowed with age. Her black tongue snaked out just as a spire of white light appeared. Three more joined it to form a prismatic shield between me and the horrific thing above me.

Her tongue snapped back with a 'snick' and she snarled, "You've quite put me out of the mood with your meddling, Millicent!" she

62

screamed. "I'll make you all sorry!" and with that said she shot upwards and disappeared through the ceiling.

Cinda jumped back in bed just as the shield broke down into rainbow orbs that disappeared as suddenly as they had come. All but one.

"That must be you, Millie. Thank you for saving us," I told her, "You and the others."

"I could not save you without their help. She is stronger than any one of us," she replied in a hollow voice that seemed to come from everywhere. "She will never rest till she has your soul and brings an end to the one you call Cinda."

"I need to be here. In this place."

There was a long sigh followed by, "I know. She will not be back again tonight. You are safe for now."

For a brief moment, I saw her again as she had appeared in the mirror and then she, too, vanished. The light came back on, and I looked around the room. It was just as it had always been. No stench. No sign at all that anyone had ever been there.

"What just happened? Did I dream the whole thing?" I asked Cinda. "Am I even awake now or is this a dream within a nightmare?"

She stretched out one paw as if to reassure me then yawned. Moments later, she was asleep. I listened again to the sounds around me. All was quiet. The wind had died down... the clock was silent. Drowsiness slowly overtook me when I had been willing to bet I would never sleep again.

***

Cinda had a very unnerving way of waking me up when she thought it was past time for breakfast. Ever so carefully, she would bat at my eyelids till I opened them. A loud meow usually followed. Today was no exception.

"Okay! Okay! Okay!" I told her as I stroked her soft black fur then poured myself from bed and padded to the bathroom with her right on my heels. Wrapped in my thick bathrobe and wearing my fuzzy warm slippers, I headed downstairs a short time later.

Instead of running on ahead, Cinda stayed close and seemed unusually agitated which left me wondering if the incident last night had been real after all. I so wanted to believe it was nothing more than a nightmare. I had had them in the past. Things that lurked in my subconscious would appear in my dreams and scare the crap out of me. My imagination must have conjured up last night's horrific episode from what I now knew about the house and its previous occupants. To believe otherwise would send me flying out of Greystone as fast as I could run with a fifteen-pound cat. Nightmare or not, I had been truly terrified.

It was another heavily overcast day. A gray wash of light found its way through the windows in the kitchen as I punched the button on the coffee maker then washed and filled Cinda's bowls.

"An oatmeal with walnuts and raisins kind of day for me," I told her as she chowed down on a can of Tasty Tuna.

64

The memory of my supposed nightmare tugged at me all through breakfast like its own kind of ghost. Refilling my coffee mug, I carried it down the hall towards my study. Cinda reached it first and pawed, frantically, at the door till I opened it. It was cold in there. Far colder than it should have been and the scent of roses lingered in the air.

"Allison!" I called. There was no answer though the cold intensified. "Allison, I know it's you. I had a dream last night...a nightmare that terrified me. I know you want me here for some reason, or everything wouldn't have fallen into place the way it did. I wouldn't keep sensing and seeing your presence. If what I saw was real, I don't want to be here anymore. Allison? Please answer me!"

A cold wind rose out of nowhere scattering the pile of receipts and house repair estimates I kept in a box on my desk. One sailed to the floor at my feet, and I picked it up just as the rose scent faded and the temperature rose. Allison was gone, but for some reason she wanted me to see what I held in my hand. I looked it over carefully. It was Joe's estimate on repairing the cellar wall that he must have left for me before he headed out. From what I could see, he wanted to jack up the left side of the house and fix the foundation before it collapsed. It was a higher priority item than most he had tackled, and I wondered why he hadn't done it earlier.

"Maybe I should screw up my courage and check things out," I told Cinda who now sat loaf style on my laptop. I was really, really hoping she would disagree, but she merely stared at me with her fixed golden gaze. "Okay, that's not at all helpful. *If* I'm going down there, I should probably get dressed first in case I have to make a run for it. These floppy slippers would not be helpful in a quick getaway."

I swilled down the last of my now cold coffee and headed back upstairs with Cinda running on ahead this time. My bedroom looked *so normal*...so untouched by horror ...that once again I thought it had been nothing more than a nightmare.

"Everything is fine up here, and there's nothing in the cellar that can hurt you. It's broad daylight for heaven's sake," I told myself which made me feel calmer until I remembered Alice telling me that my restoration had "awakened the devil".

I dressed quickly while Cinda fiddled about in her litter box until its contents were arranged to her satisfaction. A few minutes later, we headed down the back stairs to the laundry room where I kept the key and flashlight I would need. Joe had told me the new wiring in the cellar only covered the furnace, water heater and one light in that area. The rest had been put on hold till he could find another electrician. I never learned what sent the last one running out of Greystone, which was probably a good thing considering what I was about to do.

Taking a deep steadying breath, I headed to the cellar door I kept locked for no sane reason. It just made me feel safer which I guess was reason enough. Easing it open, slowly, I flashed my light down the steep steps into the cavernous space below that smelled moldy and dank. I remember Joe telling me about the toxic black mold they had found when the furnace was installed. It was supposed to be gone, but it didn't smell like it. Not that I was a mold expert.

I started down, but Cinda refused. I was glad she didn't want to come with me and would have closed the door to keep her out if I dared. That open door was my escape route. The thought of being trapped down there was beyond horrific. Who knew what was waiting for me in the dark?

"Okay. Allison wants me to do this. It's just a cellar. No big deal," I told myself out loud as I continued on down. "A quick in and out and it's handled. Sure, it smells funny, and it's almost pitch dark, and there's a funny sound off there to the right that sounds like a moan or a groan but not quite. If Joe was here, he'd tell me it's the plumbing or something else I don't need to worry about, which would be immensely reassuring right about now."

Reaching the bottom step, I paused and looked around. Pale gray light filtered through the small windows sparsely embedded in the stone walls as far back as I could see. The floor was hard packed dirt and wet in spots where water had either leaked from above or oozed through the foundation. I flashed my light over the piles of discards that had been stored down here for more than a hundred years. Joe had promised that he and his crew would clear it out later and donate anything of value. What couldn't be recycled would be dumped. I wanted none of it.

I picked my way through, carefully, as I headed towards the west wall. The floor was littered with bits of stuff half buried in the dirt. A broken bottle tore a jagged hole in the side of my sneaker, but my

67

thick socks saved me from a nasty cut. A quick glance over my shoulder to check on Cinda almost caused me to trip over a length of rope coiled on the floor between two battered trunks. I flashed my light over it. There was a makeshift noose on one end.

"I wonder if someone killed themself down here, too," I muttered then noticed the pentagram scratched in the dirt. Still more evidence of satanic worship that went wrong. It was a very unsettling thought, and once again Alice's words came back to haunt me.

It took a few more minutes to reach the area Joe meant. Whatever they had used for mortar a century ago had eroded away, and the wall bulged inward though imminent collapse seemed unlikely. Through every crevice, pale, yellow offshoots from the climbing rose had forced their way inside and still lived while winter had claimed the rest. A sudden thought occurred to me.

"What if the rose scent I've been smelling since I got here isn't Allison's?" I murmured to myself. "That massive, tangled mess outside that wall was planted early on by the first Mrs. Grey who went insane and added to by the second wife who was equally afflicted if not worse judging from what Henry shared. Both loved roses. Maybe it was one of them who lured me down here with that stunt in my study?"

I was beginning to feel nauseated and light headed by then. Was it the smell or something else? I only knew I had to get out of there fast! I was hurrying to the stairs, when I noticed a wooden door in the right wall. It had a slide bolt...a big one...the kind meant to keep someone or something inside.

Curiosity overcame both my fear and discomfort. Pushing my way through the piled up crates and rolled up moldy carpets, I opened the door and flashed my light inside where I *saw* nothing more than a rusted cot and a tin bucket, but *felt* a burst of pure terror and a paralyzing sense of loss. Was this where Millie's mother kept her? Where she was forced to stay when her pregnancy began to show? It was a horrifying thought that came out of nowhere just as a cold chill raced up my spine. I was not alone.

Trying to stay calm, I hurried back the way I had come. Instinctively, I knew that, if I ran, I would regret it. Whoever was with me wanted me to run. It was playing a game I had no chance of winning if I panicked. All around me I could feel the darkness growing thicker and blacker with every second that ticked past.

Suddenly, I felt drained. Every step became an effort as I struggled to reach the stairs. High above me, I could see Cinda on the landing. Her back was arched and every hair bristled as she uttered a prolonged 'yowl' then headed my way.

"No!" I shouted but that didn't stop her.

Shaking off my lethargy as best I could, I had almost reached her when something grabbed my ankle from below. Desperation lent me strength. I kicked hard then harder still. By some miracle, I broke free then followed Cinda to the top of the stairs at a flat out run. I was breathing hard, my heart hammering wildly, when I slammed the door shut and turned the key.

A still terrified Cinda followed me to the laundry room where I snatched up the throw rug then stuffed it under the cellar door. From there, we headed to the kitchen where I gathered her in my arms and held her close as tears ran down my face. Losing her would have been the worst thing that could have happened to me. Despite her terror, she had tried to save me a second time, and I loved her far more than mere words could ever say.

I sighed as I thought about what had just occurred. Had I just encountered the same horrific entity I wanted to believe was a nightmare? She had called Millie by name when she'd come to my rescue last night. Was she Millie's mother? Had she pretended to be Allison, so she could trap me? It was the second time that thought occurred to me, and I was beginning to think I was right.

I found myself calling Henry a few minutes later. I needed to hear his voice...a friendly voice attached to a living person I liked and trusted. It was either that or stuff Cinda in her carrier and beat feet for anywhere but here. He answered on the fourth ring.

"Sorry. Not buyin' whatever you're sellin'," were his first words before I could tell him, "It's just Jodie, and I've nothing to sell unless you're in the market for a very haunted house."

I had tried to keep my tone light, but I wasn't fooling him. "Somethin' happened. Be right there!"

He hung up, and I waited by the kitchen window with Cinda next to me. His truck pulled up just a few minutes later, and I found myself running out to meet him.

"Haven't had a pretty gal this glad to see me in a long time," he told me with a grin that didn't reach his worried eyes. "Let's get inside out of the cold, and you can tell me all about it."

70

Once we settled at the table, I started with my possible nightmare and finished with the horrific incident in the cellar. He listened quietly to the very end then told me, "You shouldn't be here. This place ain't fit to live in. Too much evil happened under this roof."

"The more I think about it the more sure I am that the red entity is Millie's mother."

"Her name was Varna. Could also be Hannah…the first wife. She'd know who else haunted this place. Both were bat shit crazy. Them 'spires of light' with Millie must have been others who died here."

I nodded. "I think someone hanged themselves in the cellar. I found a noose and a pentagram drawn in the dirt floor."

"Didn't tell you about that. A bunch of 'em were spending the night messin' with things best not fooled around with including devil worship. His friends locked him in down there and left him. His pa was a friend of mine. Found his body the next day and ain't been right since. This place has always attracted trouble. Brings out the worst in folks who come here."

Nothing he said was making me feel better. "I know a sensible woman would leave...a sensible woman would never have bought this place...but I felt a strange attraction from the moment I set eyes on it. Does that make any sense?"

He shook his head then sighed. "That kinda thinkin' is mighty dangerous, Jodie. Means Greystone or whoever haunts this place has got its hooks into you. I don't suppose I could talk you into goin' with me right now? I'll stay here while you grab the

71

necessaries including that cat of yours. You can stay at my place till you figure out where to go from there."

I was just about to say 'yes' to all of that when the smell of roses reached me, and a voice I no longer was sure belonged to Allison whispered close to my ear, "You can't leave me. I need you here."

Henry noticed the rose scent the same time I did. "Smells like flowers in here and got dang cold all of a sudden. My grandson would say a spirit popped by. Tell you what. Let me get him on the phone and see what he thinks about all that. Used to sneak over here on summer visits when he was a kid, so he knows this place and the stories about it. Got himself in real trouble one night."

I watched him place the call to Boston. From where I sat, I could hear a male voice answer then listened to the conversation from this end.

"Hey, it's just your grandpa. Got a situation here and could use some expert help that being you. It's about Greystone. Young lady bought it and moved in. Havin' more than a few problems of the paranormal kind."

I could hear his reply quite distinctly. "Tell her to get the hell outta there!"

I took the phone from Henry's hand and told him, "It seems I can't. I feel...or maybe I just hope the spirit of someone I love and lost recently wants me here."

"Look! You're being seduced. I know what you *think* you feel but there is some very dark energy there. The kind that can do the worst kind of harm...unimaginable harm. Get out while you can."

72

"Sorry to have troubled you," I found myself saying then handed the phone back to Henry.

I crossed to the window and looked outside while they wrapped up their conversation. It was beginning to snow again. I touched the cold windowpane and felt a strange dark sense of belonging. I could never leave Greystone. I belonged here now. I yanked back my hand, but the feeling lingered. Was Simon right? Had I been seduced?

Henry joined me there and wrapped his arm around my shoulders. He started to speak, but I cut in with, "I'm staying, but I want you to take my cat with you when you leave. I don't want her hurt." It cost me everything to tell him that. I would be lost without Cinda.

"Look! If you can't leave, I ain't going nowhere 'cept back home to grab a few things and make sure the animals are taken care of. You sure as shoot ain't goin' to spend another night here alone until you come to your God given senses."

Afraid for him, I started to protest though in my heart I knew his company would be very, very welcome. He shushed me then headed out the door. I stood there watching him drive away. He was putting himself at risk for me. I didn't have a clue who my grandfather was, but had I wished on a thousand stars I couldn't have found one better than Henry North. I began to cry. I was in over my head...drowning...and I knew it, but couldn't seem to help myself.

"But he will be back, and I won't be all alone, and somehow...some way it will all work out," I told myself. Brushing away my tears, I listened to the house again. All was quiet. I very much feared it had what it wanted. I was staying.

He was back before dark, and I helped him unload his truck. Before we went inside, he handed me a plaid throw to keep in my car for Cinda. "Plugs into the cigarette lighter. Will keep her plenty warm if you need to do some shoppin' in the village and don't have time to drop her off at my place. Now let's carry all this gear to a room close to yours. Don't want to be too far away if somethin' happens tonight."

"The room next to mine shares the same heat vent. I swept it out, but there's nothing more than a bed frame in there."

"Got me an air mattress in this here duffle bag and a down filled sleepin' bag. My old bones need a bit of comfort these days."

"There is a bathroom two doors down the crew used. Doesn't have a working shower, but you're welcome to use mine."

"Can go back home for a scrub. Show me where you want me."

We both grabbed what we could carry, and he followed me into the kitchen then down the back hall past the cellar door with the rolled up rug. I expected him to say something, but he didn't. Cinda led the way up the narrow steps then down the hall towards my bedroom where light spilled through the open door.

I pointed out the bathroom as we passed it. "I cleaned it and disposed of a dead rat before Cinda found him. I haven't seen any others, but there's plenty of evidence they're still around."

To my surprise, he laughed. "Ain't no rat wants a taste of this ornery old man, so don't be worryin' none about me."

"This is the room that shares the heat vent with mine," I told him when we reached it.

...He opened the door, and we stepped inside. It was bitter cold, and our breath hung in the air like frost ghosts. Gray light found its way through the grimy windows.

"This'll do me fine," he told me as he dropped his burden on the floor and opened up the heat vent.

I added what I carried to his pile and offered to help him set up.

"No need. Could do it in the dark."

"Which will be a required skill if it gets much later," I replied with a wry grimace. "Wiring is shot in here."

He grinned back and scratched his stubbled chin, "Heard about the electrician. No locals want to work here. Joe is lucky to have found anyone who would. Either they're out-of-towners or more afraid of Big Joe than ghosts. Bet not a one...Joe included...would stay here after dark."

I sighed. "Yep! The furnace guy made record time with the installation and refused to be down there alone."

"Forgot my lantern and flashlight in the truck. Could you fetch 'em for me while I start setting up camp?"

"Glad to...be right back."

I was surprised when Cinda decided to stay with Henry. As I hurried down the hall, I could hear him talking to her and felt a twinge of jealousy, which wasn't like me. Was the house already

75

changing me? The thought made me very uncomfortable, and I shrugged it off. Once outside, I looked around at the skeletal trees where darkness was already gathering. The sky was heavy with lead bellied clouds, and the wind had a sharp, bitter cold bite. Needless to say, I made record time getting back inside.

He was pumping up the air mattress while Cinda watched when I returned. "You must have run all the way. Nifty little lantern you got there...solar...battery...and hand crank powered. Set it over there next to your cat who's been instructin' me on how to do things proper like."

A short time later, he was satisfied with the result of his efforts. "Cozy as a rat in a hole though maybe that's a bad choice of words all things considered," he told me with a grin. "How 'bout we go downstairs and rustle up some grub. This old man ain't too bad a cook if you don't mind givin' him the run of your kitchen."

It was the first time I actually heard a real person utter "rustle up some grub" and it made me smile. Everything was so *real* about Henry. So down to earth. I felt much safer already.

Working together, we pulled off a decent meal. As we ate, he asked about me, and I told him about growing up in a state orphanage and how Allison had changed my life.

He listened, carefully, then replied, "She's someone the village is mighty proud of though most won't have read her books. Looks like she did a great job raisin' you."

"I owe everything to her. She and the others who lived there with us. When she asked me to come here to Courage Cove...to write her

76

biography...I had to do it. And when I saw this house with the roses...her scent...I knew she wanted me here. That's why I can't leave. Not till I find out why I'm she brought me to Greystone."

It was the truth, but not the entire truth. I was no longer sure it was Allison who wanted me here, but the house did...or so it seemed. If I were to tell him any of that, he would think me as 'bat shit crazy' as the Horace Grey's wives. I was beginning to wonder if it wasn't a *teensy* bit true, so I steered him away from my life to his.

"Tell me about you, Henry. I want to know everything."

He leaned back in his chair and crossed his arms behind his head. "Well now, let's see. My pa was from the deep South. Was what they call a 'carny'...did the circuits from one end of this here country to another. Met my ma when she delivered the tattooed lady's baby way out in Amesville, Iowa then moved here. Never knew why. Lived in that old cabin most all my life. "

"That explains the Tilt-a-Whirl."

"He called that rusted heap of junk 'Molly'. Couldn't bear to part with her even when she broke down. He was a big bear of a man. Taught me how to fish and hunt. Used to hunt regular like till I brought down a stag without a clean shot. Never forgot the look in them eyes...the sound he made. Never lifted a gun again."

He paused then told me, "Sorry about that. Sometimes this old man's mind wanders a bit. Was tellin' you about my pa and got off track some. He never took no guff off any man. Cost him in the end. Got banged on the head in a fight with Sam Collins over in Jeffries. Come home and dropped dead on the kitchen floor. Brain

77

hemorrhage. I was sixteen and big enough...strong enough...knew enough to keep the place goin' while my ma drank herself stupid most days. Never knew where she got the liquor...how she paid for it though I had my suspicions."

He shook his head then told me, "Enough goin' back to where there weren't much mor'en misery on a good day. Best part of my whole life happened after I met my Edith at a barn dance. Prettiest thing under the sun. Had the biggest heart and cornflower blue eyes a man could drown in. All of her fit into this wee package barely reached my chin. She must of liked what she saw, too. Married six months later. Lost her to cancer fifteen years ago. Died in my arms at home. Wouldn't stay at the hospital. Wanted to see her mountains. Reckon I'll be the same when my time comes."

He swiped away his tears and changed the subject. "What's the plan for tonight?"

I smiled wryly. "Not much in the way of entertainment. There's a few books in my study down the hall you might find interesting. I usually read till I fall asleep. I really like to be up there and settled with the door locked before it gets too dark."

"Don't blame you none there. Happens I got me some reading material, and the lantern gives off good light. Let's clean up down here before it gets much later."

"About your grandson...." I began to ask until he cut me short.

"Save him for breakfast conversin'. You want to wash or dry?"

It was such a normal question. I found myself laughing as I threw the dishtowel at him and began to clear the table.

78

It was inky black outside when we headed up the back stairs not long after that. We both had our flashlights and met with nothing out of the ordinary.

Outside his door, I told him, "Good night, Henry. I can't thank you enough for doing this. I...."

"Hush, girl. No need for thanks. Might as well tell you up front my being here ain't just my doin'. My Edith wants me here. Told me so when you called me this morning."

I smiled. "So, she's still with you in spirit form?"

He smiled back. "Yep. She's waitin' for this old man. Try to get some sleep."

I left him there and followed Cinda to my room where she made a beeline for her litter box. I stood by the door for a long moment then closed and locked it. It meant Henry couldn't do much to help me, but it made me feel safer. Always had.

Despite the furnace's welcome heat, it was still freezing, so I prepped for bed quickly. Cinda joined me under the covers, and I picked up the biography I'd been reading.

"Maybe tomorrow Allison's journals will finally get here, and I can start on hers," I murmured to Cinda who looked at me under half closed lids in that adoring way that melted my heart.

An hour passed...then two. I was just getting drowsy when I noticed how quiet it was. There was no sound at all. No clock chiming...baby crying...wind howling...shutter banging or whatever that had been. Nothing. It felt very odd. Like the house was listening to us and waiting. I pulled the covers over my head to shut out the light and slowly drifted off to sleep.

CHAPTER FOUR

(Millie)

There he is. The stranger who arrived before the dark. Sleeping and dreaming an old man's dreams. I heard them talking down below. He wants to protect her, but I fear it may already be too late. I saw her by the window. Saw her touch the glass and felt her reaction as though it was my own. This place is claiming her…Mother wants her and, between them both, she will soon be trapped here forever despite all I do to help.

But she is safe now, and I will leave her for a while. Go to the sea and cleanse myself of the darkness imbued within these walls until I must return. It is easy to pass through the walls and floor in the blink of an eye…like this… then open the front door and step outside into a world of dazzling moon bright whiteness.

It is snowing again…white flakes floating through me…covering the ground beneath my feet. All around me, the bare bone trees bend in the wind as though dancing to a waltz only they can hear. I remember him humming one to me as we twirled on the sand under the full moon's smile. Laughing, we had fallen in a tangle of limbs as the tide crept closer until the water lapped over our bare legs and sent us racing to the shelter of my cave where we lay in each other's arms till dawn's first gray light found us.

80

Ah, I am here. My thoughts have carried me to the sea once more. I had lost him to that black water that now stretches out before me. The cold Atlantic is his grave. I remember the wreath of roses I had fashioned from those that grew at Greystone then floated it out to him just as life stirred in me once again. I was to be the mother of his son, for I was sure that was who I carried. Those first flutters of life became infant kicks as he moved and turned within me. Small things I cherished.

I often sang to him...talked to him in all the days that followed even in my dark cell where I was hidden from sight. I remember the wracking pain of the birth...hours that seemed like an eternity as I babbled my baby's name over and over. The name of his father. There were two of them there that night...Mother and a woman who worked over me smelling of whiskey like my father had at times. She'd shouted, "I'm losing her. I can't stop the bleeding!" just before I began to drift free of my body. As though from a very great distance, I heard my mother tell me, "It's the son you wanted born dead. Strangled by the umbilical cord. Your precious little Eric. The wages of sin is death. Yours and that unholy fruit you bore."

Still...I had thought I heard him cry then realized it must have been his tiny spirit lost and afraid. I tried desperately to reach him...comfort him... but drifted farther and farther away like an untethered balloon. I don't know how long I lingered in some kind of gray limbo. Time had no relevance. I had a choice to make. Be free and move on into the unknown or go back and find the ones I had lost. I had chosen to return.

Someday, my love will look for me here, and together we will find our son. I can wait. Now I have her to protect...Jodie and her Cinda...perhaps even the old man with the sad eyes. They need me now, and I think I may need them.

(Jodie)

Cinda's persistent prodding finally woke me. A quick glance at the clock showed me it was past 8 am and way later than I usually slept. Dressing quickly, I headed out into the hall where I found Henry's door open, and his room empty.

"Must be in the kitchen," I murmured to myself as I hurried down the hall with a hungry Cinda in the lead. We were headed down the back stairs when the sound of indistinct voices reached me, and I wondered who our visitor was. Reaching the kitchen, I was surprised to see Jennie Tanner sitting at the table.

"Got us a visitor, so I was just gettin ready to go back up there and wake you," Henry told me as he pulled out a chair and waved me to it. "Breakfast is near done. Hope you're good 'n hungry."

I took the seat he indicated then looked at them both with a puzzled frown. "What's going on?"

It was Jennie who told me, "I had a dream last night about you that scared the living crap out of me. Henry's been filling me in on what's been happening. That cellar bit was an awful lot like what I dreamt. I know I told you I'd never set foot here again, but here I am much to my surprise. Brought a few things to try."

"Like that purging thing we talked about?" I asked.

"Yep. Got what I need in my tote bag over there. Like to get started after breakfast."

"There are some good spirits here, too, like Millie Grey and my mother Allison who I told you about. I don't want them *purged*."

Jennie sighed and touched my hand. "Don't worry. We are only trying to rid this place of the negative energy inside these walls. The good souls won't be affected."

The conversation took a lighter turn as we ate. It gave us a brief respite before we began what I hoped would release the evil embedded in the bones of the house. That respite ended all too soon.

"Let's begin," Jennie told us as she lugged her bag to the table and opened it up. Lifting out the items inside, she explained their purpose, "This is white sage for burning which represents the earth element...this book of matches the fire element...my abalone shell the water element...and this feather the air element. I also brought a couple of crucifixes and a big bottle of holy water. A blending of old and new world beliefs. Now I'll give both of you a card with a smudging prayer on it. We will all say it out loud while I burn the sage in the shell."

I confined Cinda to her carrier, so she wouldn't follow us, and we began in the kitchen. The smell of burning sage filled the air as Jennie walked, slowly, around while we recited the prayer: "Begone negative energy! Give way to the Lord's healing Light. We are not afraid, for we are in the care of His angels. You are banished from this place and must never return!"

We kept saying it over and over...the mantra of protection as we moved from room to room. Some were far colder than they should be, so we stayed there longer. The parlor was one of those, and I told Jennie that Hannah Grey had hanged herself there. Moving upstairs, she felt a negative energy in the hall that passed through the walls as we chanted our prayer. We finally reached my bedroom where she spent a long time purging every corner. Afterwards, the atmosphere felt lighter in there as though something dark had been lifted.

"I saved the cellar till last," Jennie told me after we finished purging the attic where she felt several benign spirits. "From what Henry told me this morning, something truly evil is down there that wants you. Someone you think might be Millie Grey's mother. It is very important you show whoever it is that you are not afraid. Evil feeds on fear. Let it know that this house is now yours, and it does not belong here." She paused for a moment...took a deep breath the added, "Time to go down there and do what we can."

An overwhelming sense of dread washed over me. The cellar was the last place I ever wanted to be, but I forced a smile I was very far from feeling then led the way to the laundry room where I grabbed the key. A cold shiver passed through me as I unlocked the cellar door and pushed it open. It was dark and quiet below. Henry and I swept it with our flashlights then headed down with Jennie close behind waving the burning sage in its abalone shell.

"There is something down here," she whispered. "Something old, and powerful, and profoundly evil. Pray for all you're worth and above all else show no fear."

We reached the bottom and began to move around in a pattern that would eventually reach every foot of the huge space. "Begone negative energy!" Jennie shouted, and we joined her in the prayer over and over again.

Reaching the spot where I had found the noose and pentagram, she told us, "They were kids fooling with something they did not understand, but the evil here is not from that source." She picked up the noose then added, "He was terrified and took his own life because the evil here told him to. It wanted him. He is still trapped somewhere within these walls. Let's keep going."

I could sense she was getting tired...as though her energy was being drained, and I felt much the same. Henry kept pace, but I knew it was taking an effort. By then, we had come to the cell I had found, and she stepped inside then screamed. It was a god-awful scream that sent chills chasing through me. Dropping the abalone shell, she collapsed on the floor clutching her belly as if in pain.

"We gotta get her outta here fast!" Henry cried as we grabbed her arms and half carried...half dragged her towards the stairs as she muttered the same name over and over in a voice I didn't recognize. It was "Eric"...and then we heard, "I hate you, mother! I hate you! Don't you dare hurt my baby!""

Our 'fast' wasn't fast enough, so Henry scooped her up in his arms and carried her up the stairs while I covered our retreat by shouting the Smudging Prayer over and over then added a lie, "I am not afraid of you. This is my house now. You are dead and don't belong here! Begone! Now!"

I could see a seething, churning blackness following close on our heels, and it took everything I had not to hurry Henry and his burden along. It seemed like forever before we reached the hall, and I slammed and locked the door behind us. Something scratched on the other side. Long nails or old bones. I didn't know which and didn't much care as long as it remained on the other side.

I followed Henry into the kitchen where he propped a now quiet Jennie in a chair. Dazed at first, it took a few moments before she snapped out of it then told us, "Don't ever, ever go down there again! Nail one of the crucifixes above the door and pray with everything you've got that what I saw...what I felt...stays down there!"

"You spoke in a different voice. A young woman's. I think her mother kept Millie locked in that cell. That she was tortured emotionally and physically from what I felt when I was there."

A shudder passed through her. "That *thing* down there is a monster! You should leave here...burn the place to the ground! Fire is the only thing that can purge it!"

"But I can't leave. You know that."

"Then pray for protection. May God help you."

She was still badly shaken when she left a moment later and was running by the time she reached her car. I watched her drive off while Henry hung the crucifix over the cellar door then returned smiling grimly. "She's right. You need to leave."

"We've been through this. You know why I can't. When I find out why I'm here...find out what Allison wants me to do and get it done... I'll be more than happy to leave. Way, way beyond more than happy."

Henry sighed. "You're as hard headed as my Edith. Looks like we're both here for a spell unless by some miracle you come to your senses."

I had to smile. "If it hasn't happened so far, it's not likely to any time soon. Help me shove that cabinet over the back hall entry, so I can't see the cellar door when I'm out here in the kitchen."

He shook his head. "Nothin' will keep her down there if she wants to leave."

Of course, he was right, but maybe...just maybe the crucifix would keep her in the cellar for a while and buy me some much needed time. I clung to the hope that thought offered as we pushed the heavy cabinet into its new place.

***

After that, I toured the rest of the house, which felt much 'lighter'. Even all the shadowy places weren't quite as dark as they'd seemed before. It had started to snow again, and Henry went back home to take care of the animals. While he was gone, a Fed Ex truck delivered the journals I'd been waiting for, and I had them spread out on the kitchen table when he returned.

"Just made a fresh pot," I told him as he peeled off his coat and hung it on the peg by the door.

"From the tire tracks I saw, you must have had company. Whatcha got there?" he asked over his shoulder as he headed to the coffee maker.

"My mother's journals finally came. If I had Internet, I would be a very happy camper right now. I have everything I need with one very important exception...where she came from...her identity."

"All you know so far is that she had the name Allison Bogart pinned to her," he said as he shoved a mug my way then took the chair across from me. "A name not from around this 'neck of the woods' accordin' to what Alice's ma told you."

"But the Internet will give me access to databases that might help me find relatives."

"What makes you think they would drop her off like that and give her real name? Sounds like a bad idea to me unless they planned on comin' back for her."

I sighed. "Who knows what they were thinking. She was a newborn. Maybe her mother panicked and ran. But you're right. She wouldn't have left a name pinned to her unless she did plan on coming back."

"Let's get some coffee in us. While you're fiddlin' with all that, I'm goin' to shovel the walk and drive. It's getting deep out there."

"This can wait. I'll grab the shovel in the shed and help you."

"You got a job to do right here. The sooner done the sooner you're out of here, so get busy and let me handle the snow. Been shovelin' the dang stuff since I was no bigger than one of Bella's pups."

I had to smile at that image then asked him about them while we drank our coffee. "She is too old to be having a litter. Should of had her fixed years ago. Usually kept her in the house when she was... Well, you know, but she got away from me. Disappeared for two days. Turned up at Ted Barlow's place. She'd been hangin' out with his hound dog Jasper. Now enough jabberin'. Burnin' daylight, so let me get goin'."

"I'll call you when lunch is ready," I promised then watched him head out the door.

Cinda jumped up on the table and settled herself next to the journals I had yet to open. Maybe she knew instinctively that Allison had written them. I sorted them according to their dates then picked up the first one and began to read. She was older than I thought she would be when she started it...a teenager full of far more than the usual angst, and I soon was lost among the pages. Time passed. It was Henry who interrupted me.

"Got 'er done, but if the wind kicks up again it will drift back over."

I looked up in surprise then glanced at the clock above the stove. It was 1 pm. "Sorry. Let me get that lunch going. Just take a minute."

I opened two cans of soup and threw together a couple of sandwiches while Henry cleaned up. As we ate, he asked what I had found so far in the journals. They were so intensely personal I hesitated to share what I'd learned, so I summed it up with, "She was a teenager who knew she was different. She was bullied and fought back. Punished and became resentful. Came to believe that her uniqueness made her ugly, and that's about as far as I got. She did mention that Alice Cooper's mother was a friend...the only one she had trusted not to betray her."

"Sounds like she had a hard time of it. Would've broke some."

"But only made her stronger."

He nodded. "Sounds like someone else I know. By the way, think we got us some company if these old ears ain't playin' tricks."

I had heard it, too, and hurried to the window. The Blue Star Telephone and Internet truck had just pulled up.

A few minutes later, I showed him to my study and asked when I would be getting a phone upstairs in my bedroom. He told me that was a separate order and would have to wait till someone got to me. "Seems like everyone wants something right now. Can't wait a minute. Always in a hurry especially them new folks."

He continued to ramble on while he checked out my modem, computer and then the wall plug in. "All good here. Going to check the box outside. Will let you know what I find."

I waited, impatiently, until he returned and reported, "Problem solved. One of them components was fried. Should be good to go now."

"How 'bout you make certain 'fore you leave?" Henry told him, so he did.

We both watched him drive away a short time later. It was snowing much harder now, and the wind had kicked up.

"Looks like my shovelin' won't amount to much if it keeps up like this."

"What are the chances of us getting snowed in?"

"You're worried about Bella and her litter, ain't you?"

I nodded. "I know how I'd feel if Cinda was over there. It's a short drive but a long walk."

His eyes were troubled when he told me, "I'm old but I can make it. If you're thinkin' about me leavin' you here all alone, forget it."

"It's fine now. You must have noticed the difference. I'm not afraid any more." It was a lie. I would never be anything but afraid as long as I was in this house.

He shook his head. "You ain't goin' to get rid of me that easily, but it's a good idea to head on back and make sure all's good at home for a while. But before I go, I got somethin' in the truck you might find handy."

He grabbed his coat and came back with two walkie talkies. He showed me what I needed to do then told me, "We'll set them both on Channel 4. Keep it there and keep it handy. Got plenty of range. Now let me get goin'. I'll bring extra batteries when I come back."

Cinda and I were watching as he turned up his coat collar and ran to his truck a second time. That was when it happened. A patch of ice...who knew what?..but he went down hard. I flung open the door and reached him just as he pulled himself to his feet.

He was grimacing in pain when he told me, "Funniest damn thing. Almost felt like someone shoved me. Feet went right out from under me. No big deal, so quit your fussin' and let me get on home. Get back inside before you freeze solid."

I was cold all the way to my bones by the time I reached the kitchen where I shrugged into my coat and grabbed a hot cup of coffee then headed for my study. Cinda beat me there and found a perch near the heat vent while I sat down and reopened my laptop.

I was worried about Henry. He had said he was 'okay', but that grimace of pain told a different story. He was one of the best friends I ever had. If anything ever happened...

"Stop! He'll let you know if he needs you. Get busy and quit worrying!" I told myself then smiled ruefully. Like that would happen. I was a born worrier.

As I typed my questions into Google, I continued to think about Henry when something popped up on the Internet that caught my attention. My search had turned up a Bogart family during that time period including a daughter named Alicia.

"Maybe Alicia found herself with a baby she didn't want. In those days, one born out of wedlock was a huge stigma," I murmured to myself. "Was she the one who left her daughter at Second Chance? But why pin 'Bogart' to her unless she planned to come back for her like Henry and I thought?"

I dug deeper and found a death certificate for her some forty years later. She had never married. It was a dead end...literally. I continued to check out whatever I could find, but nothing more pertinent turned up.

…"So, we have a possible mother for Allison," I told Cinda who was now watching me intently. It was almost as though she was trying to tell me something. Once again, I had the feeling that it was Allison looking at me through her golden eyes.

The hours had flown past and night was closing in. Henry should have been back by now. I was about to call him on the walkie talkie when it buzzed in my hand. I remembered what I had to do to answer it. "Hello! Henry? I was just about to check on you. Over...."

"Seems this here ankle might be worse than I thought. Got things done around here, but it swelled up on me and turned purple. Keepin' ice on it. It's my right one and between it and a dad blame left hip that don't do more than go up and down drivin' might be kinda hard. Not that I'd let that hold me back if you need me...over."

"All good here. Are you sure you're okay? I can drive over there if you need help...over."

"Fine here. Got plenty of firewood inside...somethin' to eat. We'll see what's what tomorrow, but I can get back there tonight if somethin' bad happens. I'll find a way no matter what it takes to get there."

"It's quiet and warm," I reassured him. "I'll make a bit of supper then go upstairs and read. Your walkie talkie will be with me every moment."

I told him what my research had turned up, and we said our good-byes...our Roger over and outs. I felt strangely bereft...lost...like my safety line had just been snapped as I shoved the walkie talkie in my pocket and busied myself throwing together some leftovers for supper.

The house still felt purged with no hint of menace, when I grabbed the journal I'd been reading, my flashlight, and the second crucifix then headed up the front stairs since going anywhere near the cellar was not ever going to happen again. At the top, I followed Cinda down the hall then paused outside Henry's door and looked inside. I missed him and hoped with all my heart he was okay. I would check on him tomorrow if I could get through the snow that was already piling up.

I prepped for bed quickly then lit a fire. Putting the screen back in place, I headed to the window and looked out at the night. It was snowing heavier than before. If it kept up at the rate it was going, no one would get down that road any time soon, which meant Henry would be on his own for who knew how long. A thought that hiked up my worry level still more.

Scurrying to bed, I slid the crucifix and walkie talkie under my pillow, piled on the covers, and patted the spot next to me. Cinda joined me and snuggled against my warmth. I started to read the journal again, but sleep soon claimed me.

It was some time later, bitter cold and now dark when Cinda prodded me awake. Only firelight lit the room. The power must be out which meant the furnace wasn't working, I thought with a groan

94

as I reluctantly crawled out of the warm comfort of my bed. Heading to the fireplace, I poked the logs into renewed effort sending a burst of sparks crackling up the chimney then added more wood.

My frozen breath followed me like a cloud as I sped back to bed and crawled in next to Cinda. If our power was out, there was every chance Henry's was, too. He had heat and must be used to dealing with power outages by now since he had lived in that cabin since forever. I sighed. Worrying wasn't helping either one of us, so I lay there listening to the fire's crackle and pop...Cinda's contented purr. Otherwise, the house was quiet, and I hoped and prayed it would stay that way, but knew that was probably not going to happen. That I couldn't ignore forever what was down in the cellar.

A sudden thought struck me. What if I had to go down there to reset something on the furnace when the power came back on? Fear piled on top my worry, and I forced myself to think about the journal I had been reading. Soon, I found myself getting drowsy. A dream was waiting.

I open my eyes, slowly, and look around. It is warm, and I can smell the sea...hear the crash of waves breaking against the shore somewhere below. Gray light pours through an opening in the rocks... dawn's pale first offering. I can still feel the residuals of our love making that had lasted all through the night that wasn't nearly long enough. His strong arms still cradle me, and beneath my head I can hear the steady beat of his heart. He is still with me, but the new day will change all that. He will be going to the war in Europe where so many will die. Where so many have already died.

He must have felt me stir and wakes up. "I know what you are
thinking, Smudge!" he tells me in a husky whisper as he plants a kiss
on my cheek. "But it won't be forever. Nothing in heaven or on
earth can stop me from coming back to you. You know that. I'll take
you home, and we'll get married and do all the wonderful things
we've planned."

The sound of his voice comforts me...helps push back the feeling
that is overtaking me as the light grows brighter and brighter. A
ripping, tearing sense of loss. My Eric will soon be leaving me.

He continues to talk about our tomorrows as I fall asleep in his
arms a second time but not before I whisper, "I will wait for you no
matter how long it takes. Even if it takes forever."

I woke up to a new day at Greystone, but remnants of the dream
still lingered. I never saw the face of the man who had held me, but
I knew what it felt like to be truly and deeply cherished even though
that feeling had belonged to Millie. I had been inside the deepest
part of her heart. She must have sent me that dream, so I would
know how much she loved her soldier...her Eric. Know the pain she
had felt when he left and understand why she was still here at
Greystone no matter how horrific it must be for her. She was
waiting for him and would not leave till they found each other again.

Still somewhat dazed, I looked around. Cinda was asleep in the
crook of my arm, and I snuggled deeper under the covers. It was
then I noticed that the bedside lamp was now on. The power had
been restored while I slept and the room felt warmer.

"Which means the furnace restarted automatically. A very good thing. Let's make that a very, very, very good thing," I told Cinda who now blinked up at me. "Let's check on Henry and see how he is doing."

I pulled out the walkie talkie and pushed the call button. It took a moment before I heard his voice.

"Worried about you, Jodie. Power was out for a spell in case you slept through it...over."

"Woke up in the middle of it, but all great now...over."

"You can expect a lot of that out here. Mostly falling trees taking down the lines. Pines are the worst. Can't take the snow load if it gets heavy....over"

"How are you doing?"

"Swellin' is down a bit. Hobbled out to see to Bella in the shed. Somethin' got one of her pups. She got hurt trying to save it. Not too bad. Got her patched up. Brought 'em all inside here with me. They're all lovin' that old stove. You probably saw it snowed all night. Be a while 'fore a snowplow comes down these back roads...sometimes a long while. You all set for a spell?"

"Good to go. Just worried about all of you over there. Sorry to hear about Bella's pup. How is she taking it?"

"Like a mother. Keeps lookin' for him like she can't believe he's gone."

We talked a bit longer then signed off. "Time to start a brand new day," I told Cinda who poured herself from under the covers with the liquid grace peculiar to cats then headed to her litter box. I sighed wondering what my brand new day would bring. For a brief moment, I could feel his arms around me again...hear his heartbeat. Millie had known a great and powerful love, and I had to wonder if I would ever trust anyone enough to find that.

CHAPTER FIVE

(MILLIE)

I find myself smiling as I watch her rise from bed. She is remembering the dream I sent her. My last memory of him...my Eric. She wants to believe she is safe now. That the woman with her burning stick has driven the evil entity that was once my mother out of here, but she is wrong. She waits in the cellar...biding her time...growing stronger in anticipation of what is yet to come, if I can't find a way to stop her. But for now, I can walk about the house without feeling her dark presence...hearing her voice...seeing her continue to torment those who came here in the past and remain still. They are not evil. Even the one who weeps and wails. They are merely lost souls trapped inside these walls much as I am though I came back when I could have escaped. There was something beautiful that beckoned beyond the gray void that followed death, but I will not leave here till I find those I love.

Ah, there goes Jodie down the hall with her cat. She is wearing those fuzzy slippers that make a slapping sound with each step. I heard her tell the old man about her life. She was lost like me once

in a dark place that left its scars...old wounds that marked her soul.
I can feel them as if they are my own. Perhaps that is why I share
my memories with her. Maybe I want her to know what love...real
love would feel like. Both the ecstasy and the pain of loss, and yet I
sense there is still another reason I cannot begin to understand.

I follow them down the stairs and watch them head towards the
kitchen while I pass through the front door into a new day. The
snow has stopped falling now. The wind is nothing more than a
whisper not a roar. Around me, the golden rays of the rising sun
bursts through the dark tangle of winter bare trees. The sky is
washed with the colors of lavender, purple, and rose. The mountains
are still shrouded in their blue haze like a dream half remembered.

I walk through the deep snow without feeling its coldness and,
slowly, circle Greystone remembering it as it used to be. Its
grandeur and beauty in the days long past. The ancient roses are
winter dead now and seem sinister somehow. Their twisted vines
have grown deep into the wall they grip so tightly as if they draw
their life from the evil here. Reaching the back, I press against the
kitchen window where I watch her making breakfast...talking to her
Cinda. I have seen another soul enter her cat from time to time and
watch me through her yellow eyes. It is a woman who loves her. A
guardian spirit.

I will lie here and make a snow angel to let her know she has still
another who will do all she can to keep her safe in the nights to
come. A cradle of pristine whiteness surrounds me as I move my
limbs and push back the snow despite my nebulous state. My father

had often made them with me in the long ago, and I can almost hear
our laughter still lingering in the air like ghosts. He had gifted me
with the shell I left for her. He told me it was called a Mermaid's
Toenail, and it had been a cherished treasure I wanted her to have.
He is another I wait for in this house of horror and death. Perhaps
one day, he, too, will return to me.

My thoughts turn to Eric, and I smile up at the blue sky
remembering the days when I lay in his arms close to the sea where
we dreamed our dreams and made wishes that never came true. "I
don't know where you are, my love, but I will wait here till that sun
is dark forever, the sea runs dry, and the earth moves no more. That
is my promise to you. The same one I made on the day you left."

(Jodie)

Cinda was perched on the window seat watching something outside that seemed to fascinate her. Curiosity aroused, I joined her there. Someone had made a snow angel just below the window. To say I was amazed would be a colossal understatement!

"Who could have possibly done that?" I asked Cinda though I wasn't expecting an answer. "I bet it was Millie! Who else could it be?"

I decided to call Henry and see what he thought about the whole thing. He answered on the first ring, and I told him what had happened.

"Could be your Millie telling you she's your guardian angel," he replied. "Don't know who else woulda done it."

100

"That's what I was thinking...hoping anyway. How are you, Bella, and the pups?"

"All warm and well fed. Ankle is better. Made me a crutch of sorts to take the weight off some. Let's me get around a bit more. Anything you aren't telling me?"

"Nope. All quiet. Going to do some Internet research and see what turns up...take notes from her journals...that sort of thing."

"Sounds like you'll be keepin' busy. Ring me up if you need to talk. Try to save the batteries on the walkie talkie. Not sure how long they'll last and never got around to bringin' over them extras I promised."

We chatted a bit longer then rang off. I was cleaning up the kitchen when the phone rang. I was surprised to find out it was Jennie.

"Sorry about how I just ran off the other day," she told me. "Not very professional, but whatever is down in that cellar scared the living crap outta me, and I've run into all kinds of bad ass entities. Any new developments?"

"Everything has been very quiet, and I understand all too well how you felt down there."

I heard a deep sigh then she told me, "Look. I still think you should get the hell outta there."

"I have my reasons...."

"I know," she cut in. "Just sayin'. Use the holy water I left. Sprinkle it outside the cellar door...outside your bedroom door...heck, sprinkle it on yourself and that cat of yours. Whatever it takes. And keep that other crucifix under your pillow."

"Already do that. Do you really think all that will help?"

I heard a second sigh and knew her next words would be a lie. "Yep. Should do the trick. Just remember not to show fear. They love that."

I smiled as I remembered her mad dash out of here, but kept my mouth shut. We finished up talking about the snow, the church bazaar, and something about a Christmas Ball. She did ask if I had ever called the number she gave me. I told her Henry had, and Simon had the same advice: "Get out!"

We hung up after that, and I looked around the kitchen feeling more alone than ever. Usually, that wouldn't bother me. I was used to being alone...my innate shyness made it hard for me to make friends, but this 'alone' felt different. This alone made me very aware of how vulnerable I was in a place where an evil entity wanted me dead.

"She wants to suck out my soul," I whispered to myself as though saying it too loud would somehow summon her from the cellar. I thought about my snow angel and smiled. Millie was with me. She left it there, so I would know she had my back though I pretty much already knew that.

Finishing up in the kitchen, I headed to my study with Cinda. She was as vulnerable as I was...more so...and I needed to keep her close at all times. While I waited for my computer to load, she settled

102

down on the end of my desk, blinked at me twice then began to utter her strange purr.

I rubbed under her chin then continued my Internet search. Maybe...just maybe... a Bogart still lived that had heard stories about Alicia they would share with me. A short time later, I turned up a black and white photo of a group of young women wearing the long dresses from that era. It was blurry...the faces indistinct and there were no names...just a legend that read: Senior Girls Somerset High School 1915.

"No help there. She could be any one of those teens plus there's a good chance she never finished high school if she was pregnant. Her parents would have made sure no one found out. Most likely, there would have been another home delivery or a trip abroad with an aunt," I told Cinda who yawned widely.

The rest of the afternoon was both engrossing and frustrating. At the end, I had missed lunch and gotten absolutely nowhere with my research. I headed to the kitchen where I checked to see if my angel was still there. The imprint was as deep as ever, and the late afternoon sun now dusted her with diamonds.

I was smiling when I threw together a P&J sandwich and sat down at the table with Cinda perched on the chair next to me. So far, I had made little to no progress solving the mystery of Allison's birth, or why she wanted me here. *Assuming* the rose scent was hers, the two had to be connected in some way.

"Maybe, I need to list what I know so far," I told Cinda who blinked at me twice.

Grabbing a pen and pad off the counter, I began to do just that in my sloppy kind of shorthand only I could ever read.

#1- *Allison was probably born to someone around here since she was left at Second Chance. Most likely candidate was Alicia Bogart long since deceased although she wasn't exactly local.*

#2- *Allison wanted me to buy this house? Was the scent she wore and the roses outside connected? Was the scent I smelled even hers?*

#3 - *Allison's soul may possess Cinda at times.*

Even as I put those words to paper, I realized that would sound completely insane to anyone not living in this house. I sighed and continued.

#4 - *There is someone intensely evil in the cellar I think is Varna Grey and am hoping she stays there until I can get out of here.*

#5 - *At lease six people...including an infant... died here. At least one may be linked to satanic worship.*

Jennie had said they were just kids 'fooling around'. I fervently hoped and prayed she was right, and they hadn't conjured something up. I took a sip of my now cold cocoa and began again.

#6 - *Both of Horace Grey's wives were insane. The second one...the sadistic Varna... had a daughter named Millie who I think is my angel and the sender of dreams.*

#7 - *Millie had a stillborn baby boy in this very house...was kept in the cellar at times...and died in what could have been a bungled birthing at the hands of Henry's then drunken mother. What happened to both bodies is another mystery.*

I leaned back in my chair and thought about mother and son. Were their bodies still here somewhere in the walls...perhaps under the floor in the cellar? How was any of what occurred here linked to Allison, and why she seemed to want me here?

"Though I truly believe that it's Varna in the cellar, I can't rule out entirely the first wife," I mused out loud. "She lost her baby at sea and went mad. Maybe I am hearing her infant cry at night. Maybe she found him after her own death, and they're here forever. But then again, what if it's Millie's dead son I hear who may have survived the birth, but died moments later?"

I studied the list in front of me. All I had were a lot of questions, speculations, and 'maybes'. Time might help me sort it all out, but time was my enemy. Who knew when the house would become active again? It was a scary thought I couldn't shake off and another night at Greystone was fast approaching.

After supper, I carried the bottle of holy water upstairs. Jennie's suggestion to sprinkle some by the cellar door was not going to happen since I wouldn't go near it. Per her suggestion, I *did* sprinkle a few drops on Cinda which made her less than happy then on myself before I climbed into bed where I continued to read through Allison's journal.

She had often fantasized that her parents would come to claim her. Made up scenarios that would explain their desertion, or ones that featured her as the kidnapped infant of wealthy parents or even royalty. I could feel her insecurities and pain as if they were my own. I had created the same sort of wild imaginings. Anything to ease the sense I had been unwanted and unloved. Might even have deserved being dumped like a load of rubbish.

Despite my best efforts to divert them, my thoughts drifted back to my own corner of hell. I had been taller than most kids my age...both boys and girls...which made me slouch a lot and feel awkward. My clothes were donations or hand-me-downs and often a bad fit. I was a target for ridicule...a carrot top... a giant...a scarecrow and worse. Tired of being their victim, I had punched more than one, which only made things worse. I ran away when things got too tough. I had even tried to run away from me, which needless to say didn't work out though I saw others on the street who had lost themselves in drugs or whatever it took to shake loose the demons that haunted them.

Allison's life had been much like mine in the beginning, including her attitude, until she discovered her true worth...her purpose with the aid of a much loved English teacher who recognized both her talent, and what she needed to achieve her potential. She had passed on the hard earned wisdom she acquired to me. Through her eyes I began to see myself differently. Being tall became regal and something to be proud of. My hair was not carrot colored but a rich copper. My lips were full not fat. My eyes were unique and beautiful not weird. Even my pale ivory skin became an asset and not proof I was a vampire as some had called me.

I listened to her words and believed because I wanted with all my heart to believe. In time, I came to be my own mirror. I was not exactly movie star gorgeous, but I had a smile that came from my heart...good teeth...and eyes that even I had to admit were pretty great. Silver gray with a black rings around the irises and fringed with natural dark lashes and brows.

"Overall, I'm not a half bad package outside and comfortable with whom I am inside thanks to the woman between these pages," I told Cinda who had snuggled up against me.

Suddenly, I felt a kiss brush my forehead and a whisper close to my ear, "Your beauty comes from your warrior's soul...your survivor's soul...your wonderful, caring heart. Your journey has taught you compassion, empathy and the value of love. How very precious it is, and that it must never be squandered. You have yet to find your 'forever' kind, but it will come."

I smiled at her words then sighed. Had that really been her or an illusion conjured up from what I'd been reading? But then, she was the only one who could have known all that. It had to be her unless a very cunning Varna had been listening when I told Henry about my past. That was yet another very troubling possibility, so I decided to make plans for tomorrow instead of giving it more thought on another dark night at Greystone.

First on the agenda would be shoveling out the drive, so I could get to Henry's as soon as the road was plowed. I had to make sure he was all right. He sounded okay, but I was still worried and would be till I saw him in person. Slowly, I drifted off to sleep with Cinda pressed against me.

***

The morning sun was pouring through the window when I opened my eyes, sat up, and looked around. Cinda was gone. and the bedroom door was now open.

"That's impossible! How did she get out?" I muttered to myself as I threw on my robe, slid into my slippers and padded, quickly, down the hall to the stairs calling her name as I went. Finally, I found her in the kitchen looking out the window at two pickup trucks that were just pulling up. Four men piled out. One of them was Henry who hobbled my way while the others began downloading snow blowers and shovels. I finger combed my unruly hair into some kind of order as I headed to the door and held it open for him. I was so glad to see him I hugged him hard.

"Now that's the kinda greetin' that makes an old man feel welcome. Are you all good here?" he asked with a grin.

"Been quiet which is way more than good. I was worried about you, Bella, and the fur kids, so shoveling my way to the road was the plan for the day. I wanted to check on all of you as soon as the plow made it here. How did you get through?"

"Road got plowed last night. Mighty lucky it did. Them guys out there are buds of mine who cleared me out and wanted to help over here. Let me put on the coffee while you get dressed and powder that pretty nose of yours or whatever women do these days."

I thanked him and raced back through the house and up to my room where the mystery of the unlocked door was waiting for me. I

108

believed Allison had been there, but why would she unlock a door I felt kept me safe? It made no sense.

I dressed hurriedly and returned to the kitchen where I found Henry sitting at the table with Cinda in his lap. I could hear her rumbling purr and knew she was happy.

"Looks like I got me a little buddy," Henry told me as he stroked her silky ears. "Coffee's just about ready. Bet them boys out there could use some. How 'bout givin' 'em a shout? I would, but it looks like I'm not movin' for a bit."

So, that's what I did...or tried to. It took more than one 'shout' before a lanky guy with a bristling, black uni-brow finally heard me above the din and headed my way. "I'll spread the word. Be in there as soon as we wrap up this end," he told me when I delivered my message then hurried back inside.

I had decided to add cinnamon buns to Henry's coffee as a 'thank you' for their help. While waiting for the old side oven to reach the temp needed, I called him to the window and pointed out my angel. The wind had obscured much of it overnight, and now it looked more like an odd shaped depression.

"It was there, Henry. No mistake. A perfect snow angel."

"I believe you. Best not mention things like that in front of them guys out there. This place spooks 'em enough though they'd never admit it. Anything new goin' on you want to tell me?"

I started to tell him about the door mystery, when I heard voices outside. The stomp of heavy boots dislodging snow followed and then a knock. I opened the door and smiled at each of them as they filed in.

"Sorry. Looks like we brung a fair amount of snow in with us," one told me as he snatched off his ski mask and shoved it in his coat pocket.

"No worries there. Coffee is ready and cinnamon rolls are headed for the oven. Make yourselves at home."

"Not too likely in this place," he murmured nervously.

"Shoot! Never thought I'd be havin' cinnamon buns in Greystone," another added with a wry grin.

Henry made the introductions. "Boys, this here is Jodie Shield. Jodie meet Ted Barlow, that there is Tiny Black, and over there is Sam Meeks. Neighbors and friends."

They nodded and grinned while I smiled back. "Thank you so much for everything," I told them. "Find a seat somewhere, and I'll pop in the rolls."

They had saved a chair for me next to Henry, and I took it while we waited. I had never learned to be completely comfortable among strangers, so I pasted on a smile again and asked some banal question none of them bothered to answer. Instead, they had questions for me.

"Seen any spooks since you moved in?" was the first followed by "Why the black cat? Isn't livin' here enough bad luck for anyonw?"

I 'tap danced' around both of those and then the stories came. Each of them had to tell me what they had heard about Greystone. Many of them were chilling but didn't come close to the stories I chose not to tell them. It seemed like ages before they left to finish the job.

Henry heard my sigh of relief and grinned. "They're just good ole boys who don't mean no harm. They're worried about you being here all alone same as me. Now tell me what you didn't get around to finishin' earlier."

So, I told him about the unlocked door. He had no explanation either. "Just remember you're always welcome over at my place. Ankle's some better, and I can get back here if you run into trouble."

"I really meant what I said earlier, Henry, other than the door thing, it's been quiet. Working on reading and making notes for the book takes up most of my time."

"Joe and his crew might be finishin' up that job soon and gettin' on back here."

I sighed. "I'll be very glad to see them even though the peace and quiet has made me more productive."

They had finished up outside by then, and we all said our good byes. I stood by the window watching them load up and drive off taking Henry with them though he had wanted to stay. Cinda joined me there.

"Looks like we're on our own again," I told her as I reached down and gathered her in my arms. She looked at me with that knowing stare that raised goose bumps up both my arms. Was Allison trying to tell me that status would soon change in some horrific way? I laughed. The gift of imagination was a two edged sword.

I mopped the melted snow puddles off the kitchen floor...tidied up the dishes then went to my study. Cinda headed to the heat vent while I flipped open my laptop. Soon, I was looking for whatever I could find about the Bogart family, which was next to nothing. Apparently, that branch died out in the 70s. There was no one still alive I could contact for information about their Great Aunt Alicia.

The day sped past as I tackled some of the household chores that needed doing. I had missed lunch again and threw together whatever I could find for supper, which wasn't all that much. Now that the roads were clear, I could drop Cinda off at Henry's and do some needed shopping and the laundry that had been piling up. It gave me a good excuse to make sure he had everything he needed as well.

A short time later, I was headed upstairs with Cinda taking the lead. Once inside my room, she made a dash for my unmade bed while I locked the door and wondered once again what had happened. I chose to believe it was Allison and let it go at that. It was now very dark, and I didn't want to consider any other possibilities.

I read for a while...took a few notes...then slid down under the covers where I lay listening to the house again. It was quiet though an owl hooted somewhere in the trees outside my window. Not a good thing. I remember reading in Native American Indian lore that the owl was a harbinger of death among other bad things best not thought about under the circumstances. I didn't trust Greystone. Didn't believe that the malignant entity who may or may not be Varna would stay in the cellar for much longer...though I really hoped I was wrong about that. One such horrific thought followed another and I was sure I would never fall asleep, but somehow I did. A nightmare was waiting.

I am cold...so very cold and hiding under my cot again because it comforts me in some strange way. This cell where she keeps me when visitors come is dark...darker than dark should be. She had dismissed the housekeeper and maid as soon as she knew I was with child. Told everyone who asked about me that I had run away and 'broke her mother's heart'. She threatens my baby when I try to fight back...starves me until I am now too weak to run. I know she hopes he'll die inside me. I hope and pray I am strong enough to prove her wrong.

She will be back soon or maybe not. Sometimes she leaves me down here for days. I remember all too well the last time she locked me in. I'd slid under the cot when I heard her returning. She'd been humming a hymn of some kind as she often did that echoed in the cavernous cellar. I shivered as she came closer and closer until I saw a thin band of light flicker under the door.

"Please no! Please no! Please no!" I had whispered to a God I hoped still heard me as the bolt slid back and the door swung open. She stood just inside holding a lantern that offered its small comfort of light. From where I lay, I only saw her shoe tips beneath the long black dress she favored and had been glad of that. Her eyes were the windows to hell.

"Come out from under there, you seed of Satan!" she had screamed at me.

A whimper had escaped me, and I heard her laugh. "Get out from under there and go to your room! Now! Our company has left. The Marchands and their lovely Julia Ann. An accomplished, God fearing, and devoted daughter while I am cursed with a sneaking, filthy sinner...a whore...a harlot! Come out now, or I will lock you in for the night. It promises to be a very cold one. You and your brat may not survive down here without the blankets I'm taking with me."

I had begun to crawl out from under the cot, but was already large with child and awkward. She laughed again and kicked me in the ribs knocking the breath out of me as I struggled to protect my baby. She had left then...taking the light with her. The door slammed shut, and the bolt slid back into place. She hadn't been back again that night. There had been no supper, and I had feared for the health of my son.

Now I wait again for her return. May a merciful God deliver us from evil.

It was Cinda's persistent cries that woke me. I gathered her close and waited for the horror of that nightmare to pass. I had been Millie again in a new and terrifying situation. Her mother had starved her...kicked her...and I had felt the blow. Varna was the devil incarnate. A creature of pure evil and....

My thoughts were interrupted as once again the ghostly clock struck the midnight hour. Somehow that was part of the mystery I may never solve before I grabbed Cinda and made a run for it like the devil was on our heels. The one called Varna Grey.

I don't think I fell asleep again after that. Well, maybe I dozed a bit. From the warmth of my bed, I could see the early morning sky streaked with pinks and lavenders. It was going to be another bright, crisp but cold day.

Plans for that day raced through my head as I dressed then headed downstairs. It was too early to call Henry, so I put on the coffee pot...took care of Cinda's breakfast needs then noticed something strange about the cabinet we'd shoved across the back hall entrance. It looked like it had been moved...not much...just a few inches, but now I could see the cellar door. A shiver shot up my spine.

"You're being ridiculous," I scolded myself. "It's always been like that, and you just noticed." It was a lie I really wanted to believe.

Taking a deep breath to steady my nerves, I sprinkled holy water on it then braced myself against the wall and shoved it back into place. Cinda was watching from across the room. Every hair on her body was bristled which only reinforced my own fear. It was beginning again.

"Let's just get out of here for a while," I told Cinda as I headed for the phone and called Henry. Trying to keep my voice steady, I asked if he would look after Cinda while I went shopping and caught up on my laundry.

"Mor'en happy to," he told me. "Come on over. We'd be mighty glad of the company."

I didn't waste much time shoving all the laundry that had piled up in my bathroom into a black garbage bag then dragged it down the stairs with Cinda running on ahead. We were headed to Henry's a short time later as fragments of my nightmare drifted through my mind.

A tail wagging Bella greeted me when I pulled up in front and downloaded Cinda's carrier. Henry was waiting at the door. "Grab a seat by the fire while I fetch us some coffee and maybe make us both somethin' to fill our bellies if you got room for it."

Suddenly, I was ravenous. "We got out of there sort of in a hurry, so that would be great," I told him as I shrugged out of my coat.

There were puppies now wandering everywhere, and several came to greet me while Bella checked out Cinda in her carrier. To my surprise, they seemed to like each other. Henry had been watching, too.

"Might want to open that thing up and let them get better acquainted. If the pups get too rough, she can head for high ground. There's plenty of that around here, and I ain't fussy about where she lands."

I released Cinda but kept a close eye on her as I helped Henry make breakfast. She had settled on top the wood box and was taking halfhearted swipes at any puppy nose that came too close. Suddenly, she jumped down next to Bella who licked the top of her head, which she didn't like but tolerated.

116

Henry smiled. "Cats and dogs aren't natural enemies like most folks think. It's how they're reared up. When Bella was a wee pup, our cat nursed her some after her own litter was born dead. Now tell me what's going on back at Greystone that sent you over here so early."

So, I told him about my nightmare and then the discovery in the kitchen. He was silent as he listened, but the worry lines in his forehead deepened. "You sure about where that cabinet was?"

"Absolutely! You helped me with it, and I made sure I couldn't see the cellar door."

He nodded. "Yep. I remember now. You would have walled up the whole dang hall if you could. Got any ideas on how you'll manage?"

"I shoved it back for starters and sprinkled some holy water on it. More and more, Henry, I feel like I need to find out what happened at Greystone...find out its connection with Allison and why she wants me there. I can't let whoever or whatever she is down there scare me off though she is doing a pretty good job of it so far"

He looked at me then shook his head. "Stubborn as they come. Maybe it's the red hair. I'll come on over tonight. Ankle's okay enough to get me there with no problem, and I ain't letting you stay there alone, so best forget arguin' about it."

I wanted to tell him that wasn't necessary...that I would be just fine...but it would be a lie he would see through in a flash, so I told him, "Then I'll make dinner for us though I should warn you my culinary expertise is nearly nonexistent."

117

I left Henry's not long after that with a list of supplies he needed added to my own. The snow was piled high on both sides of the road, but the pavement was now clear except for a few icy patches the sun didn't reach. It was a beautiful day in a wonderland of white, and I found myself enjoying it. Everything seemed so bright in contrast to the habitual darkness that seemed to linger at Greystone.

Reaching the village, I pulled up in front of the Buzzy Bee Laundromat and lugged my garbage bag inside. It wasn't busy, so I had my choice of machines and chose the huge ones at the far end. The whole process took far longer than I liked. A few people came and went. Some ignored me completely. Some murmured a greeting. Some whispered to each other, and I was sure they knew my connection to Greystone. Almost two hours later, I left with clean sheets, towels, and everything else I would need for a while.

The grocery store tucked behind the gas station was next on my agenda. There were no big chain stores of any kind in Courage Cove...all were of the 'mom and pop' variety owned by locals. The only place for groceries was the one run by Sarah and Bill Hunt. Today, they were both there and greeted me with a smile and the usual, "Give a shout if yah can't find something!" I smiled back, grabbed a cart, and began loading it. By then, I knew where everything was, so it didn't take long.

I was just pulling away when Alice drove up next to me, and we rolled down our windows to talk. She'd been worried, and I realized I should have called her. Jennie had told her about what happened at

Greystone, and she offered once again to let me stay at her place. I politely refused then asked about her mother.

"She's about the same which is good all things considered. Don't forget about the bazaar at the church. If you want to bring some of those famous cinnamon buns I heard tell you bake, they'd be welcome."

I had to laugh. The local 'grapevine' had been active. "Pillsbury did most of the work, but maybe I can bring something."

"Anything would be great and don't forget about the Ball."

I only *vaguely* remembered it had been mentioned, and she knew it judging from her next words.

"You *did* forget! It's our famous Christmas Ball and the biggest event here in Courage Cove. Residents...former residents...and relatives of both attend to play fancy dress up and dance. You might meet someone you'd like. You'd be surprised how some of these good old boys clean up. Being a couple isn't a requirement. Lot of folks go as singles. Two weeks from this coming Saturday night. The Bazaar's this Friday in case you didn't remember that either."

I don't know what we talked about after that as I mulled over what she had just said. A Christmas Ball...baking...normal stuff. Well, the 'Ball' wasn't exactly an every day thing, but there would be living people there having a good time instead of evil entities wreaking havoc.

"Well, I guess I will give you a call to confirm my contribution to the Bazaar," I finally told her with a smile.

"And I'm holding you to it. Do you good to get out of that place for a little while if you won't make it permanent."

We said our good byes, and I watched her drive up to the store in my rearview mirror. More than ever, I was beginning to realize the value of friends. Without the ones I had made at Courage Cove, I would be in deep trouble. They kept me grounded in reality, or there was a very disturbing possibility I might lose myself in whatever was happening at Greystone before I could get out of there.

As I drove back to Henry's, I thought about all the book signings, formal soirees and balls of one kind or another I had attended as Allison's protégé and then her daughter. Almost as soon as I entered her house, my education had begun...the right fork...the right clothes...the right walk...the list went on and on.

"You'd make a perfect hermit living in some cave, Jodie," she had told me with a smile more than once. "But in the world you are destined for there are things you must know."

So, it continued. I was her Eliza Doolittle, and she was my Henry Higgins even though hermit life sounded much more appealing to me at the time. I learned how to dance and the 'art' of small talk, which was most definitely not my forte. I was told I was 'too intense'...that I needed to lighten up. Enjoy what life now offered.

Bit by bit, I became all that she wanted with the help of teachers hell bent on making me a 'swan'. It hadn't been *quite* as bad as I expected though I still hated large parties...mingling...and the inevitable idle chitchat with strangers whose interest in me varied.

Some were curious about my connection to Allison. Some just needed attention or a sympathetic ear. Some wanted to seduce me.

I remember Allison telling me on my sixteen birthday...though the actual date was unknown, "You don't realize it now, but you are becoming a very beautiful and desirable woman. The kind that could attract the wrong kind of attention."

So another lesson was added. Self defense. Something I was quite good at to everyone's surprise but my own. I was told to never let a stranger get me alone though past experiences had already taught me that. I must not ever accept a drink from anyone but the waiter and never leave it out of my sight. I learned how to discourage a wandering hand and fend off an unwanted embrace or kiss without body slamming them into the ground though I now could do that if necessary and might even enjoy it.

As Allsion's health declined over the past several years, we had remained secluded. I often took notes as she told me about some of her adventures when she was young...those she hadn't written down at the time. She loved reliving every moment, and I was more than happy to indulge her. Anything to ease the pain that even the strongest meds did little to control. Her desire to spend her last days in Greece hadn't come as a surprise. She had stayed long ago in the very villa we rented with the man she deeply loved. Perhaps she felt his presence there. I tried to learn more about him, but she would smile enigmatically and say, "Read my journals. Find my past."

"I miss you so much I can't bear it!" I found myself screaming as I slammed the heel of my hand against the steering wheel again and again. I had thought I had reached a point where I dared remember those final days, but I was wrong. The thought...the *belief* that she was still with me was all that kept me going. I had a promise to keep and nothing was going to stop me even the 'hurt' I would relive again between the pages I was reading.

I pulled off the road till I regained my composure then continued on to Henry's where I hauled in his supplies...refusing the payment he offered.

"Then let me make us some lunch while you let Bella and her pups out. Will be the first time for them young'uns of hers."

I held the door open as Bella's puppies followed her outside. Since it was their first adventure in the white stuff, most didn't quite know how to handle it. Some borrowed under...some tried jumping over amid excited puppy 'yips'...one just sat on the steps and howled. Watching them helped relieve the pain that still lingered. They were alive and joyful. Something I knew in my heart Allison would want for me.

"No tears, Jodie," she had told me more than once. "Promise me." So I had, but even then I knew it was a promise I would break. How could I not?

Once we were all back inside, I asked about the Christmas Ball while we ate, and Henry told me much the same thing Alice had.

"It's a big deal. Used to go with Edith before she took sick. Rented a tux and all the rest. You should go."

I smiled. "Only if I can talk you into being my date."

He grinned back at me. "Mighty glad to be asked, but I only danced with one woman in all my years. Mostly stepped on her feet, but she never once complained. You go on. Do it. Be good for you seein' a bit of somethin' besides that mausoleum you live in. I'll make sure Cinda is safe."

I told him I would think about it then changed the subject. We talked about the upcoming Bazaar and my lack of baking skills. To my surprise, he laughed.

"You can use Edith's recipe. Was her annual entry and won most every time though that was some time back. I watched her make it and can talk you through what needs doin' best as I can recollect."

"Isn't that some kind of Church Bazaar cheating?"

He laughed again. "No one gives a hoot. It's all in good fun."

By then, Bella and her tired pups had fallen asleep in a big heap by the fire with Cinda on the wood box above them watching the flames through the grate. I could feel myself beginning to nod off. "Guess I better get going. It's so nice to be really warm for a change it's making me drowsy."

"Long as it's not the company," he teased then helped me load a reluctant Cinda back in her carrier. Though I begged him to stay in the kitchen where it was warm, he walked me to the car leaning heavily on his makeshift crutch, and I made sure he was safely back inside before I drove off.

It felt so good knowing I had him in my life that I was still smiling when we reached Greystone a short time later. Parking the car behind it, I looked at the sprawling house hunkered in the snow with its watchful window eyes. It felt like it had been waiting for me and was pissed off I took so long.

"Too bad for you," I shouted. "I have a life. I am living, breathing, and going to enjoy every minute of it." It was at that precise moment I made up my mind. I would attend the Christmas Ball. I would mingle, and chitchat, and do whatever was necessary to prove to myself I was not being seduced by Greystone.

I unloaded everything in the car and carried it to the kitchen. It took several trips. I made Cinda's carrier my last one. Setting it on the floor, I looked around. Nothing had changed as far as I could *see.* The cabinet was still in place, but something *felt* different. Since Cinda seemed unafraid when I released her, I wondered if perhaps I was overreacting. That being 'free' for a few hours had shifted my perception in some weird way. But despite my efforts to shrug it off, the feeling lingered as I put away the supplies then dragged the over stuffed laundry bag up the stairs and dumped its contents on my bed where it could wait till I got to it later.

Cinda had shadowed me everywhere and was with me when I reached my study. Opening what I thought was the journal I'd been reading, I was surprised to find it was a much later one. Had Allison been there while I was gone? Was I supposed to read something inside these pages? As if in answer to my question, Cinda knocked it out of my hand. It hit the floor and landed upside down were I scooped it up and began to read:

Over the spill of white stucco covered buildings, I watch the intense blue of the Aegean Sea roll up on shore. I have never felt so alive...so joyful. I had danced like a wind blown leaf around the room while he still slept in a tangle of white linens and limbs. I adore every inch of him...the way he looks...the way he tastes...the feel of him. There is a gentleness in him...a light in his eyes when he looks at me that tells me he loves this woman with all her faults...with all her past sins. That love cleanses me. I feel fresh and new. Reborn. I had never thought I would want to belong to any man. Valued my freedom above all else and then he was there one bright morning as I gathered shells along Aquinnah beach in Martha's Vineyard. He had picked up one that I had discarded then said, "Sometimes the beauty is not apparent. It can only be seen when we look with our hearts."

We talked very little. Just walked along the edge of the water. I don't know when his hand found mine. It just happened. I had no idea where any of it was heading and my uncertainty must have shown in my face, for he pulled me to a stop...tipped up my chin and looked deep into my eyes. "Don't be afraid. We are fated to have found each other."

He never told me how he knew that. I had thought at the time it was just a line, but the more time we spent together I began to believe he was right. It felt so natural. I felt complete in a way I had never known. Soon, I was desperately in love, and it was returned. I have never known such happiness was possible.

Tears blurred the words I was reading, so I stopped and closed the journal. She never told me what happened to him...just that he had been killed. Some part of her hadn't survived his death. Her life had changed from that point on she had told me more than once. I thought again about her dying moments. Her smile as her eyes lost their light and hoped he had found her again.

"You're just a silly romantic," I told myself, but I wanted to believe it with all my heart.

I began to read again. The words were so intensely personal I had to stop. Not once had she mentioned his name, which made me wonder if he had been married. I knew she had taken married lovers in the past because it avoided 'messy entanglements', but somehow I knew there had to be more to it than that. Her words echoed in my head once again, "Read my journals...find my past."

Time passed quickly as I continued to read. It was late when I checked the clock. Henry would be over soon, and I had promised him dinner. Easing a sleeping Cinda off my lap, I headed to the kitchen the late afternoon sun had infused with a golden glow then crossed to the window and checked out my snow angel. She was almost gone, and I felt a sharp sense of loss.

"Please don't leave me," I murmured as I pressed my hand against the cold windowpane. For the briefest of moments, a translucent hand returned my touch then vanished. It could have been a trick of the light, but I chose to believe Millie was still with me when the phone rang. Henry was on his way.

He arrived a few minutes later. I had decided on the homemade chili Anna had taught me to make, French bread, and a mixed green salad. My shopping trip had supplied everything I needed including the wine we opened and shared. He insisted on helping, and while

126

we worked, I told him I had decided to go to the ball after all. "My idle chitchat is a bit rusty. Might have to practice on you *if* I'm not going to be a complete wallflower."

He shook his head. "Not too likely with some of the boys around here. They won't much care what you say or think, but…"

"That's the very problem, Henry," I cut in. "Those are the things that are important. They are what makes me...well, *me*. Not some *body* I was born into."

He shook his head a second time. "You didn't let me finish. They ain't all like that. The right man will find his way to you some day. Just wait."

My sigh was heavy. "I won't wait for some *prince* to appear in my life and sweep me off my sneakers. I am fine just the way I am. That kind of love opens the door to the pain of loss. The gut wrenching kind I don't ever want to be mine. I've felt Millie's. I've read about and seen Allison's. I don't want it to be me. "

He was quiet for a long moment before he answered me. "Once you get past that part of it, you start rememberin' all the years in between that you wouldn't have missed a moment of no matter what the cost."

"Your Edith is still with you," I reminded him.

"She came back for me. Love is forever. It's the findin' each other again that's sometimes hard."

His words kept nudging my mind as we ate supper where our conversation was about the village...the renovations Joe would tackle next...his plans for Bella's pups. Normal...ordinary things. Time

127

passed quickly. After clean up, we took our time heading upstairs. Henry's ankle slowed him down, but he refused my help and kept going while Cinda raced on ahead. She was waiting for us at the top of the stairs then led the way to our rooms where I thanked him again for staying.

"Shoot! Think I'm going to let somethin' happen to the belle of the Christmas Ball?"

I drew him into a hug and left him there. My eyes were wet with tears I didn't want him to see. Inside my room, I locked the door and looked for Cinda. I could hear her in the bathroom tossing her litter around and headed there to shower and get ready for bed. Afterwards, I dealt with the laundry piled on top of it then crawled beneath the covers. I was asleep in a matter of minutes.

Some time later, Cinda's 'yowl' woke me from a deep sleep. The room was dark except for the glowing figure bent over me. It was a woman whose long, wet hair brushed my cheeks as she peered at me closely with eyes that looked like black holes burnt in white paper. I was beyond terrified. Suddenly, her mouth opened wide in a long, drawn out, ear-piercing wail I was sure must have woken Henry as well as the none too dead.

Sliding deeper under the covers, I looked for Cinda. A hiss from under the bed told me where she was just as the woman wailed again...a long banshee screech. In the flickering light of her glow, I could see the rope burn around her neck and knew it was Hannah clutching something in her arms I hoped was the doll Henry had told me about...but it wasn't. It was the skeletal remains of an infant wrapped in a sodden blanket.

She must have seen my revulsion and horror, so she began to whisper, "I didn't want to marry that old man. They forced me to the altar, and he made me give birth to the heir he wanted. Shall I tell you a secret no one else knows?" I shook my head but that didn't stop her. "I drowned this one I carry. Locked him in a trunk when the ship was going down then told Horace he'd been swept out of my arms by the sea. I had to do it. I couldn't stand his cries. His neediness. His demands, but I found myself missing him when I hadn't thought that possible. I went back to the wreck of the *Morning Star* after I ended my life. He was where I had left him, and I brought him home. He's quiet now...a good baby. See how he smiles? You understand. I know you do."

When I didn't answer her, she began to float above me in frenzied circles then dropped down till her face was only inches from mine. "They think I am mad, don't they?" she hissed.

I found myself nodding though that soon became apparent it wasn't the answer she was hoping for. Uttering another long drawn out wail, she and the tiny skeleton in her arms began to liquify then dissipate slowly. I watched the last of her disappear and felt a twinge of pity despite the horrible thing she had done. Her guilt must have driven her insane. Perhaps she'd always been fragile, and her circumstances pushed her over the edge. I would never know the truth.

Wondering how Henry could have slept through all that, I crawled beneath my now sodden bed and gathered Cinda in my arms. Her warmth and reassuring purr gave me the comfort I needed in the worst kind of way.

"I think she was the one in the hall by the back stairs on our first night," I whispered to Cinda. "I just hope she doesn't plan to drop by again any time *ever.*"

I drew Cinda closer. I was wet and cold. Would probably expire from hypothermia before morning, but even with that dire prospect looming over me, I couldn't seem to budge.

CHAPTER SIX

(Millie)

She is hiding under the bed again with her cat. Frightened by the other who means her no harm. Hannah...the watery one who gnashes her teeth and wails as she carries what remains of her murdered child in her arms. I would have given anything...everything to have had my baby live...grow to be a man like his father. The gnawing ache in the deepest part of my being comes from my need to hold him...love and nurture him...protect him from all harm. I still wonder if the cry I hear at night is his tiny spirit looking for me as I look for him though I have almost come to believe it is the cry of Hannah's son trapped within these walls that haunts me.

I see her shiver. She and her cat need warmth to see them through the night. I can do that for them...that and keep my mother at bay for the moon is full, and she is restless. Was she ever sane...ever able to love me if only a little? Ever felt for me what I feel for my son? Not that it matters now. She will never give up until she has what she wants. All I can do is protect these two as best I can and pray Jodie finds what brought her here before my mother destroys her, or she succumbs to the evil embedded in the very walls of this place. I so want her to be happy. To know the kind of love I had with a 'happy ever after' instead of the ending I had known. May God give me the strength I need to keep her safe.

(Jodie)

I awoke the next morning still under the bed, but warmly covered with Cinda next to me. The memory of what had happened swept over me. Had any of that been real? Crawling out from underneath, I looked around. My bed was dry. There was nothing out of the ordinary. Had it all been another horrific nightmare? And if it wasn't, why hadn't Henry heard the wails?

Throwing on my robe, I unlocked the door and bolted into the hall. Outside Henry's room, I hesitated then knocked lightly. There was no answer, so I opened it a crack and peeked inside. No one was there! A wave of panic ...fear swept over me until I heard his cheerful whistle coming from the bathroom down the hall.

Returning to my own room, I sat on the edge of my bed and thought about what had just happened. I had been terrified that

131

something very bad had gone down. "I can't lose him, too! He can't stay another night in this house of horrors," I told Cinda who was headed towards the bathroom.

My troubled thoughts stayed with me as I followed her there and prepped for the day while she perched on the edge of the sink and systematically knocked everything on the floor. A short time later, we caught up with Henry in the lower hall. He was way too chipper when I was anything but.

"Where's that smile?" he asked as he held the kitchen swing door open for me and my 'shadow'.

"Still in bed where the rest of me would like to be," I mumbled as I made a beeline for the coffee maker. I could barely look at him knowing what I would have to tell him before night came.

I waited until we had settled down at the table before I asked as casually as I could manage when I still felt the residual horror, "Did you happen to hear anything out of the ordinary last night?".

"Nope. Read for a while then slept like a rock. Somethin' happened I missed, didn't it?"

"Unless it was all a nightmare, I had a visitor," I told him then went on to tell the rest.

Henry was horrified. "Good God almighty! Didn't hear a peep! This old man ain't worth crap if I can sleep through that!"

I shook my head and pasted on a smile. "More than likely, I dreamt the whole thing so don't worry about it. I'm going to be tucking into my research for most of the day, so...."

"You don't need me hangin' around, so I'll scoot on home and take care of a few chores that need doin'," he cut in before I could finish. "Let's get them dishes done and then I'll head on out."

Cinda and I watched him drive away not long after that. He would be back before nightfall. I hadn't been able to tell him what I needed to tell him. Making him leave would not be easy. It would mean hurting someone who meant a great deal to me, which was the very reason he had to go. I must keep him safe.

I headed to my study hoping work would divert my thoughts. As soon as I opened the door, Cinda jumped up on my desk next to a journal that was already open. I sat down and began to read:

My monthly was late again. A check with the doctor confirmed it. I was pregnant. I told Edward that weekend. I had thought neither one of us wanted to be tethered, so his reaction was not what I expected. He had touched my still flat belly and smiled. "So I am going to be a father. How wonderful is that!"

Later that night, we lay in front of the fire while we discussed the changes it would mean for both of us. He wanted to marry me as soon as he had a 'few things handled'. I wasn't at all sure what that meant, and I didn't ask. Maybe I was afraid of the answer.

The idea of marriage had always been abhorrent to me, but he made it seem like a fairytale...that the 'happily ever after' kind was possible, and I ignored the small well of panic deep inside me. I was always either working like some fiend or on the road with book signings...book launches...meetings...that sort of thing that took me all over the world. Would I have time for a baby? Would I have time for him? Those were some of the doubts that I kept to myself as I lay in his arms wrapped in the world he was creating for us.

I stopped reading as I thought about what I had learned. Allison had been pregnant. To say I was shocked would be a colossal understatement. "So what happened to your child? What happened to all your plans? I know you never married," I murmured out loud as Cinda stared at me with her golden eyes.

As if in answer to my question, the pages fluttered all the way to the end where I read these words:

We were to meet at the train station at 4 pm. I waited for an hour...then two...then stayed through the night sitting on a bench where I could see the trains coming and going. During that time, I had tried calling him, but the phone had already been disconnected. We had planned on never coming back. We were starting a new life together and severing the cord to the past.

Fears nudged me. Had he decided not to leave? Did he not love me as much as I thought? There was so little I knew about him...really knew beyond the bits and pieces we shared. He had said a touch of mystery was a good thing in a relationship. That we each had secrets we needed to keep, and who was I to disagree? I certainly had my share, so I didn't press him. Just enjoyed every precious moment we shared.

The sun was bright when I stepped out onto the platform that morning and looked around in a daze. I began to walk away with no idea where I was going. I left my luggage where it was stacked, ignored the shouts of the porter, and just kept walking...and walking...and walking. I found myself on a park bench near a fountain where a young couple was tossing coins into its clear water. Making wishes. An elderly man sat down next to me and opened up his newspaper. The large photo on the front page caught my eye. The headline was: Industrialist Edward Parker Killed in Mugging.

I had snatched the paper from his hands, and read the words blurred by tears. He had left behind a wife. A family he never told me about. The "things he had to handle". Would it have made a difference had I known? Now it was all a moot point. I remember little after that as a chilling numbness stole over me. He was gone. I was alone and then I felt the first stir of life within me.

I brushed away my own tears as I closed the journal and thought about her words. Now I knew how he had died and wondered what her child's fate had been. Suddenly, I remembered something I had thought strange at the time then completely forgot.

Allison had wanted to go to a book reading by one Oliver Parker...a well-known author. His genre was sci-fi and something that had never interested her in the past. We arrived late and took a seat in the back of the room. He was tall with salt and pepper hair and a closely cropped beard. His deep voice was compelling as he read excerpts from his latest book. Allison had listened intently then got up and left before he finished. I had asked about it when I climbed in the car next to her, but she shut me down, and I had let it go at that. Now I wondered who Oliver Parker was? Could his last name be a coincidence I didn't believe in?

It was getting late and I had my own chores to do before Henry returned. I would have to put off my research until later.

***

I had just finished cleaning both litter boxes, changing the sheets on my bed and a few other necessary tasks when Henry arrived with a pot of stew he had made. "Some grub to fill you up 'cause I'm willin' to bet you didn't eat much today."

He was looking after me as he always did, and more than ever I hated what I would have to do. The moment came. While I reheated the stew, I took a deep breath then told him over my shoulder as casually as I could, "You really should be staying off that ankle more. I really appreciate you looking after me, but I think I'll do just fine on my own from now on. Your place needs attention...Bella and the pups...friends that call...that sort of thing."

"What are you tryin' to say and not doin' so great at it?"

I pasted on a smile then turned to face him. "Look! It's been great having you here. I mean beyond great, but..."

"But?"

"You're just up the road, and I have my walkie talkie. I think it's time I cut the cord. Stood on my own two feet if I'm going to be here for the foreseeable future."

"And I *think* that's a very bad idea."

I shook my head. "Won't know till I try it. I need to face my fears. Take control. That's what Jennie told me to do."

"She couldn't skedaddle outta here fast enough," he scoffed. "You're old enough to know what you want *if* you were thinkin' straight, but you ain't. Not by a long shot!"

"I know what I need to do, so let's just eat and not talk about it."

So, that's what we did. In fact, we didn't talk about much of anything. He helped me with the dishes. Told me to keep the leftovers and headed out the door a short time later. There were tears in my eyes as I watched him drive away.

Desperately needing a distraction, I scooped up Cinda and headed to my study where I began searching for information about Oliver Parker. I soon found out he wasn't a fan of social media, but there were other sources I tapped. From his bio, I learned he was the son of Maryanne and Edward Parker. *Allison's* Edward Parker. He had been born five months after his father's death, which meant Maryanne had been pregnant at the same time as Allison.

I continued to look for information and found out that Oliver had had an older sister who died at age four from leukemia. The date was two years before his father's affair. Had his daughter's death been the crisis that ended his marriage? I had read that trying to cope with the loss of a child often either strengthened or ended one. But he and his wife were expecting another child. That should have been reason enough for him to stay unless the rift was too deep to be mended.

Suddenly, I realized it was far later than I had ever been downstairs before, and I looked around nervously. Cinda was asleep near the heat vent...a good sign...but night pressed against the windows.

Grabbing my flashlight, I headed out the door with a wide-awake Cinda leading the way though her tail now twitched and the fur along her spine bristled. *Not* a good sign. My footsteps sounding unnaturally loud in the hushed atmosphere as I hurried along following the path my flashlight carved from the darkness. As I passed each door, I sensed…or *maybe* just imagined… someone or something was pressed against the other side. By the time I reached the stairs, I was running with Cinda now well in the lead. Reaching the top, I turned and flashed my light below. Someone was standing on the bottom step. A shadowy *someone* that repelled my light then dissipated.

"Be strong! Don't run!" I told myself, so I took a deep breath and continued on at a walk though my heart was racing wildly. Turning again, I flashed my light down the dark hall behind me. The shadow figure was now on the top step. A pillar of utter darkness that hissed loudly, "He would have been next. Now you are all alone."

I began to run and didn't stop till I reached my well lit room and locked the door behind me. It felt like a small oasis of safety, which I knew was deceptive. If that was Varna, a locked door wouldn't stop her.

Grabbing the holy water bottle, I splashed some over it while murmuring the prayer Jennie had used at the purging again and again. After that, I waited…watched…and listened for what seemed like a very long time. All was quiet on the other side, so I kicked off my sneakers and crawled into bed still fully dressed in case I needed to grab Cinda and get out of there in a hurry.

As I lay there with her curled up in the crook of my arm, I wondered if Millie was close by…protecting us and then remembered that someone had kept us warm when we were hiding under the bed last night. Had I done it myself in some sleep state or had she been looking after us again?

"Thank you, Millie, for everything," I whispered then fell asleep a short time later...the dreamless kind I needed.

***

The next morning, the sun was shining, and I found myself wanting a break from work. From discoveries that both intrigued and disturbed me…from Greystone and its horrors including what I had seen last night.

"Maybe we will try out Henry's heated throw thingie. You can wait in the car while I take a quick trip to the shore and wave watch. I need a water 'fix' to center me," I told Cinda as she fished the last kibble out of her bowl.

More and more, the idea grew on me till it became a compulsion. After dressing warmly from head to toe, I loaded Cinda in her carrier and took her out to the car where I plugged in the plaid throw and draped it over her.

"I'll be back in just a few minutes," I promised as she thrust one furry black paw through the bars. "I can't leave you all alone in that house and coming with me through all that snow isn't an option you would like."

A plaintive 'meow' followed me as I closed the door and headed for the trail that snaked through the trees. The snow was still knee deep in places and criss crossed with animal prints...birds...rabbits...and others I didn't recognize. Overhead, a strong easterly wind with a sharp cold bite tossed the trees about in a wild frenzy. I had forgotten my gloves, so I tucked my hands in my pockets where I felt a wad of paper. Wondering what it was, I pulled it out and scanned the few words written there: *Find my secret place.*

I had no idea how it got there. Only knew it hadn't been there when I went shopping, or I would have found it. Was it Millie who wrote those words? And where would I even begin to look for her *secret place*?

I kept thinking about what I had read, as I continued down the trail Millie would have taken often judging from the dreams I was having. The scent of the sea...the sound of the waves grew stronger with every step and then I was there. Climbing up on a granite boulder, I looked out over the immense expanse of gray, wind lashed water...awesome in its fierce power. High above, seagulls glided on the air currents...their wings flashing in the morning sun...their cries mingling with the sound of the waves. Far offshore, I spotted a sailboat heeled over...its side rail brushing the water as the wind filled its sails. It was beautiful. Like a winged creature, and I smiled until I remembered the fate of the *Morning Star*.

My thoughts turned to Millie again as I sat down and hugged my knees for warmth. Despite my warm clothing, I was suddenly cold. Was it the wind that chilled me to the bone? Maybe Millie was sitting here with me...wanting me to see through her eyes this awesome place and then a curious thing happened. I did just that.

It is no longer cold. It is a summer night, and I am dancing barefoot in the sand under a full moon...laughing and twirling...reaching for the sky. He is lying on a blanket at my feet, propped up on one elbow and playing the harmonica...a tune I don't know and then I do. It's " Moonlight Bay". I tumble down next to him, and he pulls me into his arms then kisses me. I can feel my pulse race...my body respond and..

The image was gone. I was myself again...not Millie. It was a cold winter day...not night...not summer. There was no mystery lover whose kiss shattered me though I could still feel his lips on mine. Their love was the kind that should have had a happy ending.

"Instead, she felt the kind of pain no one should feel just like Allison did," I murmured as I brushed away my tears, scrambled to my feet, and headed back to Cinda and Greystone.

***

The rest of the day passed quickly. When I wasn't working on my research, I read for a while just to relax then called Henry. I needed to hear his voice.

"Are you still angry with me?" were the first words out of my mouth.

I heard his sigh and then his answer, "Just wish you would listen and quit being such a hard head."

It was my turn to sigh. "I don't see that changing any time soon."

"Expect not. Any new developments?"

We talked for a while, and he reminded me about the Bazaar. I jotted down the ingredients I would need for Edith's recipe and promised I'd go shopping for them tomorrow. We rang off and I looked around. It was time to make supper and head upstairs before it got much darker. I remembered all too well the shadow figure on the stairs last night and what it had shouted. Now he was safe.

I had just finished up when the phone rang. To my surprise it was Joe. They were headed back and should arrive and "be rarin' to go" on Thursday. He went on to tell me he had found an electrician. I smiled. Soon there would be light, noise, and the sound of power tools.

I made it to my room without incident. Cinda had raced on ahead and was already settled on the bed by the time I got there and locked the door behind me. I had meant to replenish the firewood, but forgot. What I had left wouldn't last long, but I needed the comfort of its bright flames and soon had a respectable blaze going. As I was warming my hands, I looked around the room I had chosen.

"I'm almost certain this was Millie's room and that was her bed over there," I murmured to myself as I remembered the red hair I'd discovered under it and the image in the mirror. "By some strange twist of fate, it found its way back here." I smiled wryly. For some unknown reason, I had been that 'twist'. How it would all fall into place remained a mystery.

When I closed my eyes a short time later, I imagined I still heard the sound of the sea, and it soon lulled me into a deep sleep where another dream was waiting. I was still 'me' and now in a cave lit by a single lantern. A young woman with long red hair was writing something in a diary. I moved closer and read over her shoulder as the words spilled from her pen:

I am here now in my secret place…escaped for a time though she watches me closely. I had faked my monthly flows to buy some time, but now I am beginning to show signs of my pregnancy. God help me when she knows the truth. Her wrath will be terrible…beyond terrible, for she is quite insane. I must find a way to protect the baby I carry and me. I will run while I still can. Steal what I need to survive in an unfamiliar world. A world beyond the village where I have never been before.

I must plan carefully. It will be at night when she sleeps. I feel my heart throb wildly in my breast at the mere thought of what I must do, so I let the sound of the waves below calm me. They give me strength. The eternal sea will break upon this shore long after Greystone and its secrets have disappeared forever. Long after the devil has claimed her soul.

I awoke with a start. "Her secret place is a cave! No doubt the same one she showed me before." Closing my eyes, I tried to recapture what I had seen, but sleep claimed me again.

***

The next morning I was busy in the kitchen when Joe arrived and introduced me to the new electrician. "This here's Wiley Wyatt from Douglasville. He'll take over the rewiring."

"Thanks for helping, Wiley," I told the gaunt young man with permanent frown lines in his high forehead.

He nodded and studied the tips of his work boots when he replied, "Joe told me what's already been done, but there's a whole lot still needs doin'."

"I'd like to get both the upper and lower halls rewired and the chandelier working in the foyer as soon as possible," I told him.

"Joe told me the 220-volt plug for the dryer ain't been wired yet. Seems like you'd want that done first."

"That can wait," I replied since the laundry room was next to the cellar and not a place I would ever go again.

"Suit yourself. Ain't no skin off my nose. Where do I find the electric panel? Need to see what the last guy rigged up."

Joe told him it was in the cellar then noticed the cabinet pulled across the hall. He looked from it to me then told Wiley, "Why don't you go grab your tools out of your truck while I wait here."

I knew he wanted to speak to me privately. Knew what he would say, and I wasn't wrong. "Look...tell me what's going on here. The less that guy knows the better, or he'll be outta here like a scalded 'possum."

I gave a *very* sparse account of what happened in the cellar, but I didn't fool Joe. "Reading between them lines tells me a whole lot more happened than what you just said. Goin' to move that cabinet out of the way before he sees it. Will talk him into adding a new panel in the laundry room, so he doesn't have to go down there. You'll need to come up with an excuse why he shouldn't way, way short of telling him what you just told me."

144

So, that's what I did. If my story that the cellar steps were too dangerous sounded lame to me, Wiley didn't seem to notice or care. Soon the house was full of activity...living, breathing men going about their jobs.

I had shopping to do, so I loaded Cinda in the car and headed to the grocery store where I found everything I needed to make Edith's cake plus the calorie loaded comfort food I craved. Cinda was asleep under her heated throw when I returned a short time later and climbed behind the wheel. The day was bright and sunny. A glorious winter white paradise, and I wondered what would happen if I just kept driving. Forgot all about Greystone. Started a new life free from whatever haunted me there.

"But that won't happen. You have a promise to keep, a cake to bake, and Henry," I told myself as I headed back to the last place I should be *or* wanted to be for that matter.

The rest of the day was still chaotic. I called Henry and told him I was ready to bake whenever he was.

"Be on over in a bit. We can do the cake part tonight and whip up the fillin' and icin'. I've got all the cake pans we'll need plus the gizmos to decorate it. We'll put 'er all together in the morning."

He arrived a few minutes later and talked me through what I had to do. "Now let them cake rounds cool then wrap 'em up real good and tuck 'em in the fridge. The rest you already got a handle on, so you're on your own from here on out, since you don't want me stayin'."

He left after he helped me shove the cabinet back into place, and I busied myself following the last of his directions. It was quite late by the time I had finished, wolfed down a P&J sandwich, and cleaned up the colossal mess. Cinda had given up on me some time ago and was fast asleep on the window seat safely out of my way. Gathering her up in my arms, I left the lights on and pushed through the door into the main hall that had *supposedly* been rewired.

"Okay! We've come to the 'ta dah' moment I've been putting on hold all day," I murmured under my breath then flipped the wall switch. To my immense delight and relief, the wall sconces lit all the way down to the far end. Nothing looked *quite* as menacing as it did before. It was just a dingy, long hall with closed doors on both sides. I chose not to speculate on what was behind them.

Nothing followed us up to my room, and I heaved a second sigh of relief though I made sure the door was locked and sprinkled with more holy water. A short time later both Cinda and I were fast asleep.

***

The next morning, Henry arrived early with the cake carrier Edith had used. Together we assembled the multi layers. It was a teensy bit lopsided till we 'shimmed' up the low side with extra filling. By the time I finished decorating it under Henry's supervision, it was a work of art!

"You did Edith proud," he told me with a grin. "Got a real knack for it. Now all you gotta do is haul it on over to the church. They've already set up the tables, and I reserved a spot for you dead center."

"You're coming with me, right?"

"You don't need me. I'll just sit a spell here...check on Joe.... and keep that cat of yours outta trouble."

I protested, but he was firm. It was "my show".

Somehow, our cake survived the ride to the village where I unloaded it carefully then carried it down to the church basement that was already swarming with women setting up their own masterpieces. Alice spotted me hovering in the doorway and led me to the spot Henry had reserved.

"I halfway thought you'd bag out on me. Let's get whatever you brought properly displayed with its name and yours written on this itty bitty card."

She helped me uncover the cake and display it on its stand then studied it thoughtfully. "Looks both truly amazing and oddly familiar. If you haven't already chosen a name, 'Heavenly Wonder' comes to mind."

I had to laugh. She knew where the recipe had come from and was not surprised when I wrote on the card: *Edith's Gift.*

The rest of the day was rather a blur of faces and names. Only a very few were recognizable. The elderly judges were complete strangers. Alice whispered to me they were the Pickering twins and Madge Reinholt. Same judges every year. Even though I thought

147

my cake was magnificent, I was surprised when it won first place. All the entries were raffled off, and I was very glad to see Jennie win it.

I slipped away as soon as I could after that, but not before Alice caught up with me at the door and reminded me again about the Christmas Ball. As I left the village behind, I could still feel the warmth of the people in that room. True, I did hear "Greystone" mentioned in hushed voices...did get more than a few curious looks...but everyone was kind and welcoming. I just wished I had a better memory for names.

When I reached Greystone, Henry greeted me at the kitchen door where I handed him the small trophy we had won. While he made a pot of coffee, I babbled on and on about all that had happened.

"Them Pickerings are tough. Spiteful sometimes. You done good," he told me as he slid into the chair across from me and shoved a mug my way. "Thanks for what you named it. Edith would have liked that...been proud."

"So, what did I miss while I was gone?"

"They been busy as a nest of ants tearing up the floor and all that plaster what got wet in them back rooms. Joe's hopin' they got enough matchin' boards from some old school to finish 'em off but doubts it. That Wiley guy wanted to go down in the cellar, but it was locked so that put an end to that."

"Thankfully!" I replied with a wry smile. "That would have been the last we saw of him."

"Yep! Have to get on back home. Things that gotta be done I've been puttin' on hold till this dad blame ankle was better. Anything you need before I go?"

My eyes were wet with tears when I told him, "Thanks, Henry, for everything. I don't know how I would manage without you."

He snorted and swiped at his own eyes with the back of his hand. "You're a tough little gal in some ways. Mule headed or you wouldn't have kicked me out on my duff like you did. You'll find a way to manage, or she wouldn't have sent you here."

My eyes widened in surprise. "So you believe?"

"Come to believe your ma and Millie are lookin' after you. Edith told me so when I was frettin' and worryin' the other night. Just keep both them big gray eyes open wide and shoot on over to my place any time you need to...day or night."

I walked him to his truck and gave him a hug then waited there till he made the turn at the end of the drive. Everyone wrapped up for the day shortly after that. It was the weekend, and they wanted to be home with their families or busy doing whatever else they enjoyed on a Friday night.

Joe lingered after the others had left. After shoving the cabinet in front of the hall, he told me, "This Wiley is beginning to get real nosey about the cellar. Could be a problem since you don't want him down there. Might mention, I'll be headed there come Monday. Need to recheck that wall I told you about."

I sighed. "I saw it. Looks like it's beginning to cave in."

"Yep...and when it does there's gonna be all kinds of problems. Them supports under the whole shebang are real old...some dry rotted."

"You're telling me the house could collapse?" a very worried me asked.

"The whole kit and caboodle will rack."

"Which means?"

"Chimneys will fall...walls crack... and that's just for starters. You never did tell me the whole story about what happened to you down there. Just some tale that something scared you, and I let it go at that. I need to know more."

I sighed again. I really, really didn't want to relive the whole thing, so I told him, "There is someone truly evil...truly malignant down there who wants to hurt me. I see you don't believe me, and I can't really blame you."

"I've heard all the stories about this place...some just old rumors and wives tales...some from people I trust including you, but I just can't believe in ghosts," he told me. "When you're dead, you're dead. That's it."

"I wish with all my heart in her case that was true, Joe, but she's down there and waiting."

It was his turn to sigh. "Tried checking on the wall from the outside but that damned rose jungle covers up the foundation, so I couldn't get close to it. Like I said, I'll be going down there on Monday. See you then."

I listened to his truck drive off as I started a light supper. A quick salad with a can of tuna dumped in. "Not a culinary delight by most standards, but it gives me all I need though a piece of my cake would be more than welcome," I told Cinda who was begging for the almost empty can.

I remembered the comfort food I bought and carried a bag of chips with me when we headed upstairs. With Cinda snuggled close, I spot read through some of Allison's earlier journals and learned even more about her views on relationships. In short, she believed in keeping it light and letting it last only as long as it was mutually satisfying. A direct quote was: "I'll never shed a tear over some man no matter how good in bed. If he makes me unhappy, I'm *gone*! If he takes more energy from me than he's worth, I'm *gone*."

She was also *gone* if things got "too serious". In a short span of time by most standards, she ran through a whole string of lovers some quite famous. The details of those short lived romances were so very intimate it made me uncomfortable, so I skimmed through the steamiest parts then wondered what it would be like to have a man make me feel that way.

I remembered my dream kiss and how my body had responded then sighed. I had dated a few guys, but found myself backing away when they wanted to get too physical. Perhaps it was residual damage from the attempted assaults in my childhood. Maybe I just didn't trust them enough or care enough to take that step. I had never loved any of them. Maybe that was the missing ingredient though that certainly hadn't been a problem for Allison. Whatever it was, it had put a quick end to any budding romance.

"We're all walking wounded in some ways including my mother," I told Cinda as I nibbled on a chip...and then another. "Perhaps we will never heal." I was still thinking about that when I fell asleep half a bag later.

***

The house was very quiet with everyone gone. Cinda and I had breakfast together while I thought about how I would spend the day. I needed a break from Allison's journals...from the whole thing...and decided to strip the wallpaper off my study walls. I had watched one of Joe's men handle it in the kitchen, so I was pretty sure I knew what to do.

Cinda followed me to the room where they stored all their supplies, and I lugged what was needed back to my study then looked around for a place to start. I decided on the back wall behind the door. If I made a mess of it, I wouldn't have to look at it till Joe's crew fixed my mistakes. The corner of a seam had already lifted, so I gave it a tug. A long thin strip came off, curled up and dropped to the floor. It was beginning to look like an easy job, so I sprayed the wall with the stripper I'd found and waited for it to do its magic...all but the top. The ceiling was thirteen feet high. I would need a ladder to reach it and knew where to find one.

Cinda took refuge under my desk when I disappeared out the door and came back carrying a nine foot stepladder with difficulty. It was

152

aluminum and not that heavy but awkward. I had banged it into more than one thing or another on the way there. After setting it up, I looked it over. It was a long way to the top, and I had never liked heights or ladders though I had managed to tackle the rose pruning job despite my fear. This should be easy by comparison, I told myself when I should have remembered from past experiences that kind of thinking was a recipe for disaster.

I searched my computer for a YouTube Christmas album and cranked up the volume then lugged the sprayer up the ladder as high as I dared climb. I sprayed that section liberally then took a deep breath and ventured still higher. I was at the top when a slight tremor shook the ladder. The one that followed was stronger. Dropping the sprayer, I clung desperately to it with both hands as I looked below. There was no one there. Had the basement wall collapsed? Was it an earthquake? I began to clamber down just as a cold hand grabbed my ankle. Way beyond terrified, I tried to shake free with disastrous results. The ladder tipped to one side, and I fell. Expecting to land in the clutches of something truly horrifying, I was more than surprised when a pair of strong arms caught me, and I was looking up into furious brown eyes framed by horn rimmed glasses.

I had to say something, so I asked, "Was that an earthquake?"

He smiled grimly. "No. It was you being an idiot. What are you still doing here? I thought I told you to leave."

He had to be Simon North who hadn't been at all helpful when I needed him before. Now he was holding me longer than was necessary, and I found myself telling him rather sharply, "You can put me down now. If you don't, I can make you very sorry."

"I'm already more than sorry. You aren't exactly a feather weight, you know," he replied as he set me on my feet rather hard.

"I am tall and willowy...neither a *feather* nor fat," popped out of my mouth as ridiculous as that sounded, and I returned his intense gaze with a glare.

To my surprise, he laughed then plucked a chunk of wet wallpaper out of my hair. "You'll have to do better than that if you want to scare me off. And 'willowy' suggests a gracefulness you sadly lacked when you landed like a lump in my arms. I meant what I said. This is no place for you...for anyone."

I sniffed derisively. "Then what are you doing here sneaking about uninvited?"

"I knocked but there was no answer, so I followed the music. I'm looking for my grandfather. He's not at home, and I figured he might be over here considering the interest he's taken in your well being."

"And you didn't notice his truck wasn't here?" I scoffed then added rather reluctantly because he was all kinds of irritating, "I suppose I *should* thank you for catching me."

"But you won't. I get it. That's why you're still here. You're a stubborn little ninny who doesn't have any idea what she's messing with in this place."

My gray eyes narrowed to mere slits. "You're wrong about that. I know all too well what haunts Greystone, but I need to be here."

"You do know that renovations stir them up even more. They like things just as they were."

"So, I've heard...somewhere or other...but I'm wanted here. There are mysteries I need to solve."

"Sounds to me like this place has already infected you. You have delusions that the house wants you...needs you, right?"

I certainly hoped not, but I feared the very same thing. Not that I'd admit it to him. "That's a load of rubbish. Your grandfather knows why I'm here. Talk to him. I have work to do, so *please* get the hell outta here. That's me asking as nicely as I can."

He smiled grimly again. "As I said, that was no earthquake. I saw something grab your ankle. It's broad daylight, and you're not alone here," and with that said he turned on his heel and left.

I followed him, and Cinda followed me then we both watched him drive off. The idea of going back in the study was extremely unnerving, so I decided to abort my wallpaper efforts, load up on some firewood, and head back upstairs. Cinda led the way as I looked around nervously. There hadn't been any daylight evil manifestations to date. Now that had changed.

Reaching my room, I dumped the firewood and thought about what I was doing. I was hiding up here...letting whoever or whatever that was drive me out of where I needed to work. That would have to change as soon as I screwed up enough courage though I didn't see that happening any time soon.

Since I had time to kill, I decided to see if Millie had brought her diary back here and concealed it somewhere, so I spent an hour knocking on walls looking for secret panels and hidden places. I checked the floorboards looking for the same thing, but turned up nothing. I was about to give up when I found a faded message above the mantel: *May a merciful God deliver us from the evil that is here.*

Tears filled my eyes. She was a young woman whose dreams and thoughts I shared for some unknown reason. She had saved me more than once even though she was terrified of her mother, and I was hiding in my room instead of facing my own fears. Taking control like Jennie told me to do. That would have to change, and now was the time.

Taking a deep breath, I ran downstairs to my study before I could change my mind...hesitated for only a moment...then flung open the door and shouted, "I am not afraid of you! I live here now! Do not ever touch me again!"

Of course, the 'I am not afraid' part was a complete lie, but I thought it had sounded *believable* until I heard someone laugh. A maniacal laugh then sent a chill racing through me. Whirling around, I searched for the source, but there was none. Both the study and the hall behind me were empty.

Somehow I managed to get through the rest of the day though I was annoyed at how often Simon haunted my thoughts. I had imaginary 'conversations' with him where I skillfully put him in his place while I came off looking a far cry from the frightened 'lump' that fell into his arms. Some were out loud. Cinda ignored me for the most part then yawned and went to sleep.

I was throwing together another indifferent supper when I decided it was time to call Henry and check in. He answered on the first ring and, when I told him about Simon's visit, seemed more than a bit surprised. "He's outside with Bella and the pups. Plans to stay on for a while. Never mentioned a word about being over at your place."

"Well, he was. We didn't exactly hit it off."

He laughed. "He can be a mor'en a bit intense some times. It took a lot for him to go on over there."

"And why is that? I know you mentioned he came here when he was a kid."

"Did until he got the bejabbers scared out of him. Felt some kind of energy wantin' to harm him. Keep him there. Wouldn't say mor'en that."

Liking the comfort his voice gave me, I kept him talking for as long as I could. When he asked for the third time if I was okay, I repeated the same lie: "I was fine". We said our good nights, and I looked around the kitchen where we had spent so much time together. I really missed him a lot, but he was safe and that was all that mattered.

By then, the kitchen was beginning to make me feel uneasy, so I grabbed a flashlight off the counter and followed Cinda through the house to the main staircase. It was dark at the top. There had been no mention of when the rewiring up there would be finished. Maybe never if Wiley went down in the cellar, I thought, with a wry grimace.

Reaching my room, I built a fire, prepped for the night and settled into bed next to Cinda. I tried reading but couldn't seem to focus. Suddenly, the walkie talkie I kept close buzzed. To my surprise, it wasn't Henry on the other end.

"So, you're still there after what happened today...over," Simon told me.

"Seems like. Why are you using the walkie talkie?...over."

"Because I wanted to see if you had smartened up by now. Apparently not...over."

"I told you I had to stay. Did you talk to your grandfather about my reasons?...over."

There was a long pause before he said, "We talked after you called him, which is why I'm coming over...over."

"Now who's the idiot? This is the last place you want to be...over."

Another long pause, and then, "I'll use Grandpa's room. I'm not letting you stay there another night alone...over and out."

I tried to reach him, but it was useless. He would be here in just a few minutes. "Let him just try," I told Cinda. "Both doors are locked and even he won't stoop to breaking and entering."

By then, I was wide-awake. My room faced the back woods, and I wouldn't see his headlights when he pulled in...*if* he dared. He could have been bluffing. The minutes ticked by...nothing...and then the walkie talkie buzzed again. I answered it and heard, "I'm outside the back door. Unlock it...over."

"Go away! I don't want you here!"

158

I forgot the 'over' part and he cut in with, "I'm coming inside. Deal with it!"

My heart was hammering wildly as I jumped out of bed and pressed my ear against the door. All was quiet on the other side. The silence seemed to grow more intense with each passing moment and then I heard the muffled sound of footsteps headed my way. The doorknob rattled and then his fist thudded on the door.

"Look! I don't much care if you want me here or not. I'm here. I'm staying. End of subject," he shouted through the door.

I was furious by then. Forgetting the cat paw print pajamas with the rip under the arm I hadn't mended yet...forgetting that my hair was by now a fly away disaster...forgetting everything except my anger, I unlocked the door and threw it open. He was taller than I remembered, and I had to lean back, slightly, to meet his eyes when I spat out, "You are trespassing where you are not needed or wanted. Get out of here now, or I will call the cops and have you prosecuted to the full extent of the law."

He looked me over then smiled. "I have yet to see you when you aren't a full blown mess, but somehow it suits you. The little red hen defending her nest. Do you think Chief Wilson or any of his boys will come out here at night? I might mention there was a reddish glow in the back hallway as I came through the kitchen. The one with the cabinet pushed in front of it. Do you want me in here with the nice, warm fire and what looks like a soft bed, or next door in whatever room Grandpa camped out in?"

The 'reddish glow thing' had been more than a bit unnerving, but I did my best to hide it. "The one on the left," I snapped back then slammed the door in his face and locked it.

I heard him laugh then tell me, "Just shout if you find unwelcome company."

"Which would be you!" I tossed back then headed for my warm bed where Cinda was waiting.

I was almost asleep when the walkie talkie buzzed again. Heaving a long sigh, I answered it to hear, "In the mood for some pillow talk?"

"You didn't say 'over' which is where this pillow talk is headed...over."

I waited and then it buzzed again. "I could still come over...over?"

I had to smile. "When hell freezes over...over."

"Keep your walkie talkie close in case things get worse tonight."

"Worse than having you on the other side of that wall?"

There was no answer, and I tucked it under my pillow. It took a long time to fall asleep. His presence was very unsettling.

I awoke the next morning and found a note shoved under my door. Scrawled in a very masculine hand were these words: *Had to leave. Coffee's still hot...or might be if you don't sleep in like a slug. Be back before nightfall.*

He was gone, and I was surprised by my mixed feelings. I wanted him gone, but at the same time I didn't. He was all kinds of irritating but.... I shook my head and grimaced wryly. I knew there was more to it than that, but I wasn't about to examine it too closely without the reinforcement of a strong cup of coffee.

Only a few minutes later, I was on my way downstairs with Cinda. After yesterday's experience in my study, no place felt safe...*if* it ever had. The red glow thing could mean she was finally loose. Had it been her hand that grabbed me? I couldn't be sure, but I was very glad Simon had been there.

Reaching the kitchen, I checked out the back door for damage. There was none. He must have picked the lock, and I wondered how he had acquired that skill as I cleaned and fill Cinda's bowls then poured myself a much needed mug of coffee. It was tepid by now and way too strong, so I made a fresh pot. While I waited, I looked out the window. It was a cold, overcast Sunday morning, and I wondered what had called him away so early.

"Let's check on Henry and see what we can find out," I told Cinda as I headed for the phone. There was no answer on that end and no machine to record my call, so I hung up and thought about what I would do for the remainder of what would be a very long day in an increasingly scary place.

After a quick breakfast of cold cereal and a spoon of peanut butter, I headed to my study that I had tried to reclaim yesterday. Taking a deep breath, I pushed open the door and looked around. It felt as it always had. No hint of evil.

Looking behind the door, I checked out the wall I had been working on when all hell broke loose. A long strip of wallpaper had peeled loose revealing something painted on the plaster. It was the smudged portrait of a young woman with the saddest eyes I had ever seen. I had no doubt who it was.

Touching it gently with my fingertips, I whispered, "Hello, Millie. I'm Jodie...a friend as I think you already know by now." For a fleeting moment, I felt a hand brush mine a second time. She was there for a moment then gone.

"It must have been Varna who tried to stop me finding her portrait," I told Cinda as I powered up my laptop. "Unless there is *another* evil entity inside these walls that wants to hurt me. How many of those can there be in one house? Rhetorical. No answer is necessary, but I have to wonder how someone as gentle and loving as Millie can protect us much longer from a monster like her mother." A sudden thought struck me, and I added, "What if that's all backwards? What if I'm here to find a way to help and protect her? But how does that involve Allison? Why does she want me here?"

Since Cinda couldn't answer those questions any more than I could, I worked for a while then tried calling Henry again around lunchtime with the same result. No answer. The hours were passing quickly, and soon Simon would return unless I found a way to stop him. From what Henry had told me, he was in equal danger, and for some reason I cared about that. It was that same disturbing 'something' I had thought to examine over coffee but had put on indefinite hold.

"He can pick a lock, so those won't stop him," I murmured under my breath. "So what do we do?" Cinda had been listening then yawned on her way to a warm spot in the sunlight that still streamed through the kitchen window.

Despite what Simon had said, I decided to call the Sheriff and see what he had to say. A woman who introduced herself as Deputy Ahern answered my call and 'piped' me through to the 'Chief' after I told her what I wanted.

"So, I hear you're havin' a bit of trouble out there, Miss…. What was that name again?"

"Shield, and yes I had someone in my house last night I didn't want there."

"Did he break in or was he invited then got a little too touchy feely for your taste."

"None of that! He sort of got in when I told him he couldn't."

"So, he *did* break in. That's pretty serious. Do you know who it was?"

I hesitated then managed to say, "Simon North."

To my surprise he snorted loudly then said, "Yah got to be joking! Simon would never go back to Greystone. Almost died there when he was a kid."

I remembered what Henry had already told me then asked, "What happened?"

"Something or someone tried to drag him down into the cellar. Got away, but has a scar on his leg to show for it. Makes your story sound like a load of crap if you'll excuse me saying so."

By then, I was both angry and frustrated. "Look! It was Simon. He didn't *exactly* break in so don't charge him with that, but he did trespass, and I want him stopped. He plans to come back tonight."

"Sounds like you two got a thing going if you ask me."

"Which I didn't! Are you going to help me or not."

"Might send a deputy out there. What time do you expect him?"

"Just before or just after dark. Went in through the back door last time."

I heard a sharp intake of breath then a low whistle. "I'll round up someone, but they won't be going inside that place. He'll have a talk with him when he pulls up."

"That will do nicely. Thank you and good day."

I leaned back in my chair and thought about Simon North. He had almost died here, and yet he was willing to risk that for me. He had to be totally insane and maybe I was, too. How many times had I thought about him ever since we met?

"You really are a 'ninny'!" I told myself fiercely then groaned. I had liked the way it felt in his arms before he dumped me on the floor. I had liked the way it felt to see him standing in the doorway with his dark eyes looking at me that way despite the 'red hen' remark, which had been more than a bit irritating. The kind of look that triggered a response in me I would never, ever name even if I could.

"Looks like I'm headed for another kind of trouble," I told Cinda who rolled on her back begging for a belly rub.

***

Darkness was creeping over Greystone as I waited in the kitchen with the lights turned off, so Simon wouldn't know I was watching when he 'bumped' into the two big deputies waiting in their car at the end of the drive. The minutes ticked past, and it grew still darker. I remembered all too well what Simon had told me about the red light in the hall. Most of me wanted to bolt to the 'safety' of my room, but I had to see what happened to Simon. What if they didn't just *talk* to him like Chief Wilson said? What if things turned ugly? What if they hurt him when he'd only been trying to help? My 'second thoughts' multiplied with each passing second. I needed to call Henry and have him warn Simon before it was too late.

I dashed to the phone and made the call. Henry answered on the fourth ring. "Been out all day with Simon. He drove us to the city for a fancy dinner, movie and some shopping. I was goin'...."

"Stop, Henry! I need you to warn him that the cops are waiting for him over here."

"He should be there by now. What's goin' on?"

"I told Chief Wilson he was trespassing. Let me see what I can do to defuse this mess."

I hung up and dashed out the door, but was too late. I could hear voices...angry voices and then car doors slamming. A deputy was driving Simon's car when they headed out. Shouting as loudly as I could, I gave chase but there was no way to stop them.

"They've arrested him and it's all my fault," I murmured as I watched their taillights disappear at the turn. "I'll call the station and speak to someone. If I don't press charges, they can't hold him." Somehow I had to undo what I had done

Spinning around, I ran back inside and flipped on the lights. I was reaching for the phone when Cinda hissed loudly. Every black hair was bristled, and her tail was enormous. She was scared...terrified...and I knew why. The cold was now intense, and the stench of rot I had smelled below was seeping into the kitchen.

Snatching her up, I made a dash for the main hall where I flipped on the lights and kept going at a flat out run. One by one, the wall sconces behind us blinked and went out leaving an intense darkness that seemed to pursue us. My terror pumped up my adrenaline, and I kept running till I reached the tiny oasis of light pouring from my open bedroom door.

Slamming it behind us, I turned the key but knew, if that was Varna, it wouldn't stop her for long. I was right. A black, nebulous figure began to, slowly, seep through the closed door as a hoarse voice whispered, "I have come for you!"

I sped across the room, tossed Cinda on the bed then grabbed the holy water bottle. It sizzled like acid when I flung it on her. She withdrew with a hissing sound, and I heaved a sigh of relief. It was then I noticed the strong scent of roses. Was it Allison who was with me? Had she saved me somehow? Whether it was true or not, it was a comforting thought I clung to rather desperately.

After that, I didn't dress for bed. Just lay on top with Cinda snuggled close as I watched both the door and the hours tick off on the mantel clock. I don't remember dozing off, but I did.

Light was streaming through the windows when I woke up hours later and looked around dazedly. Memories of the night returned...horrifying memories and then I remembered the scent of roses that had made me feel safe as Allison had often had done in the past. She was there. Protected me when I needed her. I needed to believe that if I was going to spend another moment at Greystone.

It was a very cautious me that headed downstairs a short time later and placed a call to the Sheriff's office. I told Deputy Ahern I wouldn't press charges. That he had been stopped before he actually 'trespassed', and needed to be released at once. She replied, curtly, "Bail's been met, and he's gone."

I sensed there was more to it than that, but didn't ask. Henry would tell me more. I placed a call to him and learned Simon had gotten into a scuffle with a bully he had known when he was visiting here as a kid.

"His name is Lance Wiggins. Six foot four of pure mean. Probably volunteered to come out to your place if it meant he had a shot at Simon. Needed back up from what Simon told me before he left this morning for Boston. Mad as hell you would do that to him. Can't rightly say I blame him none. He was only tryin' to help you."

"I know, and I'm sorry. We just seemed to.... I don't know. Is he okay?"

"He's tough. Chief Wilson knows their history and that Wiggins he shouldn't have been the one sent out there. May drop the charges. How're things with you?"

"Joe's going to be here soon and wants to check out the wall in the cellar," I told him. There was no way I would tell him what had happened last night. "I know that's a very bad idea, but how do I stop him?"

"You don't. Guess you'll just have to see what happens."

"Is Simon ever coming back?"

"Almost sounds like you miss him?"

"Not a chance. Just curious. How about I make us dinner tonight?"

"Sounds like a plan. I'll bring a bottle of that fancy wine Simon bought yesterday."

A short time later, I heard the work trucks pull up. Joe was the first through the kitchen door. "Mornin', Jodie! Always glad to see that smile. Promised Wiley a shot at the cellar like we talked about since I need to get down there anyway. He'd like to see if he can redirect the wiring from there to the new panel, so everything will be in one place."

"That would be great, but Wiley will wonder why I lied about the stairs before he even learns what lurks down there."

Joe smiled wryly and shook his head. "Maybe nothin' bad will happen like you seem to think. The man's got a job to do. Let me get that cabinet moved back where it belongs before he spots it and asks questions we don't want to answer."

He had just shoved it into place when there was a knock on the door and the others streamed inside...said their 'good mornings' and scattered...all except Wiley who asked me for the cellar key. I fished it out of my junk drawer where I now hid it while Joe watched from the back hall. A moment later, they were headed down the stairs.

I gathered Cinda in my arms as we waited to see what happened. Apparently, nothing did. They both returned a short time later, and Wiley headed back to work.

Joe locked up and handed me the key saying, "Wiley says the hassle and expense of divertin' the wiring is not worth it, and I had to agree. The wall's not worse which is good news. Might be able to wait till warmer weather before we tackle jackin' up that side of the house. Didn't see nothin' that spooked *me* down there. You're a writer. Maybe you just have a bit too much imagination."

I could feel myself getting angry...knew I would say something I would regret, so I pasted on a smile and offered him a cup of coffee. I was glad when he refused.

While his crew tackled the jobs they had started, I tried to read through more of Allison's journals. She had been everywhere...loved 'freely' as she called it...and never let herself be tied down. She never mentioned her pregnancy again, and I wondered *if* and *when* her baby had been born.

The hours sped by. Lunch was hot chocolate and a quick sandwich I ate at my desk as I studied the small portrait on the wall. I thought again about the secret place she wanted me to find...the cave she had shared with me in my dreams. Maybe Joe would keep and eye on Cinda while I slipped out and tried to find it? The more I thought about it, the more I felt the urge to go. Soon it was another irresistible compulsion. I packed Cinda in her carrier and left her with Joe in the back room where he was working then slid into my warm outer gear and headed out the door.

The top layer of snow had melted then re-froze making my footsteps crunch as I followed the trail through the bare bone trees and evergreens. I could smell the water and see the gulls circling overhead emitting their raucous cries as they searched for whatever the waves had brought in during the night. Reaching my boulder, I climbed on top and looked out over the wide expanse of gray green water. It was calmer today. Not the churning, tumultuous fierceness of my previous visit. The tide was out and the wide beach stretched for miles.

Scrambling down from my perch, I walked closer to the water then looked back up at the cliffs that lined the shore in both directions. "Left or right?" I asked out loud. There was no answer...no sign...so I headed to the right where I saw caves randomly pockmarking the granite cliffs for some distance.

I followed the shoreline exploring them as I went along. Most of the lower ones were filled with driftwood, seaweed, human litter, and sometimes fascinating bits and pieces that had washed in from the sea. At high tide, they would be underwater and many still held shallow pools that reflected the light behind me as I stepped inside. Some were deeper than they first appeared, and I climbed back only as far as I dared go. The ones near the top must have been carved out over eons of time when the sea was higher, angrier, and hungry. From where I stood, they were impossible to reach, so I moved on.

I had completely lost track of time as I checked out every likely possibility, when, suddenly, I heard someone shout, "Go back! Run!"

I looked around for the source. There was no one there, but I was shocked to see that the tide had turned some time ago. The beach had already narrowed to a thin strip of sand. If I didn't make it to the gap, I'd be trapped against the cliff.

I began to run. Only a few moments had passed and already the incoming waves had almost reached me. The sand and my boots made it tough going...my legs felt like lead, but I kept running. A wave larger than most hit me broadside, but somehow I managed to stay on my feet. I was already hugging the sheer cliff wall with no more room to go. A second wave battered me, and water filled my mouth. I was choking...gasping for air when a third knocked me down. I was struggling to my feet...fighting the pull of the wave that would drag me out to sea, when an invisible hand grabbed mine, and a voice that could only be Millie's shouted, "Come on, Jodie! We can do this!"

With her help, I managed to get my feet under me and keep running. Reaching the gap, I climbed to higher ground then fell to my knees on the snow-covered sand. It had taken both a miracle and Millie to save me. My heart was still racing wildly as I watched the incoming waves slam into the rocks just below me. I had almost died. Now I had to make it back to Greystone before I succumbed to the numbing cold that was overtaking me.

It had to be pure adrenaline, Millie, and another miracle that kept me moving. I don't remember much of what happened on the way there, but somehow I made it to my room and into a hot shower. I stayed under its wonderful heat for as long as I could then toweled off and slipped into my robe. Back in my bedroom, I was surprised to see the hall door ajar and Cinda waiting on the bed when I had left her in her carrier with Joe.

"You almost lost me," I told her as I gathered her in my arms then wrapped the covers around us both until I stopped shivering. It took a long while, and I almost dozed off, but knew it was a luxury that would have to wait. Exhausted as I was, I had things to do. I needed to be the 'tough little gal' Henry believed me to be even though I knew better. I was still badly shaken and that wouldn't change any time soon.

I layered on my clothes and headed downstairs a short time later. I was on my second cup of hot coffee when Joe's crew began to pull out for the day.

"See you found that cat of yours," Joe told me as he came in from the back hall. "Got the door open on her carrier and disappeared on me. Figured she'd be okay. Looks like I was right." Again, he waited till the others had filed out the door then added, "I kinda didn't tell you the whole truth earlier. There was somethin' down there I hadn't seen before and made sure Wiley didn't."

My heart seemed to stop. "Like what?"

His smile was grim: his eyes troubled. "There was a message scrawled on the wall that read: *She must die.* Look...I never believed in ghosts like I said, but someone wrote that there, and I can't imagine it was you. Lock this place up and throw away the key!"

"I can't..." I began until he cut me short.

"*I can't* haul you outta here, but someone should. I saw the crucifix above the cellar door. You might want to get another one and keep it handy though I got me a feelin' it's goin' to take a helluva lot more than that."

He kept trying for a while to make me see "sense" and all he got out of me was "I'd think about it."

I watched him leave then began Henry's supper preparations as I thought about what he had said. He hadn't really told me anything I didn't already know. Millie's mother wanted my soul and, for that to happen, she needed to kill me. That message had certainly *rattled* Joe, but he hadn't seen...felt what I had down there, or he wouldn't be coming back...ever!

Henry arrived not long after that. While we ate and sipped the rather excellent Pinot Noir, I told him a *modified* account of the tide incident, but nothing else that had happened. He would insist on staying overnight, and I couldn't let that happen.

Strangely enough, the house didn't seem all that menacing when he left. While Cinda batted the wine cork around the kitchen, I did what was necessary then we both headed upstairs. All was quiet in the halls, and we reached my room without incident. While Cinda slept on the pillow next to me, I began roughing in an outline for Allison's bio even though I still had no beginning.

I worked till late... jotting down ideas...making notes...sometimes balling them up and tossing them across the room. I had no idea when I dozed off. I dreamt of the sea...just a collage of images at first, but that changed:

I was pressed against the cliff again with nowhere to run. Incoming waves battered me then sucked me out into deeper water. I no longer struggled. Just let it happen. I would join the other ghosts that haunted Greystone. It was my fate. Had always been my fate. Why hadn't I known that? Suddenly, I heard Simon shout, "Get the hell outta there, you little idiot! Swim! Dammit! Swim! Don't make me come in there after you!"

I woke up...smiled...turned over...and fell back into a dreamless sleep.

CHAPTER SEVEN

(Millie)

She's warm and dry now. Tucked up in bed for the night with the one she calls Cinda who is more than a cat. She had almost died today. It had taken a miracle to save her. I don't know what brought me there when she needed me though I often returned to the sea hoping each time I would find him there.

Sometimes it felt like time hasn't passed at all. That it was only yesterday when he held me in his arms and told me, "I'll be back. I promise" then walked away down the beach leaving behind the imprint of his last kiss, those words, and his footprints in the sand.

We had often talked about going away together and getting married before he had to report, but he had wanted a real wedding with his family there. I remember his words...every one. "It needs to be done properly in the eyes of God surrounded by all those who wish us that happy ever after we both want so badly."

I had been thinking about that precious time when I saw a distant someone walking along the shore and thought, for the briefest of moments, he had returned to me, but it was Jodie exploring the caves. Perhaps looking for my secret place I wanted her to find...had shown her in the dreams I sent her. She seemed unaware that the tide had turned some time ago and the water was coming in swiftly as it did along this stretch of coast. I had to get to her before it was too late.

I had sped down the beach shouting her name, but she was too far away to hear me above the sound of the incoming waves. It seemed like forever before I reached her...helped her. I ran with her as the incoming water pressed her closer and closer to the cliff. I never thought we would make it, but somehow we did, and now she sleeps.

I brush a strand of hair back from her forehead then plant a kiss in its place. Why have I felt such a deep connection to a stranger from the first moment I saw her? Why does she seem...well, necessary to some mystery that is unraveling? She stirs but doesn't wake. I can only hope she is safe in a dream ...not lost in a nightmare.

(Jodie)

It was a persistent Cinda who woke me the next morning. The nightmare fled quickly in the morning light. Little remained. Just the feel of the icy water as it closed over me, and Simon's words then those, too, were gone.

Cinda and I reached the kitchen a short time later. She ate while I searched through the fridge for something that wouldn't take a lot of effort and settled on a yogurt with strawberries. The coffee was still dribbling into the carafe when Joe and his crew arrived. It was another workday at Greystone for all of us.

And so it went...days flew by...the book progressed...and the house with its ghosts remained quiet...thankfully.

It was Friday when Alice called to remind me the Ball was next Saturday. I had already decided to go. To dip my toes in 'normal' and leave the paranormal behind for a while. Another part of me didn't at all like the idea of walking into a room full of mostly strangers. Allison had always been with me in the past. This time I would be all alone unless I could twist Henry's arm.

So, that is what I tried to do next time I saw him only to be told, "I'm babysittin' that cat of yours while you have a great time. Do you good."

"I really don't want to go by myself."

"You'll be danced off them feet and won't have time to think about it. It's a tradition and folks set some store by it. I'll come pick you up and drive the belle of the ball there. It would be an honor."

I didn't give up that easily, but nothing I tried budged him even the promise of a homemade apple pie, which would have been my first attempt. In the end, I told him I wouldn't go without him and that was that.

The weekend was quiet. Henry dropped by both days. He tried each time to change my mind without success. I would only go if he came with me, but then he told me something that changed my mind.

"Looks like Simon will be there. Bringing a date. Mallory Shubert. She used to be someone he knew back in the days when he visited his grandma and me as a kid. Was the Apple Princess two years in a row. Bumped into her in Boston. She's some kind of paralegal and one thing led to an invite to the ball."

"Well, how delightful for him to be dating a 'Princess'," I managed to say lightly though I didn't mean a word of it. I wasn't exactly sure what I was feeling and hoped it wasn't something as petty and ugly as jealousy though I very much feared it was.

He left shortly after that, and I headed upstairs to look through my wardrobe. Tucked in garment bags were two beautiful gowns I had worn when Allison and I had attended other balls and soirees. Designer labels she had bought for me in scrumptious fabrics and colors I hadn't been able to part with even though I knew I'd never wear them again. There was one more I had never seen.

Reaching into the very back of the armoire, I pulled out a black garment bag then told Cinda, "This is Allison's ball gown she wore when she first danced with the man she loved, but you probably already know that."

I had never opened the bag. Had promised her I wouldn't until the right time came to wear it. Maybe it was now? I would be competing with the Apple Princess for Simon's attention, which seemed idiotic when I thought about it. True...I found him reasonably attractive in an obnoxious kind of way if that was even possible. At the moment, he was furious with me and rightly so when I came to consider how it all went down. He'd only been trying to help me at great personal risk from all I had learned and spent the night in jail as a reward instead of receiving my thanks.

I should just let him have his Apple Princess and be done with it. Spend Saturday night working on the book instead of fantasizing I was some kind of Cinderella, but the thought of showing him I could look like something besides the 'lump' that fell into his arms was compelling. There was still plenty of time to think about it. I could always make some last minute excuse and bail out if I changed my mind. Alice would understand, or so I hoped.

I sighed and put the unopened garment bag back inside the armoire. I was being childish. But even knowing that, the idea stayed with me as I went about the rest of the day. It even followed me to bed that night. As I watched the flickering fire, I wondered what it would be like to come sweeping down the stairs like Scarlet O'Hara in her remodeled drapes. I knew my gown would be fantastic. Allison had a flair for fashion and had done her best to impart it to a 'me' who usually preferred jeans, tank tops, and

178

sweatshirts though I had learned to play 'dress up' with the best of them.

I could feel myself getting drowsy and then sleep must have claimed me because, suddenly, I was standing at the top of a marble staircase looking down at a lavishly appointed ballroom full of people dressed in formal wear. The music stopped, and a hush fell over the room, as everyone looked my way. A tall figure pushed his way through the silent crowd without taking his eyes off me. He was dressed like the prince in Cinderella, but his face was out of focus...a blur.

My hand lightly brushed the rail as I held my head high and began my 'regal' descent. I made it all of three steps before I tripped on my train and slid down the rest of the way on my rear end...bump...bump...bump till I reached the bottom where I was looking up into a pair of amused brown eyes that were all too familiar.

"Princess Lump, may I offer you a hand?" he asked with a smile.

I felt myself begin to melt into the marble floor...dissolve into nothing and then I heard Alice chide me, "You do know that will leave quite a stain!"

I woke up with a start...checked to see if I was a puddle...then looked around. Cinda was gone, but I could hear her in the litter box. I closed my eyes and tried to recapture the dream before the fall when there was a chance of a happy ending. I don't know if I succeeded before I woke up much later to a dark, cold Monday morning.

I dressed quickly and hurried downstairs just as Joe and his crew pulled in. Coffee was almost ready when the phone rang. It was Henry. He asked the usual "am I all right" question then said, "When you get a chance, come on over. I got somethin' to show you."

He wouldn't say any more despite my prodding. Intrigued as I was, I made quick work of breakfast then checked with Joe to see what was planned for the day.

"Tony would like to finish strippin' the wallpaper in your study. The others are doin' some window repairs on the south side. Might need to get my hands on some more of them floorboards before they run out. Turns out you have a lot more dry rot and termite damage than first estimated. A lot more."

I sighed. Greystone was a money pit and then some. I 'okayed' everything but the wallpaper stripping then loaded Cinda in her carrier and headed on over to Henry's. He greeted us at the door along with Bella and her excited pups that seemed to have grown inches since I last saw them.

"Get warm first while I fetch us both a cup of hot chocolate," he told me as he helped me out of my coat then hung it by the door.

Cinda scrambled to the top of the wood box when I opened her carrier while I sat on the floor and gathered an armload of wriggling, yipping puppies in my lap...felt their tiny teeth through my sweater sleeve...smelt their puppy smell. It was a little piece of heaven, and my face must have shown it.

"Them pups love you, and it ain't hard to see why," Henry told me with a grin as he plunked two mugs on the table. "Come on up here and take a chair while I fetch what I got to show you."

I sat down at the table and sipped the hot chocolate with tiny marshmallows on top as I looked around the room that was the definition of 'cozy' right down to the matching rockers and Edith's basket of yarn. A half finished striped wool scarf lay on top that I hadn't noticed before. Tears filled my eyes just as Henry told me from the doorway, "My winter scarf. Always was losing 'em somewhere or other. She knitted me a new one each year. Wanted me to stay warm. Kept on knitting even when the pain got real bad. Ran out of time before it was done, but she still keeps working at it."

He handed me a very old photo. "That's my Edith when we were young and full of dreams. That there dress was the one she wanted to be laid out in."

I studied the black and white photo of a very young Henry and the woman holding his hand. Her smile was radiant. It transformed her from pretty to truly beautiful. He was looking at her as though she was the most precious person in the world. Theirs was the kind of love that would last forever. No wonder she was still with him.

He had been waiting for me to say something, so I brushed away my tears with the back of my hand and told him what I saw, "She shines from within."

His own eyes were wet when he replied, "She did indeed. All the days of her life. Still does."

He touched her face with the tip of one callused finger then tucked the photo in his pocket close to his heart. "Thought you might like to see her. She wanted me to find something for you. Here it is."

He dropped a gold locket in my hand, and a sudden chill raced through me as I studied the small rose etched into the surface. The back was engraved. *E.S. loves M. G.* Very carefully, I opened it up and found a tiny lock of red hair intertwined with black. I was beyond surprised. "Where...how did you get this?"

He sighed. "Seems my ma took it off Millie while she were cleaning her up afterwards. Couldn't see letting it go to waste, so she took it. That's what she told me when she'd been drinkin'. Plum forgot about it till last night. Edith showed me where she hid it."

"Did your mother ever tell you what happened to the bodies of Millie and her baby?"

"No...never did. Did say there were stories that Millie had run off and no one was too surprised considerin' what her ma was like."

"This is a very important clue, Henry. We have his initials now. Adding that to what we already know from my dreams and what your mother told you, his name was Eric S. A soldier whose ship was torpedoed just before Christmas. There must be records of transport ships that went down."

"That's a whole lot of ground to cover!"

I smiled. "Thank God for computers! Research needed big time."

He smiled back. "Then you better get goin'. I'm cookin' up a pot of goulash that might free you up some, if I drop it on by later. I'm willin' to bet you hardly ever take the time to fix a decent meal."

I had to smile. It wasn't a bet I would take. I had the locket with me when Cinda and I left a few minutes later. Reaching Greystone, I carried her straight to my study where I opened her carrier and punched the power button on my laptop. While it loaded, I thought about what I needed to do. Someone must have kept records of ships that sank even as far back as then. If so, there must be a list...manifest of the crew and the troops on board...or so I hoped.

Google came online, and I got busy. His ship had been torpedoed just before Christmas. From what I learned, it *had* to be the Christmas of 1917. The United States hadn't entered the war until that year, and it had ended in November of 1918. I found one that had been sunk by three torpedoes on December 21st. There had been others, but I found myself drawn to this one for no reason I could name. It had formerly been a German ship that had been commandeered by the US Navy and re-purposed. Many of those on board made it to the life rafts that were attacked by a U boat once they were in the water. I didn't find anyone who matched the sketchy information I had among those lost. A further check found a possibility among the wounded. Eric Sanders, age 26, Private First Class. There was even an address...one in Baltimore on Park Street. It had to be him or the biggest coincidence in the world! Millie believed he was dead. Perhaps he had died later of his wounds. I checked every possible lead, but found nothing more.

Next, I used Google Earth and found 124 Park Street in Baltimore. His home was still there...a two story brick surrounded by what looked like a rose garden in the satellite image I called up. I shook

183

my head. *That* had to either be a figment of my imagination or another impossible coincidence. Ownership had changed often over the years. Now the Bentleys lived there.

I leaned back in my chair as I thought about what I had found. There could have been other ships that went down. Other soldiers with those initials, but somehow I knew that I had found him. *Hoped* I had found him. If that was true, I might be able to turn up relatives who could tell me more. I was making progress, but why in that direction? How did any of that bring me closer to finding Allison's roots?

I took a break to rest my eyes and scrounged up a way late lunch. Joe found me in the kitchen and reported, "Going to fetch them boards I need from that old schoolhouse in Turner. Stoppin' by the Home Depot while I'm there. Got a long list of things I need, so I'll be gone for quite a while."

His cheerful whistle followed him out the door as he headed to his truck. I went back to washing the lunch dishes until Cinda's loud hiss told me something was wrong. Whirling around, I found Wiley standing just behind me with a peculiar smile on his gaunt face.

"What do you want?" I managed to ask as I waited for my heartbeat to normalize.

He was clearly amused that he'd scared me. "A might jumpy ain't cha. I need to go back down in the cellar. Left some of my things there. Need 'em."

"Maybe Joe can go down with you when he gets back."

184

"Need 'em now," he told me as he headed to the junk drawer where I kept the key.

He grabbed it and brushed past me, but I pulled him to a stop. "Give it back to me! Now!"

He shook free and, for a moment, our eyes locked and held. There was someone else behind those eyes, and Cinda knew it, too. Yowling, she made a leap for his back where she dug in deeply. He tried to yank her loose, but she hung on like a thing possessed.

"Stop! Don't hurt her! I'll get her off!" I shouted. He was cursing me loudly as I loosened her hold and cradled her in my arms. "Get out of here now! Joe will bring you your things when he pays you off."

"He hired me, and he'll have to fire me," he snarled. "Not some entitled little bitch. "

"That's enough, Wiley!" a very angry Joe shouted from the doorway. "Get your ass outta here, or I'll kick it from here to hell and back!"

"Want my pay and my things!" he replied with a sly, knowing smile that creeped me out more than anything he'd said or done.

"You already have all the pay you got comin'," Joe told him. "I'll round up your tools and bring 'em out to your truck. Now get movin'!"

"Awright...awright. I'm leavin'. Goin' to quit anyway," he muttered to Joe then whispered to me as he headed for the door, "That black cat of yours is a real menace. Would be a good thing all 'round if somethin' *real bad* happened to her."

"Touch her...harm her, and I will see you dead!" I warned him, which only made him smile again.

"Sure sorry about that," Joe told me as we stood by the window and watched him climb into his battered pickup truck. "Not sure what got into him. Never seen him like that."

I thought I knew exactly what...or rather who...had 'got into him'. He was dangerous. Now it wasn't just the dead I needed to fear. "Do you think he'll be back?"

Joe scratched the back of his head and grimaced thoughtfully. "Lives some distance away, so not too likely, but then I didn't know that guy who just left here. I'll go grab his tools and get 'em out to him. The sooner he's gone the better. Time to get some kind of security system in place. I'll stop in the village and talk to a guy I know. "

I tried a smile I was far from feeling with mixed success. "I'd really appreciate it. What brought you back at the precise moment I needed you?"

"Forgot my list of things I needed. Was sure I'd put it in my pocket before I left. Double-checked when I hit the road, and it was gone. Let me go look for it while I'm getting' them tools."

Just a short time after Joe drove off, I got a phone call from a security company. They understood it was an emergency and would be over that afternoon. I had been working on tracing any living relatives of Eric Sanders when I heard them pounding on the door. There were three of them. Tim Rawlings was in charge and let me know up front he didn't like working at Greystone.

"Cost you more if you still want us. Probably take a week to do it right, and we're not staying late. We're outta here once it gets dark. That doesn't suit you, there are other companies not so close to home who *might* not have heard of this place."

I told him I would pay whatever was necessary, and they went to work checking out any points of entry. Wiley had truly scared me, and I was sure he'd be back soon.

Joe must have told Henry what had happened because he dropped by that evening with a taser and can of pepper spray. He also wanted to spend the night, but I told him, "Thank you for your concern...and thanks for these, but I'll be just fine."

He wasn't convinced because I wasn't very convincing. I wanted him there in the worst kind of way, but he was in his 80's and in no shape to deal with a 'possessed' Wiley when he came sneaking around.

Before the security team left, I had wireless sensors on both outside doors that would emit a loud alarm if anyone tried to enter as well as alert the security company. Of course, there were a lot of windows that would allow easy access, so I used the skeleton key from my bedroom door to lock all the rooms on the ground floor. I was *hopeful* that would keep us secure, but had serious doubts I didn't want to think about.

It was just getting dark when I headed upstairs with Cinda and the things Henry had brought me. Reaching my room, I locked the door, jammed the chair under the knob then headed to the window. Once again, I wished this room had a view of the front. As it was, all I could see were the distant white-capped mountains, and the winter bare trees stirred by a strong night wind. All were brushed with the silver light of a full moon thinly veiled by fast moving, black clouds that looked like silk scarves being drawn across its luminous face. It was beautiful but eerie. The shadows deep and dark. Anything or anyone could be out there.

"Look! Stop scaring yourself like an idiot. In all likelihood, Wiley got drunk somewhere then headed home wherever that is. He's miles from here by now. He...."

The walkie talkie buzzed. It was Henry, so I told him what had been done to secure the place and that I was fully *armed* with the stuff he'd brought me.

His reply was, "Just remember to keep this walkie talkie with you every second. I got me a shotgun and can be over there in a flash if you need me. Sure do wish you had a phone up there in your bedroom."

"That makes two of us. Never fully appreciated the convenience of my cell phone till I moved here where I can't get a signal."

We said our 'good nights'. I could tell he was having a hard time leaving things the way they were, and so was I. By then, Cinda had jumped from the bed to a spot by the door and was watching it intently. Had she heard something...sensed something I didn't? I pressed my ear against it but heard nothing, and I heaved a sigh of relief. I couldn't let every little thing spook me, or it would be a very long night.

Uncapping the holy water bottle, I set it on my bedside table then climbed into bed still fully dressed. The walkie talkie was tucked next to my pillow... the taser and the fire poker within easy reach. There was no way I would sleep a wink, I told myself, but I was wrong. Exhausted by the day, I went from drowsy to sound asleep in a matter of minutes and didn't wake up until a terrified Cinda landed on my stomach. She was staring at the door and growling then I heard it, too. An alarm was going off. One of the doors had been breached.

Struggling to stay calm, I told her, "Okay. That's not so good, but it could be a false alarm. It is windy out, and it might be a malfunction. The security company will have called the cops when they didn't hear from me. They will be here any moment with their sirens blasting." It was then I remembered Chief Wilson telling me none of them "would come inside after dark", which made them pretty much useless under the circumstances.

Despite what I had been babbling to Cinda, I knew it wasn't the wind that set off the alarm that was still blaring. It was Wiley. If the noise hadn't driven him off, he was somewhere in the house and knew exactly where to find me. The only one close enough to help was Henry with his shotgun.

I reached for the walkie talkie, but it was gone. Scrambling out of bed, I had just picked it up from where it had fallen when I heard someone or *something* scratching on the door. The knob turned...turned again... and then a fist thudded against it.

"You little bitch, I know you're in there! I ain't got a lot of time. The cops will be comin', but I can be finished with you and that cat long before they get here. Open the door! If I have to knock it down, I'll make you both suffer before I make you dead."

"Get out of here, Wiley, or whoever you are now!" I shouted as I called Henry who answered immediately. My voice was shaking but I managed to tell him, "He's outside my bedroom door. The alarm should bring help. I......."

"On the way!" he cut in before I could finish just as a heavy kick slammed into the door. Another followed, but it was made of age seasoned oak and held.

Scooping up Cinda, I shoved her in the bathroom and shut the door. Gripping the taser with one hand and the poker with the other, I shouted, "Come through that door, and I'll make you regret it."

He laughed and kicked again. The doorframe splintered this time. His next kick shattered it completely and knocked the chair out of place. The door flew open, and Wiley was standing there with a claw hammer in his hand. He was all kinds of strange...Wiley one moment...then something dark and twisted the next though the eyes remained the same. Her eyes.

"Get out of here now!" I shouted as fiercely as I could manage. "You are possessed! The worst kind of evil has taken you over!"

The voice that answered kept shifting between Wiley's nasal whine and her hiss. "He is my tool. He will kill you, so I can take your soul."

190

"Not going to happen," I told her as I backed up in hopes of reaching my fast dwindling supply of holy water.

I could hear Cinda clawing frantically at the bathroom door as Wiley headed my way with a smile that sent chills racing through me. I tased him, and he fell to the floor, but the entity inside him spilled out of his mouth in a long dark coil then assumed the shape of the monstrous woman I had seen before in this very room.

Her red, malevolent eyes raked me with contempt as she hissed," The dance is over. Time to pay the piper."

Throwing the poker and taser at her bought me the moment I needed to grab the holy water and toss it on her. It sizzled like acid on flesh, but this time she didn't leave. She just kept coming.

"This is my house now! You are not welcome here! Get the hell outta here!" I screamed at her as she closed what little distance there was between us. Suddenly, she looked back over her shoulder...snarled...hissed.... then reverted to a trail of greasy, black smoke that disappeared through the floor just as I heard voices outside in the hall. The cavalry had arrived.

It was Henry with two deputies who cuffed Wiley, dragged him to his feet then hauled him off.

"You okay, gal?" he asked as I hurled myself into his arms. There were tears in his eyes as he returned my hug then held me at arms' length as he checked me over. "You look like you're still in one piece. Was already out front when I got your call. Edith told me you were in trouble. Called the cops before I left home, and they got

191

here the same time I did. Back door was busted in. We got up here quick as we could. Tell me what happened...everything."

So, that's what I did. He was silent for a long moment before he asked, "Do you still think your Allison...your ma would want you here after all that? No answer needed. Just think about it."

Thing was...I knew she wouldn't, but I still needed to stay as insane as that sounded even to me. Varna had both terrified and pissed me off. I knew, if they hadn't arrived when they did, there was a good chance I wouldn't have survived. As I had just seen, I couldn't always depend on Allison or Millie to save me. Henry was right. I really needed to rethink what I was doing before it was too late.

I followed Henry downstairs, and he showed me where Wiley had broken in through the kitchen door. Standing there, we watched the deputies' car drive away. "Might as well make a pot of coffee since I'm betting neither one of us will be able to sleep after that," I told him.

CHAPTER EIGHT

(Millie)

It must have been Jodie's fear that summoned me. I had arrived just in time to see her stand up to my mother. She showed great courage despite her fear. The kind I wish I'd possessed back when I was a living being, but at all cost I had to protect the baby I carried.

A baby who never lived to draw a single breath.

Ah, there they go down the stairs. Two men and the one Mother had used as her living surrogate. She had lured him down to the cellar again and again...possessing him bit by bit. He would have killed both Jodie and her cat without a qualm...battered them to death while she watched enjoying every minute of it before she sucked up her soul. If help hadn't arrived when it did, I would have found a way to save her...divert my mother long enough for her to grab the cat and run. Once out of Greystone, she would have been safe, for I have never known Mother to go outside its walls since her own death many years ago. She will have returned to the cellar by now to fester and grow stronger in its darkness that she loves. I sometimes wonder if the house is the source of her wickedness or it is the other way around. Not that it matters now. The outcome is the same.

I feel an uneasiness stir me. Change is coming whether for good or ill I have no way of knowing. All I know is that my mother is both cunning and vengeful. She is enjoying the game she is playing and will bide her time then strike when Jodie is most vulnerable. Strike where it will hurt her the most. May God help me find a way to save her when that time comes!

(Jodie)

The next morning, I had to go down to the police station to fill out a report and press charges. From what I learned there, Millie's mother knew how to pick her stooges. Wiley had an outstanding

193

warrant in Pennsylvania for a B&E with bodily harm. An old woman beaten with a hammer.

I had left Cinda with Henry, so I did some shopping while I was in the village. After stocking up on supplies for both of us, I headed to the library where I talked with Alice...reassured her I was coming to the Ball...then asked about the Apple Princess.

Her curiosity was aroused. "Why the interest in her?" she asked. "How did you even hear about her?"

"Little bird mentioned she was coming. Is she incredibly beautiful?"

Alice smiled knowingly. "Some might say that."

"Would you be one of them?"

Her smile deepened. "I'm one of them gals who believes true beauty comes from inside...from the heart...the soul...the mind."

"And?"

"I'll let you judge for yourself. Have you decided what you are going to wear?"

I told her about Allison's gown, and she liked the idea. "I'm betting she will love to see you in that. How about shoes...the rest of it?"

"I have shoes that *should* work though I can't be sure since I don't even know what color it is and an evening cloak. As to the rest, I have it all tucked away...the silk this and thats I wouldn't dream of making my everyday wear."

"You will be absolutely beautiful! Now we're getting a few annoyed stares from some of the patrons. Librarians are supposed to be quiet as mice. Call me if I can help with anything."

After a stop at Jennie's for a holy water refill and chat, I drove back to Henry's and delivered his supplies. He had put up a Christmas tree in my absence, and I helped him decorate it with things he'd saved over the years. Each ornament had a story that went with it. He told me how they would lie under it when it was finished and look up at the lights as they shared their memories and dreams. How they had kissed under the mistletoe she'd hung from every doorway...exchanged handmade presents they had worked on in secret. Presents from the heart like all the days they shared.

I didn't try to hide my tears, and I saw him brush his own away from time to time. We said our good-byes after we lit the finished tree and toasted it with a glass of wine. As I drove back to Greystone, I toyed with the idea of putting one up there but decided not to and wasn't sure why. Joe and his crew had left by the time I carried Cinda inside and released her from her carrier. The shadows were already creeping in and...what had not been a bright day to start with... was now even darker.

I didn't feel Varna's evil presence in the kitchen or anywhere else as I first made a slap dash meal then headed upstairs with Cinda and my laptop. Joe had repaired my door while I was out and installed a heavy-duty deadbolt. I knew It would be useless when it came to the malignant entity that could come and go at will, but it made me feel a bit more secure. There was always the chance she would send another 'Wiley' after me.

I lit a fire and settled down with a note pad and my computer. After an extensive search, I found an obituary for Eric Sanders. He had been survived by his wife, Sarah, and a daughter named Audrey. Was it possible that Audrey still lived? After an hour of digging through every bit of information I could find, I was able to trace the family tree a bit further and found out that Audrey had married a Joseph Simmons and had a baby girl name unknown. The trail went cold after that and I called it a night. Cinda was sound asleep next to me. It didn't take me long to join her.

If I dreamt, I didn't remember when I woke up the next morning. It was an ordinary day with no surprises. I worked on the book and did a few chores while Joe and his crew wrapped up things then left early. The night was quiet...thankfully. No horrific dreams...no evil Varnas and then it was Saturday morning. Tonight was the Christmas Ball.

I lay in bed for a while thinking about what I had to do and found myself getting butterflies in my stomach. I remembered my Cinderella dream that had ended in a complete disaster. Perhaps it had been a case of foreshadowing?

I knew a whole string of 'what ifs' would follow, so I jumped out of bed and told myself sternly, "You are worrying over nothing. You'll wear Allison's gown which is sure to be beautiful, have a great time mingling...which you hate...and outshine the Apple Princess...if that is even possible."

I had gone from worrying to vacillating again. A trait Allison had tried to overcome. "Make a decision and live with the consequences," she often told me. I sighed. That was a lot harder than it sounded coming out of her lips.

As I went about the day, Alice called twice to make sure I hadn't 'chickened out'. Henry dropped by mid afternoon to pick up Cinda and told me he'd be by at 8 pm. I almost backed out then but didn't. I had made my decision and was sticking to it.

With Cinda gone, everything felt different. It was the first time I had ever been completely alone at Greystone. It wasn't a good feeling though I couldn't *sense* anything overtly wrong. I was still mulling over what Henry had told me. I knew I should leave...*had* to leave, but kept thinking I could squeeze out one more day...one more night. Nothing had happened last night. Nothing had *felt* out of the ordinary since the Wiley incident. Maybe it would stay that way...at least for a while. I knew that was probably just wishful thinking, so I forced myself to focus on my writing as the minutes ticked past.

Finally, the hour arrived. I had given myself ample time to get ready starting with a long, leisurely bubble bath where I soaked till the water grew tepid and my fingers and toes were 'pruney'. Wrapped in my robe, I laid out the silk undergarments that had been kept in a box in my bottom drawer for the 'some day' that hadn't come till now.

Now for the 'unveiling', I thought as I carried the garment bag to the bed and unzipped it. The scent of roses followed the drift of sage green tulle lined in silk that I lifted out. It was what the designers called an 'illusion gown'...a column silhouette with sheer nearly invisible long sleeves and bodice covered in artfully arranged spills of brilliant deep green sequins that hid what was necessary and left the rest apparently 'exposed'. It had a beaded waistband and quite probably a floor-sweeping hem. It was the perfect color for my coppery hair, which was no surprise since Allison had once been a redhead.

I looked it over slowly... breathing in her favorite fragrance...loving the feel of the fabric...the way the sequins and jewels sparkled in the light. From the back of the armoire, I found the perfect shoes with low heels that wouldn't be a trip hazard to a habitual sneaker wearer. My Cinderella dream had haunted me off and on all day despite my best efforts to shake it off.

Makeup was minimum. I accented my unusual gray eyes...plucked a stray eyebrow hair or two...then added a tiny trace of peach blush to bring some color to my ivory skin. My favorite, if seldom used, lipstick was the finishing touch..

"Now for some hair magic," I murmured to myself as I brushed out its long, copper length.

I had often played with hairstyles in the past and chose now to part it down the middle, roll both sides to frame my oval face, then coil the ends in back with a series of intricate loops that I pinned in place with the emerald and diamond clips Allison had given me some years ago. Almost satisfied with the result, I loosened a few wispy tendrils to soften the effect then fastened another of her gifts to the beaded belt on her gown. Her mermaid pin. Tears filled my eyes as I remembered the first time I saw it, and I dabbed them away quickly.

It was almost time for Henry to pick me up, so I slipped on my silk undies and thigh high hose then donned the gown I hoped would fit.

I had kept my back to the mirror the entire time I was dressing, but now was the 'tah dah!' moment. Turning around, slowly, I looked at the fairy tale princess grinning at me in the glass. The gown was a perfect fit...a froth of green, twinkling jewels and sequins. I couldn't believe that was really me!

Humming a waltz, I twirled in front of the mirror a few times then slipped into my shoes. After one more glance in the mirror to see if I was real, I headed down the hall to the top of the stairs where I waited till Henry's truck pulled in a moment later. The chandelier was lit. The stage was set. My heartbeat quickened still more when I heard the front door open and then his shout, "Your coach has arrived!"

"Ready or not, here I come," I called back then took a deep breath and began my descent.

His eyes were bright with tears when I reached the bottom. "Good Lord Almighty, gal! You are goin' to knock 'em dead!"

I had to laugh. "That would certainly spoil the evening, but thank you for the compliment. It means everything to me. Let me grab my outerwear, and I'll be set to go."

He didn't say much on the ride to the village, and I wondered why. Finally, he told me just as he pulled up in front of the Village Hall,

"Edith said tonight was the beginnin', but wouldn't say mor'en that. Have a dance or two for both of us. I'll pick you up whenever you call. There's a phone in the reception hall. Don't worry about the time. Just have fun."

As I exchanged my boots for my shoes, I looked around for Simon's car, but didn't see it. Henry helped me and my voluminous skirts out of the truck then escorted me to the double doors decorated with holly wreaths. The distant sound of a waltz spilled into the night, when he opened them...kissed my cheek... and left me there.

Taking a deep steadying breath, I looked around the reception hall with its dramatic mural of the famous shipwreck along the back wall. A young man dressed in an oversized tux took my cloak then whistled softly. "You are really hot! Where have you been all of my life?"

"All sixteen years of it?" I replied with a smile. "Is everyone already here?"

"They'll trickle in for awhile. Name's Harry Williams. Maybe I can grab a dance later when I finish up here?"

I nodded then headed down the long hall where the sound of voices and music poured from the open doors at the far end. I paused just inside and looked around at the sea of strangers. I didn't know a single soul and then I spotted Alice standing next to the twenty foot Christmas tree ablaze with multi-colored lights.

"You are a knock out and then some," she told me with a warm smile when I reached her. "That is some gown!"

"I was afraid I'd be overdressed, but I see some designer labels here including the one you're wearing which is awesome. You look amazing!"

"It's a splurge for many of the women here. They go as far as New York City to shop the big name stores and if the same gown is seen more than a few years in a row, nobody cares. You should see Jennie's. She'll be here later. Look! You have a lot of admirers already headed this way."

It seems I did. They murmured their names; I smiled back and let one of them lead me out on the floor. There was still no sign of Simon and then I spotted him dancing with a blonde in a stunning black gown that clung to her like paint. At that very moment, he saw me, too. Our gaze locked and held across the crowded room until the waltz swept us both in different directions. Someone cut in...a Jeff *something or other*. He was good looking with a nice smile and a great dancer, which gave me enough time to regain my fragile poise. Seeing Simon again had rattled me more than I thought it would. Was he still angry with me?

I was still wondering about that as I danced with someone named Robert or Roger, when Simon cut in. As he swept me into the dance, I asked him up front, "Are you still upset with me?"

"Yes. Though 'furious' would be a better choice of words."

"Then why are you dancing with me?"

"If I knew why, I'd tell you. I will tell you three things."

"Which are?"

"You are the most dazzling woman here, but....."

"But?"

"I rather prefer you in jeans and whatever you were wearing."

"Instead of a ball gown that must have cost thousands?"

"Yep. Surprised even me, which leads to number three. You dance really well considering.... Well, you know what I mean."

"You mean I dance really well for a 'lump'."

"Well, you *did* manage to fall off a ladder and into my arms."

He was really beginning to irritate me. "I fell off that ladder because someone grabbed my ankle! You saw what happened!"

He smiled. "Did you know you turn pink when you get angry? Sort of like an anemic radish. Looks like I'm getting the evil eye from my date, so perhaps we can continue our tete a tete a bit later."

"I don't think so. It looks like I'll be really busy," I told him just as a tall man with smiling green eyes cut in and swept me away. It was Joe, and I almost didn't recognize him.

"Looked like he was pissin' off the belle of the ball," he told me as I watched Simon disappear in the crowd. "That's my wife Linda over there waving at you. Told me to go step on your toes for awhile and give hers a break."

As one hour followed another, my dance partners became a blur of smiling faces. Simon and the Apple Princess often swept past us. His intense gaze found mine for that very brief moment, but he never cut in again. Finally, I had had enough. It was getting late. I was tired, and my feet were begging for the comfort of my fuzzy slippers, so I said a quiet good bye to Alice and Jennie then slipped into the reception hall that was now empty.

I was about to place a call to Henry when Simon grabbed my shoulders and swung me around. "You are quite possibly the more irritating...aggravating female I have ever encountered, and yet I can't get you out of my mind," and with that said, he pulled me into his arms and kissed me. Surprised by the sensations that kiss was conjuring up, I struggled for all of a second and then just let it happen. What might have *happened* after that never did. The Apple Princess found us, uttered a screech of outrage, and stormed off.

Simon sighed. "Guess I have to see what I can do about her. By the way, I'm here by her invitation and not the other way around. I couldn't say 'no' to an old friend."

I pretended it didn't matter. "Whatever. I'm going to call your grandfather and head home."

"Wait right here. I'm taking you there though that's the last place you should be," he told me then headed back inside.

It didn't sound like a good idea to be alone with Simon after that kiss, so I placed the call. Henry had just picked up on his end, when the receiver was grabbed from my hand. It was Simon who told him, "It's okay, Grandpa. I've got it handled. Guess I'll be staying the night at your place."

They said their good byes and hung up before I could utter one word of protest.

"Now that that is settled," Simon told me, "Let's find our coats or whatever and get the hell outta here."

"What about your date?"

"Found her dancing with her boyfriend. Seems my role here was to make him jealous. Mission accomplished. Let's go."

Some part of me wanted to turn him down cold...while another part didn't. It was the latter that won out. We didn't say much at all for the first mile and then he broke the awkward silence. "You didn't look like a radish...*exactly*. More like a rose. I was just teasing you because.... Well, just *because* and then there's that kiss that shouldn't have happened. I..."

I cut in before he could finish with, "No need to mention something I barely remember."

He shot a sideways glance at me then frowned. "That's funny. From the way you kissed back, I..."

I cut in again with, "Pure reflex. Nothing personal. Do you mind turning up the heat? I feel cold."

"You should have worn something a bit less skimpy."

"It's called an *illusion* gown. You do know what an illusion is? All my parts are well covered, and why do you even care? You had the Apple Princess drooling all over you."

I could see his smile in the lights from the dashboard. "Are you jealous?"

"In your dreams! She's perfect for you right down to that fake smile. Not an 'anemic radish' like someone else you know."

He sighed. "I've already explained about that."

"I wouldn't call '*teasing me because*' an explanation or an apology."

He sighed a second time. "I did amend it to 'rose' as you might remember. I didn't know you were so thin skinned."

"Well, I am, so remember that in the very short future we'll share."

Silence descended again and then he said, "When Grandpa and I talked about you, he told me that you think you have a mystery to solve...a purpose. Something to do with the writer Allison Shield who was your adopted mother?"

"Mother and friend," I replied having largely got past my snit. "I had been an orphan living in foster care, which was a microcosm of hell for me. Had run away four times...lived on the streets till I was hauled back and labeled 'incorrigible'. She took me home, helped me live up to my potential, and adopted me. She wants me to write her biography. I'm here trying to unravel the mystery of her birth and ran into a blank wall."

"And Greystone? How does that figure into it?"

I sighed. "I just knew when I saw it that I'm supposed to be there. I don't know the connection. I *do* know that Allison is still with me...protecting me. So is Millie Grey."

"The daughter of the man who built Greystone."

"Yep. She's still inside those walls as is...."

"A malevolent entity that wants to suck up your soul. Been there. Saw and felt her intense evil."

"I heard you almost died there."

He pulled over and stopped the car. "I had made a few friends back when I was a kid visiting my grandparents. We often would go there...never inside...until one night on a dare we all did. Whoever

205

could stay the longest would win. We began to hear things...creaks...rustling...and then whispers. The candles we had lit and placed in a circle were blown out one by one, so we pulled out our flashlights and swept the room. Something oily and black was pouring under the door and began to reshape. It was the distorted figure of a woman...bone thin with malevolent red eyes that sliced right through me. I could hear the others scramble for the door while I stood rooted to the spot. I couldn't move. She drifted closer and closer while I kept the flashlight trained on her and then I felt a curious sensation...a pulling...sucking kind of thing just as she said in a raspy whisper, "I want your soul. You need to be punished. 'The sins of the father....'"

He paused and took a deep breath before he continued, "I didn't stick around to hear the rest. To this day, I don't know how I got away. I just ran and ran and ran. Grandpa found me lying in the woods not far from his cabin with a deep gash in my leg. He had to carry me home. I guess I can say that incident is what pointed me in the direction of paranormal research. At the university, I studied the psychiatric and neurobehavioral sciences. After graduating, I formed a group to study Near-Death experiences, Neuroimaging or PSI, and children who reported memories of previous lives. Those memories tend to fade past age 7, but you would be astounded by the similarities in their statements. Statements we could collaborate with post-mortem reports and interviews with relatives of the deceased."

"After what I have seen and heard at Greystone very little would *astound* me. You do know that your Grandfather sees and speaks to your grandmother? I always get a sense of her presence when I'm there."

"I see her, too. Just a glimpse out of the corner of my eye and then she's gone. She's always smiling the way I remember. Theirs was a classic love story. She died in his arms in that very house."

I could feel more tears coming on as I said, "I know. I think she's waiting there for him. He has Cinda, and I would like to pick her up before I go back to Greystone. She was Allsion's cat...another stray she adopted...and I believe she possesses her. Is inside her from time to time and looking out of her eyes. I know how all kinds of crazy that sounds."

"Would to most anyone else. You're shivering again. Let's get going. "

He turned up the heater...glanced at me from time to time...but was silent. We were both lost in our own thoughts. I couldn't begin to guess what his were, but mine made me say, "I know you have every reason to turn me down, but I really could use your help."

He pulled off the road again then said, "Okay. I'm listening."

"You obviously have had a lot more experience with the paranormal than I have. My sum total is what I've found at Greystone. Perhaps you have some idea about what I should do next to find my answers."

"What you should do 'next' is never go back there, but since that won't happen, perhaps I can help. My team has done some

207

paranormal investigating in haunted places. Our goal is to find hard-core evidence that there is 'life' after death. Something tangible for all the skeptics out there."

"And did you find what you were looking for?"

"Found a lot of manifestations, but they were tricky to film and record. What we captured could just as easily be faked. The skeptics will always think the worst despite our credentials. Some of those fraudulent paranormal investigative TV shows only made things far harder for us."

"So what are you saying exactly?"

He brushed back one of my artfully arranged tendrils and tucked it behind my ear then said, "I have the team and the equipment to do a full scale investigation including a séance that should rattle that old place."

"That would be great except for the risk involved. Have any of those other places harbored an evil like that at Greystone?"

"No. Not even close. I would have to ask for volunteers only."

"I don't want anyone hurt. You've probably heard about some of the other things that happened there, but you don't know that Horace Grey's son didn't die as was reported. His mother, Hannah, locked him in a trunk and let him drown. Heard it from her own lips one night I will long remember."

He nodded. "Grandpa mentioned her visit. I'll tell them all they need to know to make an informed decision. I'm going to stay over at Grandpa's and go home Monday morning. He's worried by now that we're taking so long, so let's get you there."

We pulled up in front of Henry's a short time later, and Simon helped me inside. Cinda greeted me with a 'meow' and a *knowing* look then headed back to her warm spot by the stove."

"Well, seeing you two together would have been a surprise," Henry told us with a chuckle, "If Edith hadn't already told me it would happen. Pull up a chair and tell me all about the Ball while I rustle us all up some hot chocolate."

Sitting around the table, I gave a sketchy account of the ball, which wasn't enough for Henry.

"Would like to know how the two of you linked up?" he asked as his gaze swept us both.

It was Simon who told him, "Let's just say it happened, Grandpa, and let it go at that. It seems we are going to collaborate on finding some answers she needs."

I took a long swallow of my now tepid chocolate and added. "I asked him, and he agreed. Now we've kept you up long enough. I just came to collect Cinda and then head back if Simon wouldn't mind driving me."

Simon frowned. "Your house will be very active now. Have you ever been downstairs after midnight?"

"No. I hide in my room as soon as it gets dark."

"Good plan. I think you should stay the night here, and I'll drive you back in the morning."

Henry added, "Can put you up in Simon's room while he sleeps in the loft. No problem findin' you somethin' to wear. Even have a new toothbrush you can use."

The thought of returning to Greystone in the midnight hour had absolutely no appeal, so I agreed. Wearing an oversized T-shirt, I crawled into Simon's bed a short time later. Cinda joined me there, and I slept the best I had in as long as I could remember. I felt safe for the first time since I came to Greystone.

The next morning I awoke to the heavenly smells of coffee and bacon. Donning the robe I'd been given, I did what I could with my hair then padded out to the kitchen to find both Simon and Henry already there.

"Wondered when you'd be getting up," Simon called. "Grandpa makes the best pancakes on this planet."

"With real maple syrup. I know. I need to feed Cinda and....."

"Been fed already, " Henry told me with a grin. "Picked up a bag of her kibbles and some litter the other day for her stay overs. Grab a chair."

As I devoured my stack of pancakes, I listened to Simon and Henry's accounts of their fishing trips and sailing adventures. Apparently, Henry had been an avid sailor and still had a sailboat in storage down in the marina.

"Grandpa taught me how to sail when I was about 8 years old. I used to take her out whenever I visited. Still do when I get a chance. How do you feel about sailing?"

"Never been, but I love the sea with the same passion Millie Grey still has. I've been having dreams that she and her lover had a secret spot...a cave somewhere along the shore. I tried looking for it a few days ago and almost drowned. The tide came in before I noticed, and I was almost trapped. It was Millie who saved me in the nick of time."

"I'm staying over today," Simon told me as he added another pancake to his plate." So why don't the two of us go looking for this secret place you dreamt about?"

"We'll use my computer to check the tide table first. That's one mistake I won't make twice. I'll need some clothes to wear to Greystone."

 Simon nodded. "There's plenty of stuff in the closet and dresser. Just let me know when you're ready."

We left Cinda where she was and headed to Greystone not long after that. I was wearing Simon's sweat pants and a sweater that were way too big for me, but it felt strangely comforting at the same time. A dangerous feeling. Being with Simon was doing all kinds of worrisome things to my thinking.

Reaching the house, I carried my ball gown upstairs with him close on my heels. I had told him to wait in the kitchen, but he had insisted on coming with me to check out my room.

"It's broad daylight, and you won't find anything but dust balls under my bed," I warned him.

He reminded me it was daylight when the ladder incident occurred, so I waited in the hall while he did his thing. A few minutes later, he reported my room and bathroom were both clear "if a bit messy". I told him I liked it that way. That my creativity sprang from chaos, which made him smile and shake his head.

He sat on the edge of my bed while I hung up Allison's ball gown then headed to the bathroom to do something with my hair. One thing led to another, and it was some time before I re-emerged. I found him asleep with his head on my pillow. Bending over him, I brushed back a strand of dark hair from his forehead and had the strangest feeling I had done that very thing before. Suddenly, he opened his eyes and looked into mine.

A puzzled frown furrowed his brow as he murmured, "I dreamt I was your mystery man, and you were this Millie and then I woke up to find you standing there just like you did in my dream. What's going on?"

I sighed then told him, "I don't know. I'm feeling all kinds of weird, too. Let's go find that cave and see if it has any answers."

We left the house right after we checked the tide table and headed down the trail to the beach. The wind had picked up since we left Henry's, and the trees around us stirred in a wild frenzy. I could hear the pound of the surf long before we reached the shore.

"We've got plenty of time till the tide turns. Where did you explore before?" he asked as we stood on my rock and looked out over the dark, teal green water at the huge breakers rolling up on shore. Ominous, bruised looking clouds raced across the sky in our direction.

"I went to the right for some distance and found nothing."

"There are only a few caves that would be suitable. Never been down this way before on foot, but I used to sail along the shore. Let's see what we can find. Just be careful."

"Because I'm such a klutz?"

"Because you could sprain an ankle, and I'd have to lug you out of here. Let's go."

CHAPTER NINE

(Millie)

Through the window, I can see her head down the trail to the sea with a tall stranger. She had been gone all night and came back with him this morning. Perhaps together they will find what I want them to find. My cave...my secret place. I had watched her get ready for her ball last night wearing a gown that made her look like a fairytale princess. I could feel her excitement as though it was my own then she left with the old man and didn't come back. I had waited, and watched, and listened until I finally headed up here to the attic and looked through the trunks that held so many precious memories. Bits of the time I spent with my father. The little horse he had carved for me...the books he had read to me as we listened to the howl of the wind on long winter nights. The treasures we had found together on the shore. I had loved feeling close to him again as I lifted out each one and remembered when and where we discovered it. He always seemed so sad even then. I knew he had lost my baby brother at sea and wondered if that was the heartache that lingered. I asked him once, but he only smiled and said I made him the happiest he had ever been.

I had felt the same way. He had been the only happiness my childhood had ever known and then he left on my sixteenth birthday and never returned. I had waited up for him all night and all the long nights that followed. She had mocked me. Told me it was my fault he had left. Did all she could to poison my memories. Neither of us had known how much she resented our closeness. How much she hated me.

So much time has passed since the day he disappeared from my life. He must have died somewhere long, long ago. All are gone now. All those that meant everything to me...Father...Eric...and my precious son. I have no inkling where their spirits might be though I have never given up the hope they will come back to me. Now I have Jodie and her cat to love and look after, and I have to wonder who the stranger is who walks so close to her. I sense he has been here before, but his identity is a mystery. I can only hope and pray he is not another living one who means her harm.

(Jodie)

The wind battered us with its icy force as we headed down the shore. The tide was still headed out, and what it had left in its wake was exposed...seaweed...driftwood...a plastic bottle and a single shoe. Seagulls squabbled over the carcass of a dead fish then took to flight protesting loudly at our approach.

214

"That one is a possibility," Simon told me as he pointed to a small opening almost concealed by a rock.

"Too small. I don't think Cinda could squeeze through there."

"Let's check it out. That rock might be concealing some of the entrance."

As it turned out, he was right, but the cave was shallow and empty, so we moved on. The second cave was also a bust. We were headed farther down the coast when I spotted another possibility up above. Threading our way among the rocks, we picked up a trail of sorts that led right to it. High as the cave was, the mound of debris trapped just inside the entrance was proof the sea had invaded it often in the past. Snapping on our flashlights, we stepped over it and looked around.

"This has to be it," I murmured as we flashed our lights over the remnants of a makeshift bed...a stack of crates...a rusty lantern, and a shelf made of driftwood and bricks. Its mildewed, crumbling books were scattered across the floor.

"Not much left in here," Simon murmured, "But there's another opening in that corner. I'm going to check it out."

I followed him to a second, smaller cave that was more protected from the elements. Near the back wall was a crate covered with an old, mildew spotted sail. Pulling it back, I discovered at least a dozen rolled up canvasses. One was on a stretcher and wrapped in oilcloth to protect it from the damp and time.

Simon trained his flashlight on it while I unwrapped it ever so carefully. I don't know what I was expecting, but it wasn't a portrait

215

of Simon smiling back at me dressed in the clothes of another era. Millie had captured his essence as only someone who loved and knew him very well ever could.

Simon was as shocked as I was. "That's me without my glasses! This can't be happening!"

"It must be Eric. Millie thought he was dead though I don't know why she believed that. His transport ship was torpedoed, but he survived. From my dreams, I know he loved her deeply. He would have come back here after the war ended, but by then Millie and his baby were dead. I wonder if he even knew he'd been a father?"

Simon smiled grimly. "You can be sure if he talked to her mother, he would have known. She'd want him to suffer. What else do you know about him?"

"He married late in life and had a daughter named Audrey who married a Joseph Simmons. They had a baby girl but Audrey never survived the birth. I lost the trail after that."

"Is there any possibility that the records were wrong? Could his name have been Joseph Simon? It was my mother's maiden name which is how I ended up with it."

"I'm willing to bet that's exactly what happened," I murmured as a cold shiver shot through me. "That would explain Varna Grey's interest in you the first time you came to Greystone. Somehow, she must have known who you were."

"She started to quote a Bible verse that I looked up later. Something about how the Lord would visit the sins of the father on the children and the children's children, to the third and the fourth generation.'"

"Well, that would make you a target if she believes herself to be the instrument of a vengeful God. She wants me, too, and I have to wonder how I fit in."

"In my dream, you were this Millie."

"And in my dreams, I see through her eyes. I don't know who my parents were, or where I came from. The only thing I do know is that I was found as a toddler without any ID and taken to the state orphanage till someone claimed me. No one did."

"So anything is possible. There could be a tie to all this we haven't discovered."

"Maybe...though that would be a big leap. I only know for sure we're on to something here, Simon. In one of my dreams, I was in this very cave and saw Millie writing in a diary. I looked for it in her bedroom, but didn't find it there. Maybe its still here. "

"One way to find out. I'll start looking over there."

It was Simon who found it hidden in a hollow spot and covered with a rock.

"Pure luck led me to it," he told me as he handed it over.

"Not *luck*, Simon. She wanted you to find it. Let's see what we can learn from it that might help us."

Unfortunately, it had also suffered from the damp sea air. Most of it was ruined and crumbled when I turned the pages, but here and there something remained intact enough to read. There was no date except the year 1917:

I can't believe he really exists. That he would take an interest in me. He called me Smudge because of the blue paint daub on my nose, and I had to laugh then realized I hadn't laughed since father disappeared. She.....

The rest was undecipherable, so I carefully turned the pages till we saw:

He has to report in less than a week now. So few days left. How is it possible to fall in love so fast and yet we have. Madly...deeply...passionately...

It continued on with a description of her euphoria in finding the love of her life...the time they shared safely away from the house...the time spent right here in her secret place. She had found what few ever did...her soul mate...and then we read:

I saw the car pull away from the house when I was returning from the sea. The two men inside wore army uniforms. I knew why they had come. There could be no other reason. I ran back here. Was going to walk into the icy sea and join him when I felt the first flutter of life. The quickening had come. I remembered that I had a reason to live. A reason I must live! I walked back to the house hoping to escape to my room, but Mother was waiting for me. She took great pleasure in telling me he was dead. That a U-Boat had sunk his transport ship...that he had been hideously burned then drowned...his body never recovered. She screamed at me and called me names, but I barely heard her. The great bubble of grief I'd been feeling grew larger and larger. He was dead. Buried by the sea. He would never return. We would never have our happy ending, but

218

I had his child to love. A piece of him that death wouldn't take from me.

Many pages were too damaged to read and then we read:

I'm not allowed to be seen. Am kept in my room or locked in the cellar when someone comes to the house. But sometimes I manage to escape with a skeleton key she doesn't know I have. I come here where I can feel him close as I grow big with his son who kicks and squirms in his tight berth. I love him so much it terrifies me. My baby Eric. What will happen to us after he is born when she already starves and hurts me? I must take him and run away as soon as we are able. Perhaps I can find Eric's family. They will take us in, for they loved him dearly and must feel his loss. A grandson might help heal their grief.

The last page read:

This will be the last time I can come here. She watches too closely, and I have grown too cumbersome to make the climb safely. I pray to God my son will be a healthy boy despite the way she treats me. I have been told a midwife will be there at the birth. A woman named Nora North who has an unsavory reputation in the village. Mother said that women often die in childbirth, and Mrs. North's numbers were unusually high. She was smiling when she told me that. Should I die as I fear I might, I pray that I will find Eric's spirit...that we will be together again for eternity. My love for him and my son is greater than any force on earth. With God's help, I will find a way to bring us together again no matter what it takes.

I felt an enormous sadness wash over me as I read those words. Simon was experiencing much the same thing then he told me, "Nora North was my great grandmother. I had heard she was a midwife back in the day when home births were common. Hadn't heard the 'unsavory' part."

So, I told him what Henry had confided about the birth and his drunken paternal great grandmother. He was silent for a long time then said, "The mystery is unraveling. I'd like to talk to my grandfather and see what else he can tell us."

He wanted to take the canvas with us, but I knew Millie would not want that. Knew she must still come here often and would want to have it here.

The tide had just started to turn as we headed back, but there was still plenty of time to make the trail. We were both lost in our thoughts...deeply disturbed by what we had learned. Reaching the car, we were at Henry's a short time later and found him bringing in wood from the shed with a trail of puppies following him.

We each grabbed an armload and headed inside where he told us, "Plunk it in the box, and I'll fix us all some lunch then you can tell me what you found."

"Lunch can wait, Grandpa. We found Millie Grey's diary in a hidden cave and there was a painting."

Henry nodded. "She was an artist. Pretty good from what I remember hearin'."

"She was great!" Simon told him. "Had painted a portrait of this man she loved. This Eric. He was almost the mirror image of me."

Henry's blue eyes widened, and his mouth dropped open. "I'll be a blue nosed gopher! That ain't possible, is it?"

Simon and I exchanged glances before he continued. "Keep in mind that I was named 'Simon' after my mother's side of the family though she never talked about them. Just told me her mother had died during childbirth and the past best forgotten. Jodie will tell you who we think they were."

"I traced the family line from this man...this Eric Sanders. He didn't die at sea. Married late and had a daughter named Audrey who married a Joseph Simmons. We wondered if the Internet had it wrong. If his name had been Joseph Simon. That would explain the connection."

Henry nodded. "That's not such a big leap. You could be right."

"If I am a direct descendant of Eric Sanders, that would explain why Varna Grey tried to grab me that day. She wants to punish me for the 'sins of my fathers'. Her words that night."

Henry's eyes were troubled as he looked at us both then asked, "What about you, Jodie? She wants you, too. How do you fit into all this?"

"I only know that in my dreams I *am* Millie. Is it possible her son survived? If so, maybe I'm connected to him in some way?"

"Only know what my ma told me which weren't all that much. Don't rightly know how I can help, but........."

A smile lifted the corners of his mouth, and his eyes lost their focus. I could feel a presence close to us and knew Simon felt it, too. It had to be Edith. His next words confirmed it. "Edith just reminded me there's a trunk in the tool shed what belonged to my ma I plum forgot. Go take a look."

He insisted we get some "food in our bellies" before we left. I was so excited I scarcely remembered what we ate. It seemed like forever before we reached the tool shed and began digging our way through stacked boxes overflowing with castoffs and clutter. The old leather bound trunk was in the far corner buried deep beneath it all. It was mildewed, rat chewed, and locked though Simon soon handled that. It felt like we were entering a crypt when I lifted the lid on its rusty hinges.

"Looks like it's mostly old clothes...that sort of thing," I told Simon as I lifted out each item. At the very bottom, there was a book wrapped in a long, age yellowed apron. I carried it to Henry's workbench then opened the cover.

"Seems to be some kind of log," I murmured as I turned the first page.

Simon read over my shoulder as we looked through it. The entries were printed, professional, and well written...the outcomes mostly good for both mother and infant, but that changed as the years passed. For many reasons, more and more mothers and infants died.

We flipped through to the early part of 1918. There were almost no entries for that period and then we saw it. A very lengthy one that began with:

At 3 pm, I was called to Greystone to deliver the baby of Millicent Grey where I was sworn to the utmost secrecy. She was very frail and undernourished. She told me she knew it would be a boy, and she wanted him named Eric. At 12 am, I delivered a baby girl in poor condition. The mother hemorrhaged, and I could not stop the bleeding. As she was dying, I heard her mother tell her that the baby had been a boy and born dead "so there would be no living seed left of their sin". She died before I could tell her the truth. Varna Grey ordered me to "get rid of" the infant. I remember her exact words: "It is an abomination and should be drowned." There is no doubt in my mind she meant for me to kill her. I was also ordered to prepare Millie's body for burial since she wouldn't touch it. I was not surprised to find numerous bruises and other marks...some quite old...that showed she had suffered at her mother's hands for a long time. She had never run away as it was rumored. When I left Greystone, I took the infant with me after telling Mrs. Grey that the infant was too weak to live more than a few hours, and I would dispose of the body when she died. She was well bundled against the cold when I left her at Second Chance just after daylight and kept watch from hiding till they took her in. I had pinned a note to her that claimed she was Allison Bogart. It was the name of a good friend I had known in Iowa before I ever heard of Courage Cove. I'm not sure why I did it. Maybe I wanted her to be more than a nameless scrap of nothing dumped on their doorstep. I saw true evil that day, and it will haunt me the rest of my life. She lives close by, and I fear for my own safety should I ever tell the truth. I don't know what she did with Millie's body. I only know I did my best to keep her baby safe. She has red hair like her mother, and I hope she will fight as hard to live.

I closed the log and looked at Simon. "Allison Bogart must be Allison Shield. There can't be any other explanation for what's going on here."

"Was Cinda with you when you first saw Greystone?"

"She was in the car with me. Are you saying that Allison somehow recognized it?"

"Could be some instinctual awareness. Remember her rose scent and the roses outside those walls? She probably didn't know the role Greystone had played in her life, but knew it was necessary that you be there."

If that was true, it would explain the weirdness that was happening between us since the moment I fell into his arms. I was Allison's adopted daughter and Simon was Eric's direct descendant. Perhaps we were destined to be Millie and Eric's 'happy ending'? That what we were feeling belonged to them? That would also explain why Varna wanted us both dead.

We brought the log back to Henry and showed him the entry. "Looks like the pieces of the puzzle are startin' to fall into place," he told us as he squinted at the fine print. "Where do we look next?"

"I wish I knew," I told him. "Maybe Millie will share another dream, or I'll uncover more in Allison's journals. I need to get back and get busy."

224

"And I'll be there helping you with that, " Simon added. "Which means I'll be staying the night. When I leave for Boston in the morning, you'll be coming with me."

"And if I would rather just stay close to home and see what develops?"

"Did that sound like an invitation?"

"It sounded like an order."

"Good. Then you understood perfectly."

From there, I told him he was overbearing, a control freak, and thoroughly obnoxious. In the end, I *sort of* won the argument. He was going to Boston alone, but planned on staying the night.

We loaded Cinda in her carrier and headed back to Greystone. Once there, Simon went upstairs with me to collect the material I had been working on then followed me to my study where I powered up my laptop.

He'd been studying the little portrait on the wall when he said, "She looks a bit like you...especially the eyes. If you look *really* close, you can just make out that black ring around the irises like you have."

I peered at it. "I didn't notice that. The whole thing is so faded and damaged it could just be some defect."

"Or I *could* be right which you have a hard time ever admitting."

"When and *if* that ever happens, I will be the first to acknowledge it."

He looked at me closely then murmured, "Is it even remotely possible we could have been lovers in a prior incarnation?"

I snorted derisively. "Not likely. You would be the last man I would chose to wail and weep over let alone have...."

"My baby? That does seem a big stretch, but then I remember that kiss. Let's see what we can find out in those journals before I make that same mistake twice."

While Cinda slept loaf style next to the heat vent, we both read through Allison's early journals in hopes we would catch something I had missed but learned nothing new. By then, it was getting dark, so we headed to the kitchen, threw together a hasty meal, and finished off a bottle of wine. He seemed fine, while I was feeling a bit tipsy, when we wrapped things up then made our way upstairs. I didn't want to tell him that I felt something dark and evil was right behind us.

As I prepped for bed, I could hear him whistling in the next room. It was immensely comforting to know he was there when I crawled beneath the covers. I was lying there thinking about what we had found in the cave, when he called to me, "Hey! You asleep in there?"

"Not any more!" I called back. "You afraid in there?"

"Maybe. Did you hear that thing behind us on the stairs?"

"Yes, but didn't want to mention it and scare you."

"Same here. Would you like some company?"

"I've got Cinda."

There was a long pause and then, "I could be right over?"

I smiled. "Why don't you just go to sleep? You have your Boston trip in the morning."

"Did you hear that?"

"That what?"

"That moaning sound in the hall. There is goes again."

"I don't hear anything," I told him and then I did. Someone was moaning and weeping just outside the door. "Probably Horace Grey's first wife. She's scary, but I don't think she means us any harm."

"If you ask me, she sounds pissed off about something. I'm coming over."

Just thinking about having him that close was doing all kinds of strange things to me. I was more afraid of those feelings than whatever was in the hall, so I told him, "Just stay where you are. The door is locked, and I'm not climbing out of this warm bed."

"Sounds way more comfy than a sleeping bag on a hard floor, and I can pick a lock as you might remember," he called back.

His voice sounded closer, and my heartbeat quickened. "Good night, Simon. I....."

I never finished whatever I was about to babble as the door swung open. He was standing there without his glasses and looking rather rumpled. His smile was both disarming and beguiling and then he told me, "Hey, it's cold lurking here uninvited. Scoot on over and make some room. Don't tell me you're a bed hog, too?"

"Yep. Add it to the list. Why would you even bother with me?" I asked him wryly.

He had locked the door behind him and was headed my way when he replied, "One wonders. Whatever was in the hall has moved on...for now. Your Cinda will have to relocate a bit. Let's try and get some sleep."

Pulling back the covers, he yanked my second pillow out from under my head...plumped it up...then climbed in next to me.

My heart was hammering, and my mouth felt dry. "At no time...under any circumstances...will you budge even an inch closer than that. Understood?"

"No worries. Your cat has now wedged her fur body between us, so you *should* be safe."

"*Should* be?"

He laughed. "If I am the reincarnation or whatever of this Eric, and you're the new version of Millie, who knows what might happen in our sleep."

It was then we both heard the mystery clock chime twelve times. The time Millie gave birth.

"Now I know why I keep hearing that," I murmured.

"The pieces of the puzzle are falling into place as my grandpa told us. Now how about less talking so I can get some sleep?"

He turned on this side away from me and was asleep a short time later judging from his breathing. It was not that easy for me. I lay awake a long time thinking about those 'pieces' and all too aware of his closeness. I heard a baby cry and then silence. I must have dozed off shortly after that.

A long time later, a pale winter sun was shining through the windows when I woke up and looked around. The bed next to me

228

was empty. Both Simon and Cinda were gone. The indented pillow was the only indication he had ever been there until I headed to the bathroom and found it had been tidied. Even my toothpaste tube had been rolled from the bottom, and I smiled. We were so different and yet....

I didn't like where my thoughts were going or where they had been much of the night, so I dressed quickly and sped down to the kitchen where he was busy making breakfast.

"About time you got up. I need to head out shortly. One egg or two?"

"One. You slept the whole night and missed the baby crying."

He shoved two plates at me. "Here! You get to set the table. It wasn't Millie's baby since she lived, so it has to be the one the first Mrs.Grey drowned. If I wasn't going to be back before nightfall, I'd drag your ass to Boston with me."

"My 'ass' stays where it is. I have work to do today and will be fine."

As we ate, we talked about the team he'd be bringing back with him...a bit more about his work including the studies of children who had lived past lives. I found the subject fascinating. When he left a short time later, Cinda and I stood at the window and watched him drive off. I wanted to see if he would look back. He did, and I was surprised to find how much that mattered to me.

After a slap dash clean up, I headed to my study and began reading through the journals again. There had been no further mention of the daughter she'd conceived for some time and then there it was. My interest revved into hyper drive, and I was soon lost among the pages.

I often think about her...my Jillian...the daughter I gave away. The responsibility of raising her had been more than I could manage with my lifestyle. I believed I had her best interests at heart when I arranged a meeting with Edward's widow and been surprised she would agree to see me. Apparently, he had told her about his plans and my role in them. She attributed their estrangement to the death of their daughter and welcomed a chance to have his child. It was a good arrangement that satisfied us both.

I continued to read and found that Allison's life had changed dramatically after the birth of her daughter. She was no longer the hedonist she had once been. Sadness often edged her words, and I wondered how many times she regretted giving her away.

She had kept track of Jillian through the years that followed but never revealed her identity. She became a 'family friend' that appeared in her life from time to time. She wrote at length about her accomplishments at school. Had been there when she played a sheep in her kindergarten Christmas Pageant...rooted from the sidelines at her athletic competitions and cried with pride and joy when she graduated from Vassar summa cum laude. Shortly thereafter, she attended her wedding to Charles Manning...the son of a prominent Boston family.

Needing a short break, I headed to the kitchen and scrounged up a mug of hot chocolate then carried it back to the study with Cinda right on my heels. She was watching me intently when I picked up the journal and began again. More than twelve years passed before the birth of Aurielle Manning. Allison had been at the christening of her granddaughter:

She was so small...so tiny with a fuzz of red hair and an angel's face. I found myself desperately wanting to hold her, and when my daughter put her in my arms, I found myself bursting into tears. Everyone must have thought me quite mad or else a sentimental old fool, but I suddenly hated all the lost years when they both could have been mine.

Several years passed and then I found a clipping that horrified me. The headline read: "Wife and Daughter of Financier Charles Manning Feared Dead." It was a *Boston Globe* article that gave an account of a kidnapping gone very wrong. Jillian had been shopping when the car was hijacked. A $2 million ransom had been demanded and was paid, but mother and daughter were not returned.

I opened my computer and searched for more information. Jillian's body had been found in her burned out car near Worcester, Massachusetts. There was no trace of the child. Her bloodied, toy black cat was found in the woods some distance away. Everyone feared the worst. After a thorough search of the area, the case went cold.

Suddenly, Cinda jumped in my lap, and I gathered her close. "Allison, if you're in there, please let me know how that fits in with all that's been happening? Is there a chance that Aurielle is me?"

I knew the odds were against it, but some things just seemed to click. The age of her missing granddaughter corresponded to my

231

own as best I knew, and Worcester was only two states away from where I had been found walking down the street with no memory of the past. I wondered why no one had made the connection. Further research gave me the answer. Amber Alerts started in the late 1990s. Before that, law enforcement agencies often didn't share information across state lines.

An image flashed through my mind. A mere flicker at first, it sharpened into a black cloth cat with yellow button eyes clutched in two chubby hands. My hands? Why had I been shown that? Suddenly, I remembered! Allison had given me that cat on my birthday. I had named it Cinda because that was how I pronounced 'cinder'.

More memories swamped me. I was in some dark place that smelled funny. Moonlight streamed through an open door, and I could hear my mother shouting and calling my name, "Aurielle! Don't touch her! Please don't hurt her!" and then all went black as something was thrown over my head. Pure terror gripped me. I could hear a struggle. Things crashing to the floor. My mother's muffled cry and then a thud. "Mommy! Mommy! Mommy!" I screamed and kept on screaming as I was yanked up and carried away. The rest faded and was gone. I was left with an overwhelming sense of loss. There was now no doubt in my mind. I was Allison's granddaughter.

I cried for a long time then swiped at my tears, picked up the journal, and began to read again. She hadn't believed me dead. Had private detectives searching every possible lead, but they had turned up nothing. She became interested in orphanages believing I might have ended up in one. She had been watching from the window when I was brought back from the police station that day. It had been my red hair that triggered her curiosity, and she had asked to see my records.

Her age...while approximate...matched that of my granddaughter. Close inspection of her photo revealed a slight family resemblance that might have been wishful thinking. When I met her, she seemed so...well, unexpected. So very unlike the little girl I had known. She was frightened, defensive, with a wall around her that would be hard to penetrate. I hope and pray she is my missing Aurielle. I will take her home...care for her...heal her if that is possible. Even if she is not who I hope she is, she will be my second chance."

I wondered why she hadn't told me she believed I might be her granddaughter and then I read: *I still don't know for sure if she is my Aurielle, but it no longer matters. I have come to love her completely and unconditionally. She means everything to me!*

Tears were running down my face again unheeded. I wished with all my heart I could tell her that her instincts had been right. That she had found and saved her Aurielle. Cinda head butted me three times and began to purr. I smiled. I didn't need to tell her. She already knew.

My head was filled with thoughts of the past as the next hours flew by. Cinda and I were in the kitchen when Simon's car pulled up followed by a black van. Two men and a woman piled out then joined Simon as he headed to the door I held open.

"Back as promised," he told me as he and the others stepped inside. "Hey, everyone, this is Jodie and Cinda her friend. Jodie, I'd like you to meet Wendy Lu, Mike Jeffers, and Todd Billings. Mike and Todd will set up the equipment we need. Wendy is a multi tasking all around electronic wonder woman and clairvoyant/medium. She will be holding a good old-fashioned séance with your permission. We have an Ovilus that synthesizes spoken words out of the environment and electromagnetic waves, but most of it is worthless since it doesn't answer the questions we ask. She nearly always gets amazing results."

"Permission granted," I told her with a smile. She was probably of Eurasian descent and quite beautiful. Stunning was closer to it, and she worked with Simon every day. Once again, I felt a twinge of what might be jealously but hoped not.

"Do you mind if I pet your cat? He is quite the handsome boy," she asked as she returned my smile.

"You will have to ask her. She was my mother's, and I kept her after...after her death."

"Simon told us a bit about Allison Shield's connection to you," she replied as she hunkered down next to Cinda and extended her hand, which was sniffed and rejected.

"Did he now?" I murmured wondering how much of my personal life he had shared.

Simon noticed my reaction and smiled reassuringly. "Only a few highlights to help them understand what they were all volunteering for when they came here."

"Whatever will help," I replied as my gaze swept them all. "I really appreciate what you are doing."

Simon's smile deepened. "There's pizza in my car that will make a quick and easy supper. We are going to unload the van and be right back."

"Is there some way I can help?" I asked him as they all streamed past me a second time.

"Hold the door."

So, that was my role as everyone trooped back and forth lugging large cases into the kitchen they then stacked in the corner. Last in was Simon juggling three pizza boxes and a case of beer he plunked down on the table. "Beers cold. One each allowed. Pizza is still hot...I hope...so grab a seat everyone."

We were a chair short, which Todd handled by upending one of the cases. I supplied napkins and paper plates. It was a no muss no fuss meal for five. As we ate, there was a lot of good natured ribbing among the crew. Wendy gave as good as she got which made me like her. It was easy to tell they had worked together for a long time and were comfortable with each other, which made me ask as pizza box number two was passed my way, "How long have you been together?"

It was Mike...a tall lanky guy with sandy blonde hair who answered, "At the university, we were all in the same classes...the psychiatric and neurobehavioral sciences...and Simon thought we should hook up after we graduated and do our own research. He's a whiz at getting us the funding we need. Long and short of it is, we've been doing it for six years and have had some pretty amazing finds."

"Which brings us here on this 'field trip'," Wendy added. "Simon told us this house is very active. That we should be able to get some fantastic results."

I had to smile. "Active doesn't begin to describe this place. I just hope you all will be safe."

It was Simon who told me, "Which is why I'm giving you this. We all wear them." He passed me a silver medal, and I shot him a puzzled frown. "It's St. Benedict. He's a protector against evil. So far, we think he's helped us in some pretty scary situations."

He took it back and slipped the chain over my head. It was still warm from his pocket and felt oddly comforting.

While we finished the pizza, the group shared stories of other hauntings they had investigated. All seemed pretty tame compared to what was waiting for them at Greystone.

It was Simon who finally announced, "Not much daylight left and we have a lot of equipment to set up. Let's move!"

They all rose from their seats and began opening cases. Simon told me what the items were as they set them on the table and counter.

"Todd just hauled out our digital voice recorders."

"Which do what beyond the obvious?" I asked.

"We use them to record EVPs or electronic voice phenomena...voices we can't hear unassisted though Cinda might."

Other equipment followed including both infrared and full spectrum cameras that caught images unseen with the naked eye.

"This gismo," Mike told me as he lifted it from its case, "Is a Mel Meter and measures electromagnetic and geomantic fields."

"Which are what exactly?"

"Spirits emit an electromagnetic field as do other things like power sources, so we have to account for that. This one has a cold and hot spot detector."

I nodded. "Because cold spots indicate a manifestation. That much I know. There are plenty of them around here."

"We also have passive motion detectors we'll set up in places we won't be," he added. "The results from these and all the other equipment is fed back to our monitoring computer, which is what Wendy is setting up over there on the counter."

Simon smiled. "There's more including laser nets, replacement probes, flashlights, infrared goggles and tons of batteries since most of this place is still without power. Battery draining is one of the signs an entity is near."

"Looks like you'll all be busy for awhile," I replied. "Wish I could help in some way. I hate standing around feeling useless."

His eyes were troubled when he told me, "Just be safe. We are going to stir up a whole lot of trouble tonight."

I nodded knowing he was all too right. "I want the same for you and your team, Simon. Be safe. You are dealing with pure evil."

Since cameras and recorders needed to be set up in the most active spots, I told them my bedroom and most definitely the cellar. They weren't surprised about cellar. Apparently, Simon had mentioned my experiences down there.

"The upper hall near the back stairs has shown some activity, and there's also been a suicide in the parlor with the bay window. Hannah Grey who murdered her infant," I reported then added, "Other spirits appeared with Millie one night when I needed help. I don't know who they are, or where you'll find them."

"Looks like we have plenty of places to check out," Todd told me with a grin as he began organizing the equipment with the brisk efficiency of long practice.

While everyone came and went lugging off what they needed, I made a pot of coffee and a halfhearted stab at cleaning up the kitchen by stacking everything in the sink. After that, I paced back and forth cuddling an equally anxious Cinda. Simon returned a long time later with Wendy. They grabbed a cup of coffee then headed to the computer where Wendy scanned the remote camera feeds from the front parlor, my bedroom, and the upper hallway. They had been strategically set up for the best visual range. There were none in the cellar. No one had gone down there yet. They had decided to save it till last for a full assault by the entire team.

"What do you want to happen tonight?" Simon asked me as I put Cinda in her carrier and joined them there.

"I want the evil purged if that is possible, and the others sent to wherever they are meant to go."

"From the near death experiences we have recorded, many are reconnected with their loved ones and go into this bright Light. They describe it as a place of utter peace...love...and comfort. It must be amazing."

"That's what I want for Millie and the others, but not Varna!" I replied vehemently. "I want her to get what she deserves!"

Simon frowned as he looked into my eyes. "I can't promise any of that will happen. We're here to record the paranormal activity. Irrefutable proof of an afterlife. Wendy's séance will give you the opportunity to interact with them if they materialize. You can tell them about the Light then."

Wendy offered me an uncertain smile. "*If* it works. Not all do and some I've had to terminate rather quickly when things got out of hand. That may well happen tonight from what Simon told us."

My own smile was grim. "I'm willing to take that chance if you all are."

"We wouldn't have volunteered to come here if we weren't," Wendy replied brightly, but I knew she was already sensing something.

"I want to be on one of the teams," I told Simon.

"I wish you'd just stay here with Wendy. That way I won't have to...."

"You don't understand. I need to do this...period...end of discussion."

"Then you'll team up with me where I can keep an eye on you."

"Suits me fine. Just let me know what I need to do."

It took some time to finish the setup. It was well past 10 pm, when we divided into teams well armed with all the equipment we would need which included full spectrum cameras, EVP recorders, night vision goggles, walkie talkies, hands free flashlights, and extra batteries. Wendy manned the computer, which would receive feeds from all of us in addition to the remotes. Cinda's carrier was next to her, so she could grab it if we all needed to make a quick exit.

Todd and Mike headed down the back hall while Wendy flipped off the lights in the kitchen. With the exception of the computer screen, total darkness swallowed up Greystone.

With our night vision goggles in place, Simon and I pushed through the swing door into the main hall then continued on towards the front of the house. Almost at once, we both sensed a heaviness in the air that made me dizzy.

"Something is here, but I'm not seeing it," Simon whispered. "We'll try the EVP recorder. Ask a question and see if it picks up anything we'll hear on playback."

Taking a deep breath to steady me, which did absolutely no good, I managed to ask, "Who are you? We aren't here to harm you."

We both heard a heavy sigh and then an orb appeared in the hall just ahead. It hovered there for a few seconds then disappeared.

"I didn't get a sense of evil, Simon. Just sadness. Maybe it's Hannah's spirit in orb form though that's not how she appeared to me."

"Could be. Let's keep going."

It felt now as though the darkness had grown thicker...as though it was becoming a palpable thing we had to shove our way through. From somewhere and everywhere, we both heard the mystery clock chime again.

"The witching hour that never ends," I murmured. "The birth time of one and the death of another."

I could hear Simon sigh. "Maybe we can help them both find peace if things work out according to plan."

"I wish with all my heart that happens tonight."

We continued on...opening the doors we passed and looking inside. A rat scurried across the floor of a room yet to be renovated and disappeared through a hole in the paneling.

"Except for the orb, that critter is all we've 'seen' so far," I whispered as I looked around the surreal 'green' room distorted by the goggles I wore.

As if those words had conjured it up, a shadow detached itself from the far corner and drifted our way. It hovered close for a moment then 'zoomed' out the door leaving the smell of rot and burning candles in its wake.

"This might be the room where Joe found satanic images scrawled on the walls, Simon. That could be another kid who died here nobody knows about."

"Messing with stuff that was very, very dangerous. Let's check in with the guys and see what they've turned up."

His walkie talkie call found Todd and Mike in the upper hall checking out the rooms just past the back stairs.

"We're just hanging out and seeing a lot of moving shadows especially in this end room," Mike reported. "This place is way active. We've tried a few EVP sessions that might turn up something interesting. You guys okay?...over."

"All good here. Let me check with Wendy and see if the remotes are picking up anything. Over and out."

There was a lot of interference on the call to Wendy. We were able to make out that something had knocked over the camera in my bedroom, so we headed that way to check it out. Climbing the main staircase, I had a strong sense we were being followed by something malevolent that was rapidly gaining on us. Simon felt it, too.

"It's probably Varna. If we run, she has a clear shot at our defenseless backs. We could turn around and confront her," I whispered really hoping he would say 'no'.

"Worth a try. Stay behind me."

"Not going to happen. We're a team. On the count of three?"

"One...two...three..."

We whirled around. Behind us was a dense, churning mass of utter blackness. In its center, narrowed red eyes peered from a skeletal face with bits of flesh still clinging to it. "I have you both now," Varna hissed. "You will never leave this house."

"We're not afraid of you!" Simon shouted sounding far braver than I felt. "We know what you did to Millie and her baby. Where is her body? We know she's around here some place!"

She laughed. It was the maniacal kind I had heard way too often. "Find me in the cellar, and I will show you," and with that said she vanished through the floor.

"Okay. Looks like we have a date with the devil," Simon told me as I waited for my galloping heartbeat to somewhat normalize.

"Weren't you scared?" I managed to ask.

"I was more than that, but I couldn't let her see it. She feeds on fear."

"She'd have blown up like a puffer fish if she'd seen mine," I whispered as we continued on to my dark bedroom.

To both our surprise, we saw a glowing figure sitting on the edge of the bed. It was Millie in her bloody, white nightgown. A puzzled frown creased her brow as she told Simon, "You look like the one I love, but that cannot be. He died at sea a very long time ago. Never returned to me. I have waited and waited and now you are here. Who are you?"

Simon took my hand. "We think I am your Eric's great grandson."

Visibly shocked, she began to shiver. "But he died! That cannot be!"

"He didn't die," I told her as I slowly moved her way. "His ship was torpedoed and sunk, but he survived."

A low moan escaped her as tears filled her eyes. "But I saw them leave in their car. The men in their uniforms who came to tell me he was dead. Why else would they have come here?"

I felt my own tears welling up. "You must have been listed as his fiancée, and they came to report his condition."

"My mother told me they came to tell me he had died. Been burned in the ship's fire then drowned."

"She lied to make you suffer," I told her. "She is dangerously insane as you no doubt know better than anyone. I bet your Eric came back here looking for you as soon as he could, and she told him another lie. He married much later in life and had a daughter named Audrey. "

She smiled wanly as she looked at Simon. "I bore him a son who died. He never got to hold him...love him...and neither did I."

I so wanted to hug her but was afraid that would scare her off. "Your baby wasn't a boy, and she didn't die. She was my grandmother. Your mother wanted her disposed of, but the midwife saved her. Dropped her off at the orphanage in the village. I came here searching for her roots and never thought I would find them at Greystone."

Millie's smile was now brilliant. "I had a daughter? My baby lived?" I nodded, and she continued, "I know she must be dead by now, but you are part of her...part of me and Eric! Is it she I see inside your cat sometimes?"

I smiled back. "Yes. I think she sometimes possesses that old cat. She became known as Allison Shield...a famous author. You would have been very proud of your daughter."

"And you. I am very proud of you. That you would find the love of your life, and he would be the great grandson of my own beloved is a miracle. A happy ending for both Eric and me."

"Well, we're not...." I began to tell her.

244

But Simon cut in with, "We're not there *yet*, but we're working on it, Millie. Right now...tonight...we would like to put a stop to what's happening here. End the hold your mother has on you and the other spirits in Greystone."

Horror filled Millie's gray eyes. "She is very powerful! Nothing can stop her!"

My fingers touched the medal I wore. St. Benedict. The Protector. "It will be a fight of good against evil," I warned her. "We may not win, but we're sure going to try and could use any help you can give us without putting yourself at risk."

She closed her eyes for a moment then asked, "Where do we begin?"

It was Simon who told her. "She invited us down to the cellar and....."

She shuddered violently as her now frantic eyes darted back and forth between us. "I can't go down there," she whispered hoarsely. "There is more to fear than her down there."

"Such as?" I asked though I was afraid of her answer.

"I don't know!" she wailed then vanished.

"She's too terrified to help us," Simon told me, "And who can blame her. About what you told her. How did you become so sure you are Allison's granddaughter?"

"I didn't really get a chance to tell you before, but I found out more information in the journals that pointed me in the right direction and then I had visions...memories...that gave me irrefutable proof of my identity."

"Looks like you need to catch me up on all of that when we get the time. Let's get back to Wendy."

There were no further incidents on the way to the kitchen where the light was back on and the others waiting. As we stripped off our equipment, Wendy reported, "Just been showing these two some of the stuff we got so far tonight. The knock your socks off kind including that horrific entity you guys encountered on the stairs. Millie will have our viewers in tears."

"I don't want to see her exploited," I told her flatly. "I know she wouldn't like that."

Wendy was about to protest when a worried Mike broke in, "Sorry, guys, but after seeing that footage, I'm having second thoughts about the cellar bit."

Simon's gaze swept us all. "It needs to be done. Volunteers only."

"Let's try a séance first and see what develops," Wendy suggested. "We came here for some action, and we're getting plenty of it. Let's not chicken out now. We'll worry about the cellar later."

"You're sure you are up for that?" Simon asked. "There's a good chance you'll summon that 'horrific entity' while you're in a vulnerable state."

"I'll risk it. We need to get some answers if we can."

It didn't take long to set up the candles and form a circle in the now dark kitchen. We all joined hands. Wendy was on my left and Simon was on my right. An agitated Cinda was in her carrier on the floor next to me.

246

"There are two types of mediums...mental and physical," she informed me as I watched her in the flickering candlelight that cast her face in odd relief. "The mental kind tune in to the spirit world by sensing, listening or seeing the dead. Physical mediums use their ectoplasm or that of those at the séance to create materializations...bell ringing, knocking. Well, you get the picture. I am a bit of both. I have no spirit guide most of the time, but occasionally my brother will show up to help me. I do enter a trance state, which may be a bit disturbing to those not used to it, but before we begin I must say a prayer of protection. Let me begin: '*We pray that the power of Love encircles all those gathered here. That it will protect us and guard us from all evil and prevent any attachments that would follow us. May that Higher Power light our path and guide us through whatever may come our way this night and always*'. Now we will go around the table and all will ask for the protection of a Greater Power starting with you, Jodie."

"What do I say?"

"Your heart will tell you."

I felt a chill raise goose bumps up both arms and heard Cinda stir restlessly in her carrier. Nothing else broke the utter silence. "Please protect those who have risked so much to come here tonight. I ask that the innocent trapped in this place find their loved ones in the Light, and that Your justice finds the other."

Simon squeezed my hand, then added, "May God protect us all."

And so it went, until everyone had a chance to speak. It was then Wendy told us, "Okay. Based on what we saw tonight things should get pretty interesting. Just don't break the circle no matter what happens. Now I need absolute quiet, so I can focus."

Long moments passed as I watched the candles flicker in the drafty room. Suddenly, I heard a long drawn out moan as Wendy's hand jerked spasmodically.

In a voice I barely recognized, she asked, "Is there anyone here tonight who would like to speak to us?"

There was only silence and then a faint rustling in the far corner.

"I sense someone is here," she called. "Was that you over there?"

There was a soft "yes" and then silence.

"Can you materialize for us?"

The silence continued for what seemed like a very long time and then a spire of blue light formed that gradually took the shape of Millie in her usual attire.

She smiled at me then said, "I'm sorry, Jodie, I left like that. I heard your prayer just now and want to find those I lost. You told me Eric married. Did he love her as he loved me? Was he happy with her?"

Wendy squeezed my hand. "Answer her," she whispered as Millie's light surged and ebbed.

"I have no way of knowing that, Millie, though I can't imagine he could love anyone as much as he loved you. Perhaps Wendy can summon him, and he can tell you all your heart needs to know."

"That's not at all likely to happen!" Wendy whispered fiercely. "It would take a miracle to re-connect them."

"Then let's try for a miracle," I whispered back just as the scent of roses filled the air. Allison was there.

Slowly, she materialized not as the gaunt dying woman I had last seen, but young and beautiful. She was wearing the green gown I had worn to the ball. The resemblance to her mother was striking.

"I will help you find my father," she told Millie. "I know what it is to have loved and lost the one man who completes you in a way you never thought necessary."

A tearful Millie pulled her into her arms, and their light merged into one bright column. They had found each other again. Mother and daughter. Millie's search for her baby had ended.

Wendy's hand tightened on mine, and she called, "They are both here, Eric Sanders. Your Millie and the precious daughter you never knew. Come to them! They need you! Come!"

But the miracle I had hoped for didn't happen. Instead, there was a long, drawn out shriek as a powerful burst of wind slammed into the kitchen from the back hall. Paper plates, pizza boxes, beer bottles, even my potted ivy were caught up in the vortex. The computer was hurled high in the air then smashed against the wall.

"Don't break the circle no matter what happens!" Wendy shouted to be heard above the din as we ducked the flying objects as best we could.

A beer bottle slammed into Simon...another grazed my cheek...then all grew very still as a familiar oily blackness spread into the room sucking Millie and Allison into its core. From the heart of that darkness, the glowing red entity began to take shape. A woman made of shifting shadows that one moment concealed her gruesome remains and the next exposed what death and time had done to her.

"Look at the mess you made me make," she hissed as her red eyes swept us all. The smile that accompanied her words was both amused and horrifying. The grin of a rotting death's-head. "Here you all are. Those who have been stirring up the night with your silly pranks. Doing the devil's work. I have you all now."

"You will not harm them!" I found myself shouting. "You are the incarnate of evil and will be punished by One far more powerful than you."

She laughed...almost dislodging what was left of her jaw as she floated closer to me...step by step.

"Don't break the circle! It is our only protection," Simon whispered urgently as both he and Wendy tightened their grip on my hands.

"Don't listen to him. Break your precious circle that is less than worthless," Varna scoffed as her malevolent eyes raked me slowly. "Look at you glowering at me! I knew there was something troubling about you from the first moment I laid eyes on you. Eavesdropping supplied me with the answer. You are the granddaughter of that thing Millicent birthed. The one I now have in my grasp. The midwife was paid well to keep her mouth shut and get rid of that abomination."

"Well, she didn't!" I told her hoping my voice was steadier than it sounded to my ears. "She saved her and now there's me. Someone you don't scare." It was a lie of course, but I wasn't about to let her see I was way, way beyond terrified.

Leaving a trail of black slime on the floor, she slid even closer. Her narrowed red eyes were filled with hate as she bent over me. Her stench was nauseating as a bit of her rotting flesh dangled then dropped landing on the table just inches from my arm. "Liar! You are terrified of what I might do. Will do. You trusted your pathetic guardians to protect you like that cat that follows you around. I had wondered who the spirit was that was attached to it and eavesdropping supplied that answer as well. Where is it?"

"Like I would ever tell you!" I shouted up at her as the most profound dread crept over me.

She smiled. It was the stuff of nightmares. "No need. I see it hissing and growling down there and just a cat at the moment. An old cat whose neck I could easily snap with a great deal of pleasure or make it suffer a long lingering demise I would enjoy even more. I never did like cats. Wouldn't allow a filthy, flea ridden creature like that within these walls, yet there it is."

Despite my fear...my horror, nothing would stop me from saving Cinda. "Back off, you bitch!" I screamed as adrenaline lent me the strength I needed to break the circle and make a grab for the carrier.

Fast as I was, Varna was faster. I could hear Cinda's terrified yowls as her carrier was sucked inside the thick, impenetrable darkness she had reverted to once more.

Her voice reached us as she withdrew down the back hall. "Come to the cellar. You might get it back unharmed...or maybe not. Killing it would be such a pleasure."

The cellar door banged against the wall and then there was only silence. Screaming Cinda's name, I was headed that way at a flat out run when Simon pulled me to a stop.

"You're playing right into her hands. We need to be prepared when we go down there."

"I can't wait!" I shouted at him as I tried to shake myself free. "Every second counts! I need...."

"Stop! We need a plan. She won't do anything to Cinda till she has an audience. You said she doesn't like holy water?"

My heart was thudding frantically.... tears were streaming down my face, but somehow I managed to tell him, "She sizzled and left once but not the second time. I don't care what happens to me. I'm going down there! Now!"

"Not without me. I can't let that happen."

Wendy had joined us by then. "Sorry, guys, but after what we just saw I won't be joining the party."

Simon nodded. "Understood. There's no guarantee whoever goes down there will make it back alive."

As it turned out, Simon and I were the only ones willing to take the risk. Wendy wanted to wait in the van. Mike and Todd in the kitchen. I had thought Millie and Allison were still trapped inside Varna's darkness and was more than surprised when they reappeared together.

It was a badly shaken Millie who told us, "She forgot about us for a moment and loosened her hold long enough for us to escape. I don't want to go down there, but I won't let you do this alone."

"Nor I," Allison added. "I won't let her hurt you or Cinda."

"Then let's get it done," Simon replied with a grim smile.

Arming ourselves with holy water, flashlights and extra batteries, we headed down the back hall. My heart was hammering wildly again, and I knew Simon must be in a similar state though he hid it well.

"We will go first," Allison told us when we reached the open cellar door.

Millie added. "She still has ways to hurt us that you can't possibly imagine, but you must stay alive. You are the happy ending I never had."

Hand in hand, mother and daughter floated down the stairs into the thick blackness that waited below. The smell was rank...decay, death and something else I couldn't name. Distantly, I heard Cinda's yowl. She was still alive.

"I'm here, Varna!" I shouted as Simon and I followed them down. "I'm the only one you want!"

"You're wrong about that!" she screamed hoarsely from everywhere at once. "I know who he is. Saw the resemblance to the one who came sniffing after Millicent when he was just a boy. Listening to your chatter confirmed what I suspected. Now I have you all in my net. The sins that began with my daughter over there will be punished by..."

"By whom?" I cut in sharply. "What gives you the right to judge any of us?"

"I am the instrument of the Lord!"

"You are the instrument of Satan and this ends here and now!"

"Ah, Listen! Hear how your old cat cries for you to save it? Poor, poor thing. Come closer and I might release it, but first I have something to show all of you."

Varna laughed again as a red light seeped from the earthen floor and licked upward like flames that gave no heat. She was standing in the middle of them... a monster fashioned from darkness and death.

"Look at the wall over there!" she commanded pointing to the one scheduled for repairs...the one hidden behind the rose thicket. We flashed our lights that way. A trickle of dirt spilled out between the stones, and the floor beneath us trembled. A large rock tumbled out. Another followed...and then another. The house above us creaked and groaned as a section of the wall caved in spilling dirt and still more rocks into the cellar. Among them was a human skull... a scattering of bones.. and then a second skull that rolled close to where we stood. I wondered who they were and soon had my answer.

"That is where the rest of you has been, Millicent. Buried under the roses where no one would ever think to look if they didn't believe you'd run away like your father. By the way, that's the other pile of bones. Your father who loved you more than he did me. His mistake. His spirit escaped me, but none of yours will."

Simon's hand gripped mine tightly as he shouted, "You arrogant bitch! You claim to be 'God's instrument', but He is the embodiment of unconditional love and mercy towards all. When have you ever shown anyone that?"

Her red eyes narrowed still more as she pointed to Millie. "That one sinned and bore the fruit of that sin under this very roof. She does not deserve my mercy and....."

A furious Millie cut in before she finished, "I would have gone to Eric's family and had our baby there if you hadn't kept me prisoner...tortured me...lied to me! You told me he was dead. That he had been hideously burned then drowned."

"And I told him when he came poking around that you had found another and run off to get married. I couldn't tell him you were dead because he would have wanted to see your grave. You should have seen his face when I added a few embellishments. It was priceless."

"And you see no evil in that?" I shouted.

"I was merely punishing the transgressors in the Lord's name, and now I will see you all destroyed in the purifying fire."

With that said, she snapped her bony fingers, and the red light became real flames just as the door at the top slammed shut, and the stairway behind us collapsed into a pile of rubble. There would be no escape that way.

"If you destroy Greystone, what will become of you?" I screamed at her.

"I will have completed my mission and will finally ascend into the glory of Heaven! I will be among the angels!"

Suddenly, a low rumble shook the foundation a second time and the hole in the wall widened. We could still escape through there in time, but I wasn't going anywhere without Cinda. I could see her carrier through the smoke and flames as I struggled to break Simon's grip, but he tightened it. "We'll save her together! You're not alone any more!" he told me fiercely. "On the count of three. One...!"

"No!" I screamed as I slammed my fist into his chest again and again. "Let me go! I've got to do this! I won't let her hurt you, too!"

From the heart of the fire, Varna was belting out a hymn as Allison shouted to me, "Stay with him! I'll get her!"

I held my breath as I watched her speed through the flames and return a moment later with Cinda in her arms.

"Run like hell!" she called over her shoulder as she headed to the gap in the wall with us right behind her. Echoing through the now blazing cellar, we heard a shrill scream followed by another... and another...then nothing at all. Varna had been trapped by her own fire and was burning. I didn't question how that was possible. Maybe the devil had claimed his own. Maybe the justice I had asked for found her. The outcome was the same. Varna was gone.

Choking on the dense smoke, Simon shoved me through the hole in the wall and was right on my heels as I crawled past the rose thicket the collapsing wall had torn wide open. Millie and Allison were waiting in the moonlight. Cinda was still snuggled in her arms, but glowing now. It could only mean one thing. Allison's words confirmed it.

"I was too late to save her," she told me when I reached her. "Our Cinda was old, and I think her heart failed. The little black shelter cat nobody wanted shared her love with both of us for many years and will be waiting for you. Back there at the séance, you prayed for the Light and our loved ones to find us. How do we make that happen?"

Simon replied, "All I really know is what those who had near death experiences told my team. A bright white Light came for them. Their loved ones were waiting there for them. Maybe you just need to let them know you are ready."

Millie's smile was radiant as she grabbed Allison's arm and shouted up to the star bright sky, "We are here, Eric. Your Smudge and your daughter. Please find us! Please take us into the Light with you!"

Nothing happened at first and then what looked like a bright star appeared directly overhead. A tunnel of light began to take shape and drop closer till it was hovering just above us...a bridge between heaven and earth. Silhouetted against the intense, white Light at the top, two glowing figures appeared. One began to run down the tunnel shouting, "Smudge? That better be you down there!"

Millie was screaming his name...laughing and crying at the same time as she sped his way and flung herself into his arms. It was a mirror image of Simon who held her tightly, kissed her passionately then handed her over to the second man who had joined them by then. "Papa!" I heard her cry as she threw her arms around his neck and hugged him fiercely.

He was crying openly as he returned her hug. "Looks like I missed your birthday a few years back, but I'm here now. Now and for always."

It was then Eric told her, "You need to know that I married someone else a long time after your mother lied to me, and I thought you gone forever."

She was smiling as she took his hand. "I know about her and your daughter Audrey. There's room in our love for everyone. Let's go now. Papa's waiting

They disappeared into the Light, and I looked at Allison who had been watching their joyful reunion with tears in her own eyes. I knew what she was thinking. Knew she was waiting for her Edward. Hoping and praying he would come for her, too. Suddenly, a tall, dark haired man appeared at the top and silently descended through the clouds. His eyes never left Allsion's as she rose in a swirl of green tulle to meet him midway.

"I see you're dressed for our ball. May I have this dance forever?" he asked then tipped up her chin and kissed her with infinite tenderness.

It was a long moment before she smiled up into his eyes and replied, "If you make it a threesome. My little cat must never leave me again."

She was still holding Cinda, when he twirled her around twice, then took her hand and led her up the tunnel towards the Light. She paused at the top and blew me a kiss then vanished. She was with the only man she had ever truly loved, and I had never seen her so happy.

Other ghosts began to emerge from the windows where they'd been watching. They drifted towards the tunnel with the same look in all their eyes...hope. They were not disappointed. There were cries of joy and recognition as each and every one found those who loved them and been waiting a very long time. One of them was Hannah. Her mother had come for her and, when her daughter hesitated at the tunnel's edge, told her, "Come, my sweet child. Look at the one you hold so tightly. See him smile now! I know how much you have mourned him...regretted what you did. We are going into the Light together. You and me. Hand in hand. His love is unconditional, and He knows your true soul."

"She did a terrible thing," I murmured to Simon as her mother led her towards the Light, "But she may have been suffering from postpartum depression...perhaps had a psychotic break of some kind. None of us have the right to judge her." I didn't want to think about Varna. What had happened to her after her screams. Was she always evil or had the house changed her? Infected her? Or was it the other way around? Either way, I had felt its malignance.

We continued to watch the exodus until the last of them was gone, and the tunnel disappeared in the night sky. Simon's voice was hoarse with emotion when he told me, "That is something I will never, ever forget!"

I was smiling through my tears as I replied, "It means the end of Greystone and all the hideous things that happened here."

"It needed to end," he told me as we watched the smoke billow out through the breach in the wall. Flames followed and ignited the ancient roses that had hidden such a terrible secret. "Let's go see how the others are doing."

We circled the house and found them looking for us just as Henry's truck pulled up behind their van.

"There you are! We thought you were goners!" Todd shouted as he sped our way and gave us both a bone-crunching hug. "We tried to reach you when it sounded like things were headed south, but the door slammed shut, and we couldn't force it open."

An excited Mike took up where he left off, "We were looking for something to bust it open with when this young guy with curly black hair walked right through it. Told us not to worry... that you'd soon be outside and safe."

"I had decided to quit being a major wuss and came back in just as he appeared," Wendy added as she pulled both of us into a fierce hug of her own. "I'm so very, very glad you are okay."

Henry had joined us by then. There were tears in his eyes when he told me, "Sorry I'm late to the party. Fell asleep in that old rocker. Edith woke me and told me to get on over here. She said it had ended. That they had gone up into the Light."

I smiled as I hugged him tightly. "She was right. Millie found her lost love and her father who had been buried next to her under the roses all that time. Allison also found her love...her Edward. They all have their happy endings."

The fire had now become an inferno that was spreading quickly. We could have called the fire department from Henry's place, but nobody wanted to save Greystone, so we watched it burn. I could probably have rescued some of the journals...maybe even my laptop...but there was no way I would ever re-enter that house. I had the distinct feeling it would never let me out once I stepped through those doors.

I began to shiver violently from a mix of cold and shock. Simon wrapped his arm around me and led me to his car. We followed Henry back to his cabin while the others left for Boston. Sitting around the table with a blanket draped over me and a mug of hot chocolate in my hands, I looked for Cinda out of long habit then remembered she was gone. Tears gathered again in my eyes. She'd been my comforter. My protector. My friend. Her loss left an aching hole in my heart that she had filled from the first moment I saw her.

Suddenly, I felt something bump my knee and looked down. She was sitting there looking up at me. Two slow eye blinks followed then a rumbling purr as I gathered her in my arms for what I knew would be the last time...at least for awhile. She had come to give me a proper good bye...to let me know she was okay...and then she vanished as the scent of roses filled the room. Allison had come to take her home.

Simon smiled at me and squeezed my hand. "Yep. I saw her. She'll be waiting for you just like the others did for Millie and Allison. Looks like love is eternal."

261

I smiled wanly back and brushed away the tears that now dripped off my chin. "What happens now?"

"Depends. I need to get back to Boston. I've got a team that needs sorting out...insurance claims...that sort of thing, but I want you to come with me. I need you in my life. Never thought I would say that to anyone."

"I think that's something we need to explore a lot more thoroughly when we're past all that's happened here," I told him a lot more calmly than I was feeling. "We are no longer their happy ending. They found their own. If we're meant to be together once all this is behind us, it will happen. You go back to Boston while I sort out my life. Henry will let you know how to find me."

Neither one of us had noticed Henry slip away or heard him whisper, "Them young'uns still don't know they're in love, Edith."

"Time will take care of that. Now how about hitting the hay, old man. You've had more excitement than you can handle in one day," she whispered back as her hand slipped into his, and she led him to his bed.

(Three months later)

I was busy doing a yoga move on my mat and thinking about Simon as I did way too often even though I hadn't heard from him in months, when there was a knock on the door. Muttering under my breath as I untangled my limbs, I padded that way...peered through the peephole...then threw it open. The subject of my frequent thoughts was standing there holding a single red rose. Bella was sitting at his feet.

"Simon! What a surprise!"

"Bella asked to see you, and who am I to say 'no'. By the way, I found great homes for all her pups. Bought this for you from a street vendor before I stopped to think it might...might...."

I finished what he had tried to say. "It might bring back some memories best forgotten. It's okay. Come on in, Bella. You can bring him with you if you want."

"She insists on it."

I bent down and scratched behind her floppy ears then told him, "Grab a seat and tell me what you've been doing with yourself since forever while I make us a pot of coffee."

"Let me do that. Been meaning to tell you that your coffee sort of sucks. Haven't seen you around since my grandpa's funeral."

"Not that you looked very hard," I replied with a wry grin. "I've been busy with one thing or another."

"By the way, I like your eclectic loft. Has a great view of the harbor," he told me as he headed to the huge windows.

My own gaze swept the wide expanse of very blue water and boats. "It's the reason I bought it. I'm a sea person. The *eclectic* bit is due to all the things I had in storage. Stuff from my travels with Allison and antique store finds. As you can see, the furniture is mostly from the Mission Arts and Crafts period which seems to suit this place."

He nodded. "It used to be an old shoe factory back in the day."

"This whole building is supposed to be haunted, but I haven't seen or heard anything," I reported. "Funny you should show up today of all days. Just finished the final details regarding Greystone yesterday. Donated the insurance money and the property to a retired couple who were friends of Allison and me. They want to build a farm for intercity orphans with fresh air...animals to raise...gardens to plant...you know what I mean."

"All the things that might point them in a different direction. I get it. Do you think it will work?"

"For some...not all, but every single one is important. Heaven knows what would have happened to me if Allison hadn't rescued me when she did."

He studied me closely. "My personal opinion is..."

"Which is seldom right," I pointed out.

"Is that you would have turned out great. You have all the qualities needed to be a great human being except for a few failings I dare not name because...."

"Such as?" I cut in.

"See! You never let me finish a sentence. I'll add that to the list plus you are stubborn...willful...and pretty much insist on having your own way."

I shook my head vehemently. "That sounds both redundant and not true!"

"Too very true. Not that I let that bother me. There's more, but you will no doubt overreact when I name them, so plunk yourself

264

down," he told me over his shoulder as he headed towards my open kitchen. "I'll make the coffee, and we'll catch up."

I was close on his heels. "If I were the kind to make a list...."

"Way too organized for you," he replied as he picked up my coffee can and studied the label with a wry grimace.

"I'd put control freak right at the top of a very long one. I may have mentioned it already, but it definitely deserves a repeat."

"Hmmmm. That might be something I could work on. Sit!"

"Only 'cause I want to."

I took a seat at the table and soon was cradling the cup he handed me when I told him, "As you know, the fire destroyed everything I'd been working on, and I came to think it wasn't important any more. Allison had found her mother...reconnected with her lost love...had the perfect happy ending, so I made a change."

He took the chair across from me then leaned forward and tucked a loose strand of my hair back in place, "You do know you are sort of a mess right now? What have you been doing?"

"Do you know how annoying it is when you do that?" I asked as I slapped his hand away. "It's my hair...my mess, and I liked it just the way it was."

"That almost hurt," he murmured as he studied my lips or the tip of my nose...I wasn't sure which. "You've haunted me as surely as any ghost since the day you fell into my arms."

I could have told him the very same thing, but was afraid where that might lead, so I quickly redirected him back to the subject he'd changed. "I've written the first rough draft of another book. It's titled: *The Ghosts of Greystone*...the story of what happened there to all of us. I guess it was a way of finding closure."

"And it helped?" he managed to ask when I knew my reply hadn't been what he'd been hoping to hear.

"Yep. I have yet to add Henry's death. It's still too raw. Every time I begin to write it down, I start to cry."

"But it was the very best of happy endings...or rather new beginnings. The kind he wanted."

I nodded as memories floated to the surface. Henry had known for some time he was terminally ill...something he didn't share with anyone. He had waited till he could no longer hide his condition then confided in me one day when I called, "I didn't want no one feelin' sorry for an old man who's lived a long life...a good one...and just been waitin' around till the time came to check out. I'm fine for now. Will let you and Simon know when I ain't."

Not long after that, Henry's neighbor found him lying next to his truck with Bella at his side. He'd been rushed to the hospital. I joined Simon there after he called to let me know what had happened. I was the only one he notified. Earlier, Henry had told us both he didn't want his son told till it was over. I remembered his every word.

"Him and me have never seen eye to eye about much. Always been ashamed of his old man who made a livin' at the sawmill and farmin' this place. Got him a scholarship and took off from there. Made it big and I'm proud of him, but he won't understand I want to go out my own way. He'll want to keep me goin' with tubes and drugs and crap, so best not be troublin' him."

We stayed by his bedside...trading off just long enough to grab a coffee or a bite to eat in the cafeteria. We were not alone. Edith was with him the whole time. Monitors beeped and buzzed...the staff came and went. He never regained full consciousness until the third day when he opened his eyes...smiled at us all and said clear as a bell, "Enough of all this mollycoddlin'! I want to go home. Home to my mountains...to my Bella."

So, that is what we did. We brought him home. He died in his bed with Edith cradled in his arms and Bella at his feet. Simon and I were asleep in chairs nearby when Bella's mournful howl woke us just in time to see them pass through the open kitchen door hand in hand. Turning, they both looked back at us. "We are going home now," Henry shouted. "But this ain't good bye by a long shot. Be seeing you both again."

Edith smiled as she added, "Just be as happy as we are and know you are both loved very much."

They turned then and walked towards the rising sun with Bella following them until they vanished. Her long bugle howl echoed in the still morning air. She would have gone with them if she could and refused to leave that spot until Simon scooped her up and carried her inside then brought her and her puppies back to Boston when he left later.

I shook my head to clear the memories that had brought such intense sadness with them.

Simon had also been remembering. "I'll never forget what we saw that morning."

"Nope. Never," I replied as I brushed away my tears with my sleeve. "If we don't stop bringing up the past, I'm going to lose it entirely at the rate I'm going."

Simon brushed away a tear that had escaped my efforts. "But before we do, I have something for you. I went back to Greystone after Grandpa's funeral. Not sure why. Not much left. Been picked over by vandals...other fires set...but I found this just lying there like I was meant to find it. It's been cleaned up and the clasp repaired. Still some damage, but here's your mermaid pin. The one you were wearing the night of the ball."

I could scarcely breathe as I took it from his hand. "Allison wore this the first time I met her. It means more to me than I can ever say. Thank you so much, Simon," I told him as tears ran down my face again.

"You are the cryingest person I have ever met which I've added to the plus column," he murmured as he took it back and awkwardly pinned it to my tank top. "I should have sent it to you earlier, but it seemed to like my pocket. I carried it with me everywhere."

I swiped at my tears a second time then told him, "If we don't change the subject again and *quickly*, I can't promise there won't be more tears, so tell me what's been going on with you?"

He smiled ruefully. "The team broke up. That night shook them all up badly. I've been reconnecting with old friends I lost touch with who are scattered across the county and learned how to rope a steer in the process. Also, spent some time with my parents. They're both still a bit pissed with me for not calling when Grandpa was in the hospital. But no matter where I was or what I was doing, I kept remembering what we've seen, Jodie. The Light. The reuniting of lost loves and think maybe I could facilitate that."

"Like how?"

"Find haunted houses and see if the spirits there can be released into that amazing Light."

"Do you not remember how dangerous that was?" I asked in disbelief. "You're an idiot. You can't go traipsing into haunted houses all alone!"

"I was thinking more of a team of two. We were pretty good back there as I remember."

"I remember being terrified!"

"But the Light...the love...the..."

"Reconnection. I get that. I just don't know how we could work together. We're so different...so..."

"Meant for each other?"

"How would I ever know if what I feel for you isn't some residual...something left over from the relationship between Millie and Eric?"

He smiled, leaned closer, and tickled the end of my nose with another strand of my unruly hair. "You're wondering if you love me for just my adorable self?"

Slapping his hand away a second time, I told him as calmly as his nearness would let me, "I wouldn't put it that way, but 'yes'...in the future *should* it ever happen."

He answered me by pulling me into his arms and kissing my forehead...the tip of my nose...my eyelids...then my lips. I could feel a rush of sensations swamp me. My feelings...not Millie's. Bella howled as he swept me off my feet and carried me toward my still unmade bed then tossed me into the middle of it.

"Looks like I didn't have time to tidy," I murmured as I removed his glasses and ruffled his hair.

"So, I noticed. Failing number four or five or whatever. I've lost count," he murmured back. "Guess I'll have to make the bed when we move in together."

"Like that's ever going to happen. I'd be forced to kill you within a week and...."

His next kiss silenced me in mid reply.

The End?

This book is dedicated to all those I love.

Other Merabeth James' titles that might interest you include:
The Ravynne Sisters Paranormal Thrillers (15 Books)
The Skye Wilder Paranormal Trilogy
The Caitlin McLeod Modern Gothics

Printed in Great Britain
by Amazon

82403699R00159